WHAT'LL WE DO ON SUNDAY?

Gwen and Paul Dubov

WHAT'LL WE DO ON SUNDAY?

G. P. Putnam's Sons, New York

For A.S. and G.E., with love

WHAT'LL WE DO ON SUNDAY?

1

FOUR days a week Ron Gohdiener drove home west on Wilshire, joining the northward migration on Highland Avenue, crossing Hollywood Boulevard, avoiding the thrombosis of the freeway for old Cahuenga Pass. By leaving the office at 5:02, providing he caught the first DOWN elevator and snaked his way into the proper lanes, he generally made it home to Keefee Avenue in North Hollywood between 5:28 and 5:35.

Mondays, disturbingly, it took forever.

Not Ron's favorite day, Monday, since Mr. Meader had become a disciple and ardent advocate of Creative Corporate Togetherness, spreading the gospel with a start-of-the-week sensitivity session followed by a fellowship lunch (always knockwurst, beans and heartburn), and after a dinner grabbed on the run, the latest synod: an interdepartmental bowling tournament. It was a sport Ron felt destined never to conquer, having narrowly avoided serious injury several times when he forgot to take his fingers out of the holes. To patronize an important client of the office, they bowled all the way out in Glendale, reserved the last four alleys each week, and wore orange nylon jackets emblazoned on the back in electric blue—*The Lifers*.

Waiting out a red light, Ron mentally assessed how

many blocks before he'd get off this one-storied, colorless street; blobs of neon retelling an identical story of tacos, hot dogs, whirling tubs of fried chicken, Swiss-chaleted pancakes. Franchise Heaven, he thought. The thunder of the alley was still in his ears and the hinges of his jaws ached from "team spirit." His throat, fortunately, was only slightly raw. He was learning to save it. The first time bowling he had lost his voice for three days. Now, once the evening got under way, all he did was mouth each chorused yell and let the others supply the noise.

He wondered what the others got out of the bowling. Kemper's enjoyment was obvious, slapping asses —anybody's, male or female—at every spare or strike. And his deadly humor tonight, horsing around with the two bowling balls at his crotch ("Hey, any a'you broads wanna ball?"). Lucky for Kemper that he produced as much business as he did or he'd be out on the street in the morning. Ron could still see Mr. Meader's contorted face as Mrs. Meader, hysterical with laughter, hobbled her way, tight-thighed, to the ladies' room.

Being with the office family for sixteen straight hours was a damned imposition. A fringe benefit he could do without. It was a relief to be in the car alone. To have Monday done with.

Cautiously, he checked rear- and side-view mirrors before making a lane change and was disturbed at the tension he read in his face. Did he look forty? Over the edge. . . ? He touched where his hair was receding slightly. Barely any gray. He'd never go bald; he was sure of that. His belt had been unbuckled and the top button of his pants released ever since he got in the car. Between the red and green lights he took all the pledges of the sedentary brotherhood: diet, jog, go to the gym. They could diet together, he and Geegee. Do them both good.

GOLDEN STATE FREEWAY, North, loomed just ahead like a ribbon on a Christmas package. The hairpin turn to the on ramp slowed him and his headlights played over the graffiti on the concrete abutment like a spotlight

2

following a star performer. *Motherfucker.* He'd have to remember never to bring Geegee this way. Smut like that drove her up the wall.

He picked up speed and melted into the red and white contrails of the night. The freeway lifted him tree high and swept him past Griffith Park and Forest Lawn. He rolled down his window, inviting the wind to wash away the stale smell of smoke that clung to him, and he thought of the laughing girl in the next alley who'd kept dropping her ball into his gutter (deliberately?) and wondered if he'd find her in that same alley when next they bowled. It would be just his luck for Geegee to decide to come along with him next week. . . . That thought came and went without taking up residence.

The wind was swinging the hanger that held his dress shirt and suit jacket like a pendulum, so he closed the window and turned on the radio. A lonely saxophone out of the thirties wailed it had no place to go.

He did. It was good to be going home.

George Brent had left and Bette Davis was going upstairs to die alone. Geegee had the pack of tissues poised for the first flow over the spillway when the siren severed her concentration. A stab of anxiety impelled her out of the bed to turn down the sound. *Listening . . . always listening when he wasn't home.* Almost one o'clock and there seemed to be a night wail of disaster every few minutes.

Geegee was no fan of Monday nights either. There were only so many things you could do to fill the hours, and her bedside table was a still-life testament that she had done them all. In the clutter of magazines, dog biscuits and overflowing ashtray were her hormone face creams, hair rollers, used wads of cotton for separating the toes for pedicure, curdled coffee in a cup, and a few crumbs left over from early evening munching.

She hovered momentarily by the set, the chill of the siren in her bones. Alone like this, the room always

3

seemed too big, the corners too dark, the sounds too echoed. Aubie twitched on the floor, running in a dream. Duchess moaned a little. Geegee hungered for a cigarette but wasn't about to cross the dark house for a fresh pack. She thought of emptying the ashtray before he got home, but her image in the mirror stole her mind away. Some people used to say she looked like Rita Hayworth. She could always see it. The hair. The body. True, she was a little top-heavy, but her legs were certainly as good. She drew the sheer nightgown skintight, her hands moving over the full breasts and down the extra pounds that rounded her hips and belly. Gravity had extracted no toll from her, but as a precautionary measure she stood on her head in the corner, the nightgown falling in folds over her face as the siren bled out of earshot. When she turned the sound back up, Bette Davis was already dead, and *damn*, she had missed it.

She got into the big bed, stepping over the two dogs on her way, touching each a kiss good-night. *Wasn't that sweet, Aubie's head nestled against his mother's?* In the darkness, Geegee settled into the caress of the pillow, wondering if Rita Hayworth had put on any weight?

She didn't sleep; couldn't—ever—till he got home.

At the first rasping groan of the gates, she was anxiously peering out through the drapes. *It had to be him, who else could it be?* Yet she had no more control over the panic that welled in her at the gates whining open than she had over the thudding of her pulse. Headlights arcing through the living room sent her hurrying back to bed—door closed, night light out—before he turned off the ignition.

Home. . . . Now there was a four letter word you could live with. The night wind in the towering sycamores that formed a canopy over Ron covered the sound of his footsteps as he walked back, closing first one protesting gate, then the other. Time and rust and earth tremors had given the heavy hinges the arthritic creaks of age and the querulous voice of an ancient sentry deploring the need to move. The gates, hung from thick white-adobe walls, now illegal in height but permitted to stand in privilege, were wrought iron in the design of twisted garlands of roses, some leaves now missing, most of the blooms now rusted to death, and gowned with a chicken-wire apron that scraped the asphalt. The wire had been placed there to keep Aubie in when he was a puppy. It was still there, over seven years later, on both sets of gates that began and ended the broad circular driveway.

Like a dowager in a laundromat, the house stood, in its final subdivision, surrounded by the ordinary. Once it had been the ranch of a movie star; how it distressed Geegee to have to explain to people that it had been built by Judge Hardy when they asked, "Who's Lewis Stone?" His crest was still above the massive, carved front door. Geegee would never let it be painted out. Never.

Before turning the key, Ron stood for a moment on the broad, bougainvillaea-covered veranda and fantasized himself the *patrón* of this stately, aging Mexican-colonial hacienda. Then he went inside, noting, as always, the peeling paint and the broken shutter.

The cavernous, cathedral-ceilinged living room received him. Dull amber pools of light on highly polished pegged-mahogany floors, welcoming red on red of rugs and couches, absorbed his fatigue. Big as the house was for just the two of them, there was stability here. Permanence. And, as Geegee said the first time they saw it, "Thank God we won't hear the neighbors flush their toilets."

"Zat you, baby?"

"I'm home, doll," he called to the sliver of light that slipped under the master bedroom door.

Geegee, propped on one elbow, smile sleepy and appealing, pursed a kiss in his direction as he came into

5

the room. He smacked it back and gave his attention to Aubie, who was jumping up on him. Duchess, creaking to aged feet, lumbered over to be petted.

"Sorry I woke you, didn't mean to be so late."

"Oh, is it late?" Through an elongated yawn, she turned the clock to face her. "I fell asleep early."

Ron hooked the hanger that held his dress shirt and suit jacket over the top of the heavy door to keep it out of Aubie's reach and peeled off his bowling jacket, dropping it onto the bed, all the while fending off the dogs. "Good boy . . . yes, Duchess, good old girl . . . come on, Aubie . . . easy . . . down. . . ." The old female moved obediently off to her pallet, but Aubie kept nudging with his head, circling and slapping with his metronome tail.

"Cut it, Aubie. Cut it."

"Here, sweetie, come to mommy . . ." Geegee baby-talked the dog to her. "Is your daddy being cross to you 'cause he didn't win tonight?"

"Nobody wins, not till the playoffs." Ron, sitting down to remove his bowling shoes, found a knot in one of the laces. "Liability's in the lead, Premiums and Billing tied for second, we're trailing. The dogs been out? I want to get to bed."

But sleep was out of the question. Geegee wanted to talk. She was sitting upright, scooching backward against the headboard for support, tucking the blanket under her armpits; the feigned drowsiness disappeared, gone.

"What'ja do all day, hon?"

"Geegee," he pleaded, "I've got to get some sleep."

"Don't I deserve some consideration? You're gone all day, I'm here alone all night."

"Once a week, only once a week . . ."

"I haven't heard my own voice all day. . . ."

"You called me twice at the office."

"That's not talking."

"Okay." He was a graceful loser. "Let's talk."

"Did'ja have fun tonight?"

6

He shrugged his indifference. "Um . . . when did you take the dogs out last?"

"I didn't."

He took them out, waited for them, and on the way back brought Geegee a cup of tea, and sat back on the bed to worry the knot in his shoelace.

"Here, use a bobby pin," she suggested, noting that he'd had his hair trimmed. At noon, he told her, stealing fifteen minutes from the fellowship lunch.

"Get me my scissors."

He began the strip-mining operation of searching for the scissors in the drawer of her dressing-room table. "You sure they're in here?"

"Sure I'm sure."

There were ancient emery boards, hardened, spilled nail polish from nude to crimson, detachable garters from girdles long ago garbage dumped and serving as fill for well manicured public golf courses. "Geegee, there are no scissors here."

"Never mind, sweetie." She'd found them underneath her copy of *Mademoiselle* beside the bed. "Come, sit down. Sit closer. . . ." He inched backward toward her, tilting his chin down. With practiced habit, she began to trim the offending hairs at the neckline.

"What're the prizes? Did you find out?"

"For what?"

"The bowling."

"First is a weekend in Vegas for two."

She made a face. "Vegas? We've been. Now if it was Hawaii . . ."

Hawaii or Timbuktu, he'd never won anything in his life, why should things start getting different now? As she snipped away his barber's indiscretions, they shared their day. She told him of the prizes on *The New Price Is Right*, and he gave her his highlights: what he'd had for dinner; how one of the elevators in the building got stuck and when they finally got the two people that were in it, out, the woman had the man arrested; a résumé of his evening (leaving out Kemper and his balls and the obscenity on the concrete wall); and the office talk about a merger.

"You won't lose your job?" was her first concern.

"No, no . . . a merger'll probably even mean more money."

She hula'd in bed. "Waikiki, that's for me."

He told her it was still in the talking stages and not to go making reservations. She smoothed his hair and felt satisfied with her barbering. Duchess, trying for a comfortable spot, moaned. "She wouldn't eat her biscuit," Geegee reported her concern.

"Did you eat?" he asked.

"Can a' chili."

"I can't leave you alone, just can't leave you alone."

"I made *num-num* and played hide the box, but I just couldn't get her to eat."

Ron picked up the dog biscuits and got down on his knees. "Come on, Duchess . . . num-num, num-num-num . . ." The old dog surveyed the hard, dry thing that the man seemed to find so delectable, and turned away. "You try it with milk?" he asked of Geegee.

"You know milk gives her diarrhea."

Ron adjusted the heating pad across the bony back. "Getting old there, Duchess."

"Don't say old to her!" It was a crisp reminder he'd broken the house rule. "She's only fourteen."

"Fifteen."

"No . . ." a lost year bringing to Geegee the same chill as the siren in the night. Ron was concentrating on the futile task of bringing some order to the bedside table.

"What else did you eat?" he wanted to know.

"Can't be fifteen," she insisted. "We got her after we moved to this house. That was . . ."

"Sixteen years next March." His memory was always irritatingly exact. "She's almost sixteen." He moved the cigarette butts around in the ashtray like the beads of an abacus. "I see you smoked your dessert."

8

"I get nervous," she snapped.

"If you don't want me to go bowling, say so." His voice came back to her above the flushing of water as he emptied and wiped out the ashtray.

"All right, don't go bowling." *If he was going to be snotty and throw the years around.*

"You know I can't not go. I have to go."

"Did I ever say to you, don't go? Did I ever stop you from a night out?"

"What the hell," he said, "it's only once a week. Now I don't want this ashtray dirtied again tonight," he admonished, returning it to the table and sitting back on the bed to dump used tissues and cottons into the wastebasket. "But you eat next time. . . ." There were bristles of loose hair itching the back of his neck.

As his T-shirt came off over his head, she patted him on the stomach. "Well . . . what're we getting here? A little pottie?"

"What? Pot?" The offense brought him to his feet, tightening his rectus abdominis. Displaying triceps and biceps to the mirror. A latter-day Adonis. "Where . . . what pot? No . . . I'm in great shape. You should'a seen me tonight . . ." In an exaggerated arc he hurled the imaginary bowling ball. "*VROOM* . . . hot as a pistol . . ." and felt her eyes on him, in critical appraisal.

"You had a good time tonight."

"Well . . . not really . . ." and immediately a tinge of guilt veiled his enthusiasm.

"I get the feeling that you go for this whole cornball bit."

"Well, no. . . ." He could hear his failure to discriminate between apology and explanation, and hated it. "You know what happens . . . you get there, get warmed up, have a coupla beers . . ."

"And look over the BB's."

He felt himself tense. "What's that supposed to mean, Geej?"

"Broad behinds."

9

"Oh. I thought you meant Big Boobs."

"Don't be vulgar."

She puckered a little air kiss, hinting for a cigarette by digging into an empty pack. No dice, he told her, and sat back down on the bed, to stuff his shoes into the bowling bag. She scrutinized him as he did, sniffing audibly at his bowling jacket, which she now held in her hands, and informed him he wasn't fooling her; she knew he had a girl stashed.

"Wha—?"

"I'm broad-minded, baby. I'm not gonna toss you outa the house. Where'd you really go tonight, hmm? You might as well tell Geegee. . . . Hmm. . . ?"

When Geegee played it cute like this it always made him squirm. "I said I went bowling; I went bowling . . ." and wished he could keep it from sounding like a lie.

"This isn't your cologne. I know your smell." She held the bowling jacket out to him, the smiling prosecutor presenting incontrovertible evidence. He took it, feeling trapped, immediately aware that the heavy musky odor wasn't his scent, and for the moment he foundered, with no answers. "Oh, sure . . ." in relief, finally, "Kemper's wife . . ." explaining that Joe Kemper's wife had worn it for a while, that the air-conditioning system at the alley had been on too high and Mrs. Kemper had gotten cold and he'd offered his jacket. Geegee's face showed no change of expression. Was she just going to let him hang? "Well you met her, Geegee—the office picnic? Denise. . . ?"

"The one with the hairy armpits?"

The laughter relaxed him. "God, Geej, the things you remember." She stuck out one bare foot and nudged him.

"Had you goin' there, didn't I?"

The foot nudged again. Insistent. He took it in his hands, fingers rhythmic on the high arch, the short crooked toes. "I don't like you to stay home alone every Monday. Why don't you come with me next time?"

"You know how I love the smell a'sweat."

10

"It's not that bad, you'll enjoy yourself. There were several women there tonight beside the teams. Mrs. Meader was there."

Her toes curled, her eyes rolled under the closed lids in enjoyment of the foot massage.

"Wives, girlfriends . . ." he expanded.

"Now it all comes out. You have got a Monday girlfriend . . ." Her voice was a contented purr and he knew now it was a game.

"What d'you mean, a girl. . . ?" he played back. "Girls . . . in triplicate. You are talking to Joe Stud."

"Well Joe Stud better get his beauty sleep." She peeked through one lazy eye. "She good-lookin', your girl? Better-lookin' than me?"

He studied the smooth oval face framed by luxuriant dark-red hair flared out on the white pillow. "Baby," he said, "you are the best-lookin' broad around." He tucked her foot under the blanket, leaned over and kissed her on the forehead. "I'm going to bed." Gathering up bowling gear and the hanger that held his still uncrushed suit jacket and dress shirt, he headed for his own room. "Come on, Aubie." The dog followed him.

"Good night, Mother," he said as he went through the far door.

"Good night, Sonny."

2

AUBIE stood patiently by, waiting for Ron to remove the spread from the twin bed that was his and throw the old sleeping bag over it, then jumped up and settled down while Ron completed his nightly catechism: hanging away the suit of the day, brushing his teeth, washing himself and his sox, putting a fresh pair into his shoes for tomorrow.

There were five suits in his closet. He wore them in rotation—dark blue, blue-gray, gray, dark gray and black. Every year he bought one (off the rack) and retired one, giving it to Goodwill and taking the acceptable tax deduction. The gray had the faintest chalk stripe, the dark blue the new, wider, lapels; the three oldest had been let out an inch in the waistline. He wore black shoes, white shirts and narrow ties with all of them, saving his cordovans and vari-colored sneakers for casual clothes on the weekends.

As he hung away the bowling jacket, the hint of Denise's cologne took him back to the alley. Had she actually groped him when they were all crowded together in the booth having their second beer? A tight band formed across his eyebrows for the moment, pressing into his conscience that she was Kemper's wife and Kemper was his friend. But the fast flow of blood concentrated in his groin, the current so strong it swept him into the bathroom. Behind the locked door, he relived a memory of a day months back: The woman who worked on the fourth floor of his building—Joanne?—whose car wouldn't start, whom he had helped, finally had to drive home—no, Janelle—hadn't gone a block when she had his fly unzipped and her hand inside his trousers, quoting Kate Millett.

Quieted, he came out of the bathroom, hung the blue-gray suit on the closet door hook ready for tomorrow. Tuesday. Unaware he was destined not to wear it. He would wear Friday's black instead. A fracture in his life-style that would never heal properly.

He was in deep sleep, lying on his stomach, his breathing full and measured. Trembling fingers digging into his bare back shocked him awake. He turned, half rising, startled, confused, into Geegee's arms. She clutched desperately at him.

"Sonny . . . oh, my God, Sonny, she's dying . . . Duchess . . . dying . . ."

I did everything as though I had rehearsed it. As though death and I had an arrangement. Never expecting it to be so bloody. All those towels, reddened, while she hemorrhaged. Geegee couldn't even call the vet. I had to do that, too. She just kept saying, "Aubie is losing his mommy, losing his mommy." My voice was completely detached on the phone. I keep remembering that. Why was it? Why was it like that when I loved her?

Burdened with the limp, wrapped, life-ebbing body of the heavy dog in his arms, the distance seemed greater than his strength could endure. Ron kicked off his hindering house slippers, leaving them, twin island specks in the sea of blacktop behind the pet hospital. Dr. Camden held the emergency door open for him. It swung closed and the light was gone from the parking lot. The

13

only sound in the indifferent night was Aubie whining. Straining to follow his mother into the hospital, a place he was normally terrified to enter.

Geegee shivered. Underneath the heavy coat, the sheer tricot nightgown, usually a sensual pleasure, felt clammy. She dragged Aubie back into the car and sat with him.

"Your mommy's going to be all right, we just know that, got to hold a good thought. Sonny is going to come out in a minute and tell us Duchess is going to get all better and get his house slippers—wasn't that funny, leaving his house slippers?—then we'll all go home and come back in the day and get your mommy. . . ."

Aubie believed her. He sat, leaning against her, but still he trembled. There was a radio somewhere in the distance. Geegee's distress reached for the sanctuary of the occasional clear note. Staring ahead through the windshield, mouth slightly open to receive a word that would clue her into recognition of the tune, her attention was drawn to the pseudo-Scotch-highland towers of the decrepit motel across the street. Wee Highland Inn, that's what it used to be called. The Wee Highland Inn. Seeing it was broker to the past. They had eaten there one Sunday when Sonny was small and a bus ride out from Hollywood was a full afternoon's excursion. He wore (and she remembered how he struggled against it) his little blue long-pants suit with the fancy round-collared shirt like the one Freddie Bartholomew wore in *Little Lord Fauntleroy*. They had eaten the specialty of the house. Hag-bag-something. Whatever, it tasted rotten.

She watched two people slip into a car in the motel parking area. *Mr. and Mrs. Smith, no doubt.* The car entered Ventura Boulevard, lights still out. *Serve 'em right to get a ticket. Bums, sleeping around.*

A sudden glare from the hospital doorway exploded her distraction. Ron was stepping back into his slippers.

"There's a chance, Geegee," he told her as she ran to him, desperate for reassurance.

14

"He said that, Sonny? He really said that?"

"He's giving her a transfusion, but you've got to remember she's old."

"Don't give me old! I read about a dog lived to be twenty-two. She's only fourteen—"

"Almost sixteen."

"Fifteen! They've got new drugs—"

"Geegee, the doctor knows all about—"

"You go right back in there and tell him no matter what it costs—"

Don't press me, Mother. Don't push me. I don't want to have the trouble again. I'm telling you everything there is to tell. I did not lose it. I wasn't careless. It was in my gym locker, somebody broke into it. I know I'll never get another glove I know we haven't got the money I know you worked hard for it I know you try to do the best you can for me I know you're all I've got in the world I know you're counting on me I know I'm the only one you can trust I can't breathe, Mother, I can't breathe please please forgive me. . . .

"Sonny, you don't act like it matters."

"It matters." He squeezed the words past the tightening vise in his chest.

"He said it? The doctor said it? He really said it? A chance?"

"All things—considered—it's"— the constricting blood vessels choked off speech— "possible." The word escaped in a wheeze. Geegee dug his pocket nebulizer out of her purse and thrust it at him.

"You're not lying to me? You know Geegee does not like lies—"

"My God, Mother"— it was a plea through desperate inhalations as he pumped adrenalin mist into his throat, surrendering to gasping silence until there was the relief he struggled for—"have I ever lied to you?" She tucked the nebulizer back into her purse. "He told me she's got

15

a chance. That's all I know. A chance. He's the doctor. Who'd know better?"

Aubie told them when the moment came. He knew, the instant it happened. Even before Dr. Camden came out to tell them she was gone, Aubie let out a long howl of mourning.

They took him with them to the funeral. It was only right he should go. She was his mother.

It was a hot day for November. The sun, refusing to accommodate to their sorrow, shone relentlessly. Geegee responded to the occasion with no earrings, a touch of makeup, and the only black dress she owned, which was three seasons tight. Annoyed at not being able to find her shields, she tucked Kleenex into her armpits. Ron wore his Friday black suit, carefully hanging the jacket on the car hook so as not to wrinkle it. Aubie, who normally spent travel time with his head out the window, embracing the wind, rode the whole distance lying on the back seat.

"Simple." Ron had made his wishes known over the telephone. "As simple as possible . . ." saying no to an insulated casket. And no, not lined. Just a simple box. A return to the earth. "No, no flowers. . . . Please, Geegee, I'm on the telephone—"

"Tell him no cremation, I won't have cremation."

"Look, do you want to talk to the cemetery, or do you want to let me handle it?" One hand over the mouthpiece, he zipped her into the groaning seams while she held her breath for the terminal inches.

"I couldn't stand the thought of just being ashes . . ."

"All right, then, let me handle it. Yes," he replied back into the phone, not realizing until later when presented with the bill that he had agreed to sixty-five dollars extra for a permanent plastic remembrance wreath and perpetual graveside care.

"Fourteen years of love—"

"Sixteen, sixteen!"

"And you'd just dump her in the garbage."

"No, Geegee, that's not true."

"You told the doctor just get rid of her."

"No, I told him just take care of it. But if you want to do it this way, fine, fine."

"Then why don't you show something? You didn't love her, it comes out now, you didn't love her."

"I loved her, Geegee, I loved her. Who brought her home in the first place? Me. I did."

He turned left from the house to Burbank Boulevard, then right . . .

What the hell did they want with a dog? was Geegee's greeting, he remembered, when he first carried the handful that had been Duchess into the house. *She'll ruin the rugs. Can you imagine the stink? Flies? I'm not going to clean up all that dog do . . .*"

Left again on Coldwater Canyon . . .

"*I never had a doggie, you know that, Sonny? This is the first doggie I ever had in my life . . .*"

"*Two weeks ago you didn't want her, Geegee . . .*"

"*I didn't say that, I never said that, Sonny. Would I say that about my sweet puppy, Mommy's baby. . . . Buy her a heating pad, y'hear, I don't want her catching cold nights. . . .*"

Ron looked over at Geegee, her head pressed against the car window, eyes tightly closed, and wondered if she remembered what happened back then like he did. He got onto the freeway and into the fast lane. One-oh-one all the way. The same path they had traveled together so many times, so many Sundays: Solvang for Danish pancakes, Carpinteria for a wade in the shallow waters of "the world's safest beach," Santa Barbara for brunch in the centuries-old El Paseo and a browse at the open-air art shows, Ojai just to sit in the park, Buellton for pea soup and wine tasting in the cellar . . .

This flow of thought curtained any need to analyze his detachment at his first personal experience with death.

Geegee was right not to wear black, he decided. Black

17

drained the pink from her skin, dulled the glow of her dark-red hair. That dress was all wrong for her. When things settled down, he'd ask her to get rid of it. Too short, made her look all legs. If he were to tell her that her head rested on an extra chin, she would sit up straight. And pull in her abdomen. He pulled in his. Drawn, that's how she looked. Walled off by sorrow. He wanted to reach out, comfort her, but the Thousand Oaks off ramp rushed unexpectedly at him. Not totally trusting the rearview mirror, he swiveled his head for a look back and made the abrupt lane change, braking to diminish his speed. Only then did he become aware of how fast he had been driving.

The approach to Assisi Haven was a two-lane road bordered by sentinel eucalyptus trees. Planted by the padres, they had so far survived progress, but the bulldozers could be heard growling at their heels. The gateposts, structured between a jumble of scrub oak, were crested by dog statues painted in lifelike colors, long faded, leaf-stained and chipped. The parking lot, where Ron's Fury III came to a halt, lay beneath the extended, benevolent arms of an enormous plaster Saint Francis surrounded by his animal friends. Frozen, it seemed to Ron, as though in perpetual audition for Disney's.

As he helped Geegee from the car and fastened the leash onto Aubie's collar, the cemetery owners, man and wife, came smiling out of the crematorium to greet them. Sixtyish, suntanned from grave-tending, exuding heartiness and welcome, they informed that they were the Fretters, call them Belle and Chester, everybody did, but no live pets in the cemetery. However, in view of Geegee's imminent hysteria, in Aubie's case they would make an exception. Since the deceased was his mother.

Please follow.

They led the way upward between gravesites. "She'll be happy with us, we're dog people . . ." around plaques and markers: *We'll miss you, Faithful Buddy . . . Our friend Fritz . . . Run in peace, Miss Pookie*, mentioning, in the

event the Gohdieners had a cat, that a new Feline Haven
had just been completed on the downside of the second
hill away. But they drew the line on monkeys, Chester
Fretter said, and other exotics some people were getting
involved with nowadays—unquestionably a result of our
muddled foreign policy. As he spoke, his eyes savored
a rivulet of sweat traveling down Geegee's throat into the
shadowed interval between her breasts.

They *were* dog people. Ron recognized that. Chester
Fretter was just that: a chesterfretter. From the tip of his
nose to the end of his tail, the type people felt no loyalty
toward and simply left behind when they moved. Belle-
fretter was a different breed. Ron felt certain she bit her
husband whenever he annoyed her.

Climbing the hill, Ron's eyes were level with Belle Fretter's ample behind. With each step, it rippled. It became
a challenge to read the label. A step up on the right foot
and "Levi Strauss & Co." disappeared into a fold of flesh.
Left foot up, "San Francisco, Cal.—Original—Riveted."
They all paused for breath. Geegee's stiletto heels knifing
into the sod tortured her calf muscles. She removed her
shoes and walked stocking-footed the rest of the way to
the hillside grave with the view.

"May she rest in peace," and Belle Fretter was on her
way back down the hill. Chester intruded into their sorrow just long enough to press his bill deftly into Ron's
hand with the condolence handshake, imparting the
information that it could be paid on the way out by check,
Master Charge, B of A, Express or Diners.

The freshly turned earth that covered Duchess gave off
a warm, rich smell.

They stood alone, the three mourners, their mood
renegade to the brightness of the day. Aubie's ears, head
and tail hung down; the genes of some distant
bloodhound in his ancestry contributing to his baleful
look. Ron was aware of Geegee's voice muttering frag-
ments of prayers from the revolving door of religions
they had gone through.

19

"There is no Life, Truth, Intelligence nor Substance in Matter . . ."

His concentration was on a worm. Long, glistening, frenetically trying to find its way through the disturbed earth back into the safety of eternal darkness. His memory projected a childhood dream—of a boy baiting a hook curled from a safety pin on knotted-together string, to go fishing in a river seen only in coloring books.

"Rest in the bosom of Jesus . . ."

Geegee, sinking to her knees, sobbing, rendered Ron's memory illegible. Her tears flooded his eyes but occasioned no real sorrow in him. He puzzled about that. He had not lied to her. He had loved Duchess. When she was nine and they found out she was pregnant from the hole in the fence, *Geegee* had said get rid of her. *He* hadn't. She bore just one pup. One time. And that made Aubie special.

"Hail Mother, Mary of Grace . . ."

He almost laughed. But the supplicant was unaware of having misquoted and transposed the words. Geegee's hands clawed the earth. He felt a wave of pity.

"Come, Geegee . . ." He touched her tenderly. "We'd better go. Come, Mother. . . ."

Without protest, she permitted him to raise her to her feet. There was acceptance in her, and calm, as Ron turned her from the grave for the descent.

It was Aubie who resisted, who was reluctant to leave. Ron tugged the leash, but Aubie held back.

"Poor baby . . ." Geegee understood completely. "He wants to have one last time with his mother . . ."

Ron studied Aubie as man has studied the beast from the beginning of time, mazing at the mystique that separates them. Hadn't Aubie been the one to sense the exact moment of Duchess's death, while they, the reasoning species, clung to feeble, fallible hope? Ron tentatively tugged the leash once again. The dog was unyielding, so he unhooked it. Putting a protective arm around Geegee, he led her away. Leaving Aubie alone to solemnize this last communion. For a moment the dog just stood there. Head drooping. Sniffing. Then he raised his head, looked around at his immediate surroundings. And lifted his leg.

Requiescat in pace, Duchess.

Ron caught it out of the corner of his eye. He felt his chest cave in, the implosion draining all the blood from his face. The strangling sound that escaped him penetrated Geegee's grief. Her head swiveled: Was Sonny having an attack?

"No, no, watch your step, it's steep here, keep your eye on the path . . ."

He couldn't let her see Aubie's act of desecration. It would destroy her.

But he found himself drawn back to the blasphemy. As they descended, he stole a second look. Nothing had changed. No abruption of the act. Aubie had a large bladder.

On his own mother . . . my God . . .

Ron had no clear memory of the drive home. Lane transitions, freeway interchange, he took them all and saw nothing but the dog with his leg in the air.

And there he sits, arrogant sonofabitch, curled against Geegee. Moaning, accepting her stroking and petting as though he deserved it. *As though he deserved it?* The instant he authored the thought, logic challenged it. He's a dog, just a plain ordinary dog. Male dogs pee whenever they want to, just marking off territory. Ron had read enough to know about that. Every time he took Aubie for a walk, didn't he leave his mark on every tree and post he could get to? Just a dog, for all his supernatural howling . . .

Ron felt the chaos within him subsiding by the time they got home. Why then, he wondered, was he having such trouble opening the gates? As though he'd forgotten the formula. They were taller than he by more than a foot and sagging with their own weight. You have to grasp both sides, he reminded himself, and pull slightly

21

toward you, then shove hard backward to dislodge the heavy iron latch. Once you had the two parts balanced equidistant on their hinges, it was easy to grab the latch, raise it, and thrust them wide open. Yet here he was standing, fumbling, as though he hadn't done it thousands of times before.

"Sonny . . ." Her voice came from the car, faint and plaintive, "I'm sticky and hot and tired. . . ."

The gates reluctantly yielded up their secret. Swung open in dissonant screech. With the metal supports that would keep them open flipped down and secured, he drove the semicircle to the front of the house. As he reached to open the car door for her, the sun drilled a shaft through an opening in the trees and landed on his watch. Just past one. But Geegee, weak and pale, leaning on him for support, eroded any hope of getting to the office. (She'd gained more weight than she admitted. He'd have to get her back on the exercycle.)

"You didn't close the gates." An accusation, making him feel like a negligent child. But also a reassurance. The subpoena in her voice held promise of recovery from the tragic events of the morning.

On the way to close the gates, he talked to himself. "Aubie doesn't know who's buried on that hill. How could he? Hell, he probably never even knew she was his mother."

The rationalization didn't stop the acid that was eating at the lining of his stomach.

He prepared her favorite soup—cream of mushroom—heating it to just under hot, adding a liberal dash of sherry exactly the way she always liked it, and carried it to her bed.

"I couldn't get it down, sweetheart." She looked up at him from beneath the icebag balanced on the bridge of her nose. "You haven't had a thing in your stomach all day, Sonny, you eat it, baby, go on, don't waste it. . . ." Her cold hand touched his, "It's good for you. Go on. . . ."

Obediently, he swallowed a few spoonfuls and carried the bowl back to the kitchen where he poured it down the drain. How could he tell her, today of all days, that he'd always hated cream of mushroom soup with sherry? He took a teaspoon of baking soda in a glass of water.

Aubie had followed the soup to the kitchen.

"Get away from me!"

Ron tiptoed through the house, drawing all the drapes, closing out the late day sunlight that offended Geegee's mourning, assuring himself that his anger at Aubie was temporary, had no meaning at all, that Aubie was, after all, just a dog.

As Geegee surrendered to the Nembutol, he sat out in the backyard. Correctly, architecturally, he knew he should think of it as the *plaza* as Geegee wanted him to, but to him it was always the backyard.

The wings of the low, sprawling house surrounded him. The last of the sun he would see that day lingered for a bit on the red tile roof then slid away. With the retreat of the sun came the abrupt chill of evening. Still he stayed outside. Sitting on the low adobe wall that encased the water fountain that didn't work, observations came and went in his mind. The overgrown camellia bush was getting ragged, scraping against the windows. This light was kinder to the house, making peeling paint seem character rather than neglect. He felt the nag of guilt that he was letting the place go. The palm tree hung with dead leaves. He wondered if it was true that rats lived in palm trees. He'd never seen any, but it would have been a suicidal rat indeed to challenge Duchess. For all her walleyed gentleness, she had been a tough one. Aubie, lying over there on the walkway, absorbing the last of the day's heat in the tiles, would run from a cat, let alone a rat. Touch him wrong, he'd yipe. Ron had his own opinion of that, although he'd never told Geegee. Aubie was retarded. Seven years old and still an infant.

The dog got up and came to him as though he had been called. Pressed his wet nose against Ron's hand.

23

"What're you after?" he asked the dog. "Want me to tell you what you did was right? You've come to the wrong man. Go on, get away." He kicked out at him. Didn't come close, but Aubie yiped. Backed away. Lay down by the door, studying his master. It was dark when Ron went into the house.

Geegee's face, in sleep, was always a marvel to him. This was his mother? This unlined face that at times could look younger than his own? Awake, there were definite arrows at the edges of her eyes, the faintest track of time trying to forge its way across her forehead. Angered, there were always sharp double parentheses bracketing tight-drawn lips. Asleep, there was only innocence. And vulnerability. Her mouth was slightly open. Her too-short upper lip, raised in delicate snore, gave the illusion she was about to laugh, to speak, to amuse. Like one of their games—
I'll only be a minute—
Minute? That's a dance—
No, that's a minuet—
Minuet? That's those buildings in Russia—
No, that's a minaret—
Minaret? That's how long I have to wait till you're ready.
He picked up the icebag from the floor, tucked her foot back underneath the covers, turned off the nightlight. But he could not turn off the image of the dog defiling the grave.

For the first time in memory he did not lay out his clothes for the morning. The last thing he saw before he closed his eyes was Aubie, across the room on the other twin bed—staring at him.

He wore his Tuesday suit on Wednesday.

3

"HEY, Gohdiener—" It could only be Kemper. Vocal cords thickened from yelling *Kill the umpire* and *Get up ya bum*. From the far end of the parking lot the voice rolled again, "Friend—" competing with pneumatic brakes of the Wilshire Boulevard bus disgorging its morning complement of secretaries and clerks to populate the glassed-steel towers; "Hey, goombah—" perforating the roar of the wrecking ball splintering the Victorian building down the block that had been built when the plan for L.A. had been horizontal and not vertical.

Ron's car had found its well-traveled way into the first available opening stenciled "Reserved for Meader Ins. Agcy." He was locking the door as Kemper steamrolled toward him, beefy linebacker legs running a constant tensile test on double knit pants, bulging briefcase hanging from a meaty hand.

Ron nodded Morning, how are you.

"Keep away from my wife," Kemper growled as they fell into step and synchronized their briefcases. "What're you tryna do, kill a good thing for me?"

A grunt. A nod. And Ron satisfied Kemper that he was with it, understood he was being put on.

"Took me ten years to break that French broad in. You go around openin' doors for her, givin' her jackets to

25

wear when her ass is cold, I gotta train her all over again. . . ."

With Kemper, he could coast until he got organized, until he got rid of the tension that sleep had failed to erase. Did it show on the outside? was his concern. Could Kemper detect that he wasn't the same man he'd been two days before? Would the others see through his calm and recognize he had searched the mirror this morning and could not find his face.

He had talked aloud the whole way in to the office, causing a few curious glances at stoplights. But what did he care for them? Had any of them opened their hermetically sealed capsules to ask, Who are you? Why are you?

He felt he had lost a link somewhere of an invisible chain and was floating, filled with the helium of doubt, feet off the ground. An inch. No more. Just enough to lose contact. What troubled him even more, he had difficulty concentrating on his confusion. Passing Hollywood Bowl, he made a mental note that Geegee wanted him to renew their season tickets. Crossing Hollywood Boulevard, it occurred to him he had never seen a drag queen with purple hair before, and it popped into his mind, I'd rather see than be one.

"Heard about your dog." Kemper's voice, like a drill bit, intruded. "Sorry."

"Thanks."

Kemper paid for the coffee at the catering truck even though it wasn't his turn. "It's rough, I know. Believe me, I know—" He impulsively laid a bear's paw on Ron, then withdrew it, self-conscious at sentiment, but in the privacy between two cars, he lifted the paper cup, well laced with cream and sugar, in memoriam. "Well, here's to him."

"Her."

"Yeah. Know just how you feel. They really get to you, don't they?"

Ron ordered a doughnut rather than talk about it, wondering if Kemper knew his middle button was hang-

26

ing by a thread. Kemper was going on about some pigeon he'd once owned.

"—Homing. I wasn't more'n ten at the time. We were still livin' in Missoura . . ."

Dropping the half-full paper cup and half-eaten doughnut into the wastecan didn't deter Kemper from pelting Ron with the depressing narrative as he walked along with him to the building. "Now that was a bird. Used to crap all over everything, but, boy, did I love him. He wasn't just a pound of feathers—" Impelled to share the pain of memory, he blocked Ron at the entrance. "Know what he knew? He knew my old man hated him."

"We're going to be late, Kemp—"

"In a crowd of twenty he'd pick him out—bulls' eye—pinpoint bombing ev'ry time . . ." Kemper's limpid blue eyes, incongruous with the rocky face, brimmed with tears. "My old man got even. Forced my mother to make soup outa him."

To Ron's relief, the closing doors of the crowded UP elevator rang down the curtain on this elegy.

"Never sell a man a policy. Only his wife—*on* the man." Kemper had evidently spotted some new female faces in the elevator and was fishing for clients, making his standard pitch to Ron. "I sold a twenty-five thousand dollar straight life on this one guy—" He'd repeated the story so many times it had grown hair. "He says to me, 'I don't need insurance,' but his wife and I got him signed, got him examined. Guy passes with flying colors, leaves the doctor's office, crosses the street, gets hit by a truck. Double indemnity. Now there's one little lady well taken care of. . . ."

How did he get away with it? As Kemper oozed aside for each departing female passenger, Ron appraised him. Personality, gamey (witness the two balls crotch gag at the bowling alley). Nose, too large, pitted, slightly off center; the result, he had told Ron on many occasions, of walking into a negative opinion years back in a Texas tavern;

27

always adding that he was only passing through, selling roofing and siding. His jaw was heavy, protruding. The gap in his front teeth, Ron felt certain, must give him trouble with his bite. Forehead, a shelf of bone with eyebrows gone rank and wiry.

It had to be his eyes, Ron concluded. As dependably clear-blue as the field in the flag. Oval, thickly lashed, they said Trust me, God bless America and Pay your premiums on time.

Ron was grateful he hadn't been decoyed by those eyes into sharing with Kemper his disturbance over Aubie's irreverence at the grave. And it had been on the tip of his tongue to ask, Do you think a grown male dog knows he has a mother?

Good morning, Mr. Gohdiener, morning . . . morning . . .
He nodded through the gauntlet of condolences from the reception room, passing the wall of framed photos of Rotary luncheons, of Xmas parties and office picnics, awards dinners for the million dollar club (Kemper always right there in front), photos of the bowling teams, along with their scores, and a table covered with loving cups waiting for the engraver's burin. (His name would never be cut into one of those, but of what possible use was a loving cup?) Through the gate into the general office, losing Kemper at the new girl's desk, but not before Kemper finalized his pigeon obituary. "To this day," he said to Ron as they parted, "to this day, I can't eat anything that flies."

Ruth was at her desk, as she always was. Not at the coffee maker, or coming out of the Little Girls' Room, as the secretaries liked to call it. Not combing her hair or putting on nail polish. But organized and ready, mail opened, a welcoming smile on her face.

"Good morning, Ruth."

"Good morning, Mr. G." His letters were slit, paper-clipped to their envelopes, and neatly arranged in the in basket. He reached for them and noticed her smile was misty. "I'm sorry about what happened, Mr. G., and I want you to know I express sympathy for the entire office."

"Why, thank you, Ruth."

"If there's anything—"

"That's very nice of you."

"Just ask me . . ."

He would, he assured her, he would. Once inside his own office, he closed the door and began to arrange his desk as he dialed. Correcting, with only minor resentment, the good intentions of the cleaning crew. (How many times had he left the note, *Don't touch desk.*) Pencils: erasers toward him, points away; shortest pencil to the left, graduating longer to the right; conveying to the waste basket any pencil less than a hand's length.

"Hello . . ." Her voice came to him, thin and faint.

"Geegee?"

"Yes, sweetheart."

"Are you up?"

"No . . ."

The vital Geegee who beamed at him from the barely retouched photograph on his desk was in sharp contrast to the frail sound on the phone. Her chin rested on the palm of her hand, lips parted in a smile caught just this side of a delighted laugh, eyes reflecting some secret pleasure. Duchess and Aubie occupied the other half of the double frame. *At a happier time* . . . The phrase caught his imagination, realizing how often he'd read it in the newspapers but never applied it to himself before.

"Geegee, it's over. You can't bring her back . . ." He pressed the phone to his ear. "What did you say? I can't hear you . . . Geegee . . . are you crying. . . ?"

She was actually choking on a fragment of toast. Caught in her throat, it took a good deal of hawking to keep it from going up into her sinus cavity. "I'm all right, dear, don't worry about me . . ." She was propped up in bed, indulging her grief with calories. The tray bore the remnants of a hearty breakfast.

"Well I do worry about you. . . ." His voice came to her, heavy with concern. "Now you've got to get up, Geegee."

"Poor Aubie . . ." She sniffed again to dislodge the troublesome crumb.

"You *are* crying. . . ."

"You should see the poor baby. . . ." Her look caressed the dog, lying beside her on the bed, accepting tidbits of breakfast. "It just breaks my heart—he goes back and forth, back and forth over this whole house, looking for her—" Aubie licked off the last of the bacon and eggs from the plate, "looking for his mommy. . . ." As she nuzzled the dog she became aware there was no response emanating from the phone.

"Sonny?" Questioning. *"Sonny."* Sharp. "Did you hear me?"

"I heard you, Mother."

"—looking for his mommy." Did she detect resentment in his voice? "Sonny?"

"Yes, Mother, yes."

"What's the matter?"

"Nothing."

"Nothing? You lose a faithful friend and you say nothing?"

"Geegee, I'm in the office, what can I say—?"

"You're in your own office, aren't you?"

"Look, I've got a lot of work—"

"Sonny . . . come home early."

"You know I can't, Geegee, I took off yesterday. Now please, for my sake—force yourself to eat something."

About to put the last bit of toast into her mouth, she felt ashamed at deceiving him. "I'm trying, hon," she said, controlling a slight burp, "I'll really try. Don't be late, please, don't be late." When she hung up she rationalized that some people mourn differently from others. She would not comb her hair all day or put on makeup or open the drapes.

She turned on TV. When the set warmed up, Barbara

30

Stanwyck was telling William Holden how lousy life had been to her. *Golden Boy!* Geegee guessed it immediately, and felt sorry the big quiz programs were gone because she felt she could answer all the questions about Hollywood.

The day was dismal for Ron. Never before had he been so aware of the sterility of his office. Walls covered with actuarial charts, metal file cabinets, metal desk, metal venetian blinds—one always raised annoyingly higher than the other. He got up and adjusted them. He and his tabulator were old friends, but this morning his fingers seemed to have forgotten the melody. The eraser ends of his pencils were getting more action than the graphite, and his mind would not stay with the charts.

From the frosted glass of his door his name reflected backwards to him . . . *reneidhoG C. R.* And his title, *yrautcA.* He experimented with the sound of it: "re-neid-hog . . . yoo-raut-ca."

Restive, he made several trips to the water cooler and a subsequent number of treks down the hall. He could never, somehow, call it the john as most of the guys did, or the can, as Kemper did. He had tried calling it the head, but since he had never owned a boat or been in the navy, that seemed an affectation.

Escaping the confines of his office had its penalty. People to whom he had barely ever nodded felt impelled to commiserate about his Loss. The new girl (he really should get better with names) caught him at the water cooler. Even as she saw him moving toward it, she abandoned her filing and zeroed in. She was dressed in red, white and blue. Her breasts preceded her like headlights on bright.

"Why, thank you," she said, accepting the water as he poured himself another.

"You're welcome."

"I'm glad this opportunity came up, Mr. Gohdiener," she pulled her sweater taut, accenting her assets, "because

I want to personally tell you how sympathetic I am." He nodded and drank. "I don't know what to say," she said. "What can you say at a time like this? I mean, it happens. In a way, you're lucky. She could have been a vegetable. This way she just died. Some people say pass on. I never do. Die is die." She was definite about that. "And I feel that people who aren't afraid to say the word—say it right out loud—DIE—they're the ones who know how to live, you know what I mean?"

As he stooped to pour himself another cupful he could see her through the burble of the cooler, her patriotic outline unfurled like a drunken flag. Through one rising bubble the breast nearest the bottle threatened to engulf him.

Geegee called twice that morning. The first time to say she had eaten. The second, just before noon. "Geegee, please, could you make it brief? Bring Aubie a what—?"

"A little present. Is that too much to ask? You of all people should understand what he's going through, losing a mother."

He told Geegee no. Definitely, unequivocally no. But on his lunch hour he was in the pet store just off Wilshire and Western, resisting the large, red, rubber fire hydrant. "But it's our most popular—" the clerk attested.

"I don't want it. Is that clear?"

Was that strained, high-pitched voice his? The staring customers seemed to think so. Unfortunately, there wasn't another pet shop for sixteen blocks. There he selected a dinosaur-sized rawhide bone and felt foolish asking the clerk to gift wrap it. He came back to the office famished, and had a Mounds bar from the machine for lunch.

The boss paid his solace call late in the afternoon.

"No, no, don't get up—" R. De Vere Meader came across the room in three strides of his long legs, hands extended as for a benediction. Ron found himself thinking Meader could have been an evangelist. "Do you know who was the subject of a two-and-a-half-hour discussion

last night in our executive sensitivity class? *You*, Ron."
Under the touch of Meader's well-manicured, paternal,
boneless hands, Ron listened, but his mind unreeled an
endless tape of trivia. *Meader's hands sweat. His face doesn't,
but his hands do. Never saw him actually sweat. Not here. Not
bowling, not at the office picnic last summer when it was ninety-
eight in the shade. Maybe he sweats in bed. Do you sweat in
bed, Mr. Meader?* Ron wondered what Meader would
answer if he heard him.

"And do you know what our industrial psychologist
said when I told him of your old dog's passing to the
other side?"

*And he never needs a haircut, or looks like he just got one.
How does he manage that?*

"He said, 'Any man who cares about his animal as you
demonstrated yesterday is *summa cum laude* in the demo-
graphics of the human equation.' "

*Or age . . . in all the years I've been here, not one more
gray hair or one extra pound. While I—* Ron tried to close
the disturbing door he'd just opened, but the years he'd
passed in this chair sat with him, broken down into
months, days, minutes. Like one of his charts on the wall.
And he was depressed.

"Good man, Ron. Proud to have you aboard."

"Thank you, Mr. Meader."

"Yes, indeed. Good man." *Why didn't he go? What more
was there to say?* "Thoughtful."

"Sir?"

Meader reached out and touched the gift-wrapped
package Ron had bought on his lunch hour.
"Thoughtful," he repeated, his fingers tracing the rib-
bons to the double picture frame on his desk. "How *is*
your mother?"

"Bearing up," Ron said, observing the small bubbles of
saliva appear at the corners of Meader's mouth as he
picked up Geegee's picture.

"Remarkable woman . . ." The sonofabitch was drool-
ing. "Remarkable." Meader put the picture down, but his

eyes lingered. "Well go on, talk it out. Get it off your chest."

For a moment, Ron couldn't imagine what he meant. "Oh . . . Duchess—" and realized he was already forgetting.

"Don't be shy. Every man cries. We're family here." It was an executive order.

"Well," Ron began reluctantly, "she was old. Quite old. When we went to bed she seemed all right—" Meader wasn't listening. He had gone back to Geegee's cleavage. "Her appetite wasn't too good, but other than that she was—"

"Yes, well, it happens that way." Meader's interest span had run its course. "You'll finish up the new pension plan for the cab company, right, Ron? We want that business. Condolences. . . ." And Meader left the room, leaving Ron feeling soured. Insignificant. He worked well past six finishing the chart.

All the end-of-day things he did by rote, but as he reached to put on his suit jacket he had a moment of fragmentation. What day was this? Wednesday? There should be a chalk stripe in the sleeve. There wasn't. It was Tuesday's blue-gray he was wearing. The whole day, and he hadn't noticed. That kind of thing just never happened to him. He computed the remedial possibilities. Go right to Thursday's suit tomorrow, but then Wednesday's would go unworn. And he'd already worn Friday's Tuesday. Hell, he'd just have to go to the end of the week and start over on Monday to try to get his life reorganized.

He was the only one in the down elevator, so no one else heard him say it. "Damn you, Aubie."

So went the day. *reneidhoG C.R. yrautcA*.

Geegee heard the gates open. On their first complaint she was out of bed, padding across to the kitchen.

Ron closed the gates and leaned against them. They were the moat, he the weary knight. They the *barranca*,

34

he the *vaquero*. The ring of wagons against the marauders. . . . If any in the office could tenant his mind,
they'd find themselves in a strange land. Sometimes even
he wandered too far in the corridors of thought and
found it a difficult road back: This garden deceives. The
hibiscus bloom and it's winter. The calendar says so. I've
turned forty. The calendar says so. Who turned the clock
so fast? Inside these walls it could be any time. Forty years
back. A movie star is building this hacienda. The street's
a dirt road. There are Mexican artisans working the
forge, turning the iron, shaping roof tiles over their
thighs, while across town in a Hollywood hospital they
hand me to her. My eyes were open, she said, from the
beginning. . . . The others, what did they go home to?
Kemper cries over a pigeon. And St. Meader, for all the
family pictures bulging his wallet, itched to climb into the
frame with Geegee. It's like Geegee said, THEY're out
there. WE're in here.

"Sonny—"

She was out the front door even as he approached it.
"Geegee, you're barefoot." He pulled his tie loose without
undoing the knot and opened his collar. "Get inside,
you'll catch cold."

She stood firm. "Get rid of these—" thrusting a brown
paper sack at him.

He surveyed the contents. "Tomorrow."

"Now."

How could she look younger than he one day and a
hundred and four the next? And where had she dredged
up that shapeless flannel nightgown? When Geegee
mourned, she dressed for it.

"Get rid of it all. I can't stand these things in the house
another minute."

"In the morning, Geegee," he pleaded, "I've had a
long, lousy day—"

"Baby, please . . ." The voice was filigreed steel. "Do
it now. For Geegee, Sonny—now."

* * *

35

If he had turned right from the driveway, within six blocks on Oxnard Avenue he would have found the Cellar, the Barfly and Happy's. Right again yields up Cocktails in neon, one with a blinking cherry in a four-foot glass against a psychedelic brick wall, others offering Topless or Real Live Action.

He drove without destination, the paper sack an irritating companion. The only Goodwill receptacle that he knew of, the one in the market parking lot, had been removed. Circling the area looking for another, he thought of throwing the damned thing out the window but conscience sat on him. When the sack came to rest, it was on the bar of a storefront saloon in Van Nuys called, simply, Mac's.

Halfway through his first drink his bones began to feel easy. He swiveled an ice cube with his finger and wondered if the sullen man behind the bar reading the newspaper was Mac. The skin around Ron's eyes tingled. He blinked and saw the printing on the paper sack move: *Total Discount.*

Alpha Beta Mkt.
Geegee's in bed
The collar's inside
Duchess is dead.

Sixteen years subtracted from forty—

Sorry, too late for a generator now. No, haven't got a loaner to give you. . . . The long walk home and a puppy caught in the terror of traffic. Brakes. Cars lurching. Swearing drivers. Hold it, hold, I'll get her—

You sound like Jackie Cooper in Skippy, *only you're twenty-four. No dog! I won't have it . . . she stinks, keep her away from me.*

She likes you, Mother. Just wants to nuzzle. She likes you. . . .

"Repeat?" asked the bartender.

"Wha—oh, no—thanks—not just yet. . . ." Had he talked out loud? The large mirror over the back bar assured him that in this cavern his isolation had not been violated. The others—one man two stools to the right of him, one four down, one on the curve—each was in his own side pocket. Eyes staring into the mirror, seeing nothing. Had they searched for their faces while shaving this morning as he had?

The door made a sucking sound as the woman came in from the street. She didn't need the pause to adjust to the darkness but homed right in to a stool, two to the left of him. Her rump explored the familiar vinyl like a penguin settling to nest. A raised eyebrow, a nod, and the bartender poured a double Cutty Sark with water on the side. She pried off her shoes on the chrome footrest, put out a pack of cigarettes and matches on the counter. And waited for the absolution of the first belt.

Ron raised a finger for another and discovered in the mirror an old man, like a Rembrandt, sitting alone in a booth against the wall in almost total darkness.

"Cheers," said the woman.

To *him?* Her eyes were closed as he turned to her. On impulse, Ron opened the paper sack and asked the bartender, "You have a dog?"

The sallow-faced man studied him with the suspicion reserved for strangers. "Why?"

"Like to have a nice collar for him?"

Refilling the woman's drink, he directed Ron's attention to the prominent NO SOLICITORS sign overhead.

"No, no," Ron quickly corrected. "I'm giving it all away. Collars, leash, dog dish . . ." There was no response as he displayed the contents of the sack on the bar. Almost apologetically, he added, "My dog died." These three words seemed to bridge all the islands in this murky pond. Four Stools Down leaned in and studied him. Two Stools spoke, "What kind?"

37

"Best kind." Ron met him in the mirror. "Dog. Just dog."

"Damn right best kind. Had me a part blue tick hound back home . . ." Two Stools retreated with his memories into his drink. The old man was at Ron's shoulder, presenting his empty beer glass for refill. His heavy-lidded eyes swam with longing as he picked up the studded collar. "Can't have no pets where I live. No pets."

"How long did you have him?" the woman wanted to know.

"Her," Ron explained. "Sixteen years."

The old man put down the collar. "Had a suicide our place last week . . ." He had his beer but stood there, reluctant to leave human contact. Two Stools came out of his glass. "Sixteen, that's old. My blue made twelve."

"Well not quite sixteen." Ron leaned out to look past the old man. "We figure she was born in March." The old man nodded and walked back to his booth muttering to no one in particular, "Bet if she'd had a dog she wouldn't'a done it. Gas . . . ain't no decent way to die."

The woman and Two Stools fell into a conversation across Ron. "A dog's life is seven years for every year of a man," she said.

"No, only seven the first year." Two Stools seemed to be an authority. "Five after that. Lemme have your pencil?" he asked of the bartender and started figuring on a paper napkin.

The woman finished her second double and slid over onto the stool next to Ron. "Know just how you feel." She put a sympathetic, fraternal hand on his knee. "Lost my doxie."

Ron nodded his understanding. He could see her quite clearly now. About his age, maybe a little older. The expensive pants suit she wore was masculine enough to be feminine. She used a water filter cigarette holder. No attempt to cover the sprinklings of gray in her brown hair. That was honest, he felt. But he didn't like that short a haircut on a woman. He finished his drink,

38

ordered a refill, and told her he still had a dog at home—seven. She nodded the bartender to put his drink on her tab and confidentially told him booze wasn't what he needed at a time like this.

"Know what really helps?" she said, leaning into his ear. "What you need is a good lay."

Wordless, he stared at her through bourbon-softened eyes.

"Oh, I'm not a pro," she certified. "I broker properties at Security Trust." Digging into her purse, she presented her business card. "Trumble. Edna." It took some effort, but Ron focused on the card.

"Oh . . . yes . . ." he said, and presented his card. "Gohdiener. R.C. Gohdiener."

"I'll never let myself be owned by a dog again." She studied the small, white, embossed rectangle. "R.C.? Robert? Richard?"

"Ron."

"Insurance, huh?" The hand was on his leg again, exploring his thigh. "You must know Ryan Kirby, he's in your building."

"Kirby? No," he said, aware of the swelling inside his pants, and tried concentrating on her card. "Main Branch. Then you must know Henry Washburn?"

"Hank? Sure." Her hand aggressed into the combat zone. "Worked with Hank when he was selling Mortuary Services . . . great bunch o'guys, great bunch o'guys . . ."

"Then you'd know Joe Kemper from my office—friend of Hank's."

She navigated one of her knees between his like a boat into a slip. "Know a Charlie Kemper."

"No. Joe."

"So you're an actuary, huh? Sexiest part of the business. Y'know what the charts say—women are stronger, last longer . . ."

"I know!" His fingers snapped in recall. "Bill Hoffman!"

"Hell with him. You married?"

He shook his head.

"Good." She put on her shoes. "Married men always get nervous toward the end. . . . I'm across the street," she imparted for his ears only, stuffing cigarettes and matches back into her purse. "Pink building—Sherman Arms—three-oh-one." As she stood up, her hand ran his zipper. "Five minutes is all I need." She signed for the tariff and left.

Ron downed his drink.

"Eighty-two," Two Stools announced, returning the pencil to the bartender. "Your dog was eighty-two years old."

Four Stools turned on a transistor, assaulting the stale air with hard rock. Two Stools took exception. "Hell's wrong with you? You got no respect? This guy's dog just died."

"Up your keester."

"What're you, some kind of left-wing pervert?"

"Who you callin' left-wing?"

The bartender gaveled a shot glass on the bar, "No politics."

Ron was unconcerned with the differences of opinion stirring. His mind, ruttish, was already across the street in a pink building. He put down his money. The *whoosh* of the closing door drowned out the bartender's futile call after him, "Hey, Charley, take your dog junk or I'll throw it out. . . ."

He stood outside, rocking on his heels, his eyes on the third floor of the confection-colored apartment house. Oblivious to a swerving, angry Chevy, his penis pointed him across like the needle of a compass. But as he stepped up onto the curb the smothering scent of night-blooming jasmine altered his trajectory. That same heavy incense lived outside their kitchen window and brought him the message that it was Wednesday. His night to cook dinner.

He crossed back to his car and drove home.

40

4

"I could have lied to you."

"Ha-ha and ha."

"I could have told you I put it in the Goodwill."

"The way you stink? I could smell booze the minute you opened the gates."

"Well, if I'd tossed the stuff in the Goodwill you wouldn't have known where it went either—"

"Stuff . . . now it's stuff! That what you're going to do with my things when I die? Dump 'em in a bar?"

"Please, Geegee, let me up—what kind of logic is that? You're the one said, Just get rid of 'em."

"Oh, you got rid of 'em. They'll end up in a dump somewhere, covered with garbage."

"All right, I'll go back there, get 'em." He shoved back his chair.

"You'll do nothing of the sort. Eat your dinner."

"No, no, I'll go—"

"You want me to eat by myself, that it?"

"God, Geegee—"

"Doesn't matter. It's done. Eat."

The pronto tamale pie he had whipped up, adding his own touches to the recipe on the Bisquick box, sat uneasily in his throat. His fork nudged a wilted romaine leaf around the edges of his plate.

"You don't like it."

"I don't feel like salad, Geegee."

"Not the salad. The goodies I put out—" He nodded appreciation of the squat perfumed candles, pottery and rebozos that lent atmosphere to the table. They'd bought them in Tijuana the Sunday they went to the bullfights. "Just to please you. That's the reason I put 'em out, to please you."

"Very nice, Geegee. Looks nice. Really does. I mean it. Uhhh, really." He could hear the disinterest in his voice and was certain it must irritate the hell out of her.

"What's the use of having a Mexican house if you're going to make it look mail order?"

"I told you, it's very nice. I mean it. Whole gallery looks nice."

"*Galleria.*" Since she had learned what to call it, she liked to say it.

"Very nice," he said again. Now that the drinks had settled into his system, he felt slowed, dulled, and wondered if there had really been a woman in a pink building.

"And I dressed."

"Hmm?"

"I dressed." Did he detect a note of reprimand in the statement? "The way I felt, I still dressed."

"Gorgeous."

"You finally noticed."

"Noticed right away, Geegee."

"I can't read your mind."

"Best-looking broad around."

She tried to deny the smile admission, but it broke through. "G'wan, I'm old enough to be y'mother."

He saw her through the halo of the candle flame. Incredible. Only a couple of hours had gone by and she looked years younger. No makeup that he could detect, just a touch on her lips and false eyelashes. In this light, her hair was copper, one hairpin spearing it to the top

42

of her head. Her chin, firm. If there was a line in her face, it wasn't visible from across the table. The shades of orange in the jellaba she was wearing put gold flecks in her wide, deep-brown eyes.

His mind fell into the rhythm of counting her chews per minute. She was aware without looking up.

"I know you're laughing at me. Well-bred people always take small bites. Can you imagine a movie star ever talking with his mouth full?"

I should have been a movie star for her. The thought gave seed to an unborn bitter laugh. He, with his ordinary face and double cowlick no barber could tame, making a crew-cut the only feasible solution. He'd probably look ridiculous with long hair anyway.

The woman in the pink building, was she angry? Laughing at him.

Beyond Geegee, his eyes fastened onto the staid black umbrella hanging from the gun-belt rack. It looked out of place beside the huge *charro* hat and burro *piñata*. Hadn't rained in five, six months and the umbrella had hung there gathering dust. He questioned how he could live with something, look at it every day and not see it.

"Where you going?"

"To put the umbrella away."

She laughed. "Took you six months?"

Damn Geegee . . . not to put it away herself but wait all this time for an opportunity to jab at him.

When he came back, Geegee was stretched over the chair, arching her body, looking at the gun-belt rack upside down. "I can just see Gary Cooper when he came to dinner, hanging up his guns."

"You don't know Gary Cooper ever ate here. And it's highly improbable he wore guns to dinner. . . ."

"You have no imagination." Aubie laid his greedy mouth on her lap and again she filled it. "Sometimes, Sonny, I wonder if you have any Me in you."

His head had begun to throb. The combination of

43

booze and perfumed candles, he decided. He tried to recall the face and smell of the woman, but the memory of night-blooming jasmine got in the way. Edna. . . ? Edna—what? When he got the chance, he would check the card in his wallet.

"For God's sake, stop wiping his mouth!"

"Why? His mother did that for him from the day he was born." She dabbed her napkin at the dog's jowls. "He misses it, you know he does. And don't tell *me* about Gary Cooper . . ."

"But guns! He was a sophisticated man, educated in Europe."

"Guns," she argued back. "He was a real Westerner, came from Montana. Misses his mommy, doesn't he?" she purred, kissing Aubie between his eyes. "Poor baby . . ."

"Baby my ass!" Ron shoved his chair back with such force he almost toppled with it. "He's as old as I am."

"Don't talk like a garbage mouth. *Now* where you going? S-onnnnnn-y!" Her voice rang after him through the slam of the front door.

He sought the pain. Wanted it. Welcomed it when the hard rubber pellet stung his hand through the thin, worn leather glove. The sweat pouring from him was confession of a fermenting disquiet he could neither understand nor contain. Here, in the womb of the four-walled, windowless handball court, the running, swinging, forcing, straining, aching served as gestation to the hoped-for release.

It was finally born in the steamroom. Calm. Calm.

He lay flat on the hard bench and let the heat placate. How many times the others had said to him, You've got it all, man. The best of all possible worlds. A woman takes care of you, no real responsibility to anybody but yourself. Any broad you want to make it with, you go. And when it's time to put your pants on, you walk.

He hosed the rocks. They hissed and the mist enveloped him. Geegee hadn't meant anything about the umbrella. What did it matter, he thought as he took the sting of the crashing cold water, if it pleased her to believe Gary Cooper had set his boots under the table in their house?

But with a brace of pistols?

The chuckle that the incongruous idea brought was still with him as he bought two of Geegee's favorite candy bars from the lobby vending machine. On the sidewalk, he paused and looked back. *Welcome to your new Y.* It still felt unfamiliar to be coming out of these doors. How much shoe rubber he'd left on the steps of the old main entrance, starting back when he was twelve. The third-hand bike he'd bought from the bulletin board for six hard-earned bucks. The week at summer camp. And always different faces. Thoughts. No nostalgia. No memory of good or bad times. He was standing at the axis of his life. In any direction there were pieces of his childhood. The library on Yucca and Selma where Geegee would bring him sandwiches while he studied. The high school on Highland, but the one year spent there stirred no *alma mater* in him. Hudson was all parking lots; used to be small houses. The one he could see at the end of the street, overgrown, a gargoyle—they'd lived there once for a week between places. The bus bench was still there, advertising a credit dentist now. When he used to sit on it, waiting for Geegee late at night, it advertised saddles and things like that.

He decided to let his membership lapse. He didn't belong around here anymore. *Young Men's Christian Association—1926.* Time had almost eroded the stonecutter's words. It gave him a slight lift to realize he was younger than this commonplace, yellowed structure. His hand patted the candy in his right pocket.

The night air, fouled by exhaust, blew a parched newspaper page past him. Without thinking, he reached out, crumpled it and put it into the litter can.

45

"Hey, baby, you look like a stud, whaddya say?"

The voice had a thinly bearded face possessed of full, loose, sensual mouth and dilated pupils. Bottomless eyes stared without blinking. His tongue licked around his lips as he flexed the muscles of a compact, powerful body, cupping his wares in his hand. "I'm a left dresser, case you're hurtin'. You wanna hat job? Ten bucks."

Dirty faggot, I'd like to cut your cock off.

"I need the bread, baby." The night visitor laid an imperative hand on Ron's arm.

"Get your hand off, I'll call a cop."

"Cool, baby, for twenty I'll blow the both o' you."

Even after he was in the car with the windows closed and the air conditioning on, Ron couldn't get the feel of those predatory fingers off his arm.

There was no outside light on for him. No light in the living room.

She heard the gates, I know she heard them. Nobody touches those gates she doesn't hear.

He thought of the candy in his pocket and for the moment stood silently in the vast, dark living room. But no welcoming sliver of light appeared beneath her door. In total darkness, he unwrapped one of the candy bars and ate it himself. Then, with no regard for the thud of his footsteps, moved past her door, across the gallery, and into his own room.

Aubie wasn't there. Nor had his bed been prepared. Ron ate the second candy bar. *She's overweight as it is.* In three steps he was through the short corridor that separated their rooms, opening her door, voicing his irritation in hoarse whisper, "Aubie."

The dim light, spilling from his room, outlined the dog on the bed. Curled next to Geegee.

"Aubie."

He saw the dog's head come up. Saw her arm restrain him.

46

"Aubie," he ordered, "come to bed."

From pillowy depths, Geegee's voice, muffled and pouty, drifted to him. "You hurt his feelings."

"Christ." The word rolled up, bitter, from his gut.

"Your dinner got cold. He didn't know where you were."

"Next time he can pin a note on my shirt!"

"You can't blame the baby for worrying," her voice censured. "He just lost his mommy."

"Damn you, Aubie!"

Geegee sat bolt upright in bed. Formidable. "Don't you dare to talk to me like that!"

The deep scalding breath he took and held to bursting was no palliative to his anger. His impiety as a child had been to do just that, but experience had taught him that to stay, to argue, the mere act of breathing would become a triumph.

He was wheezing for air as he grabbed for the nebulizer that was always at his bedside. When free breath finally came, partnered with intolerable weariness, he pulled off his clothes to fall where they would, ripped back the bedspread and dropped into the bed.

To sleep. To put this day behind him.

But routine pulled him out, led him by the nose to the closet to hang away his suit. He was putting out shirt, shoes, sox for the morning when Aubie strolled through the open door and stood blinking sleepily at the light.

"She finally let you come back, huh? Well, you didn't have to, you know. . . ."

Aubie replied with a yowling yawn.

"Baby." Ron coated the word with disgust. The dog waited for the sleeping bag to be yanked from the closet floor and thrown over his bed, then jumped up onto it, circling to flatten tall grasses as his genes told him to, and settled down, looking up at Ron as though expecting praise for having done something bright. Ron met his eyes.

47

"You're forty." It was an indictment.

"What's that?" Geegee voiced from her bedroom. "What'd you say?"

"Nothing," he called back.

"I heard you. You were talking. You said something."

"Just Aubie and me, telling each other dirty stories."

"That's not funny." Her voice elevated. "That's not funny at all."

He didn't reply, but went about his structured ablutions. "Forty," he said to the mirror as he spat out the toothpaste.

Forty. The thought defeated him.

He flopped onto his bed, closing his eyes against the world but it was etched on the inside of his eyelids: 4—0

He knew she was in the room with him before she spoke, having learned early in life that Geegee was a Presence. Like—something taught way back in high school—the theory of displacement. When Geegee occupied space, she displaced air, essence, probably even dust. And *she* knew *he* knew she was there, another damned disconcerting thing about her. He could hear the slightly impatient rustle of—? His face furrowed, puzzling—what was the sound? Silk on silk? Straw. . . ?

He opened his eyes.

She was posed in the doorway. His first impulse was derision, but from what could he manufacture a laugh at this moment? Over her nightgown a vividly colored Mexican serape hung from one shoulder. On her head was the huge *charro* hat from the gun-belt rack. One hand on a rounded hip, the other languorous against the door frame, she gave him an eyelash flutter straight out of *The Cisco Kid*.

"Don' be mad to me, señor. Don' let's fight." Her lower lip trembled, her accent got mangled by a sob. "We're all we've got. . . ." The words hung there. Bleak.

"Don't, Geegee, please. . . ." Anguish cracked his voice. "Mother . . . don't . . . please don't cry. . . ." Her back to him, body convulsed, pressed to the indifferent wall,

she seemed small, hurt, defeated. "Mother . . . please . . .
it was my fault, all my fault."

It was his fault, and now he knew it. So she forgave
him. "Sonny?"

"Yes, Mother?"

She turned, face still wet with stinging tears. But
radiant. A child anticipating a treat.

"What'll we do on Sunday?"

5

CHANNEL 7 predicted overcast skies and a 30 percent possibility of precipitation. "He's been wrong before," Geegee reminded. The cartoonist weather man on 4 was even more of a killjoy with his black cloud coming rapidly in off the Pacific to collide with some cloud from the east, rendering Sunday not only wet but cold. "Look in the newspaper," Geegee urged Ron. "I trust the newspaper." He had, he said. The *Times* was iffy.

"If it rains it won't be much fun."

"How do you know it won't?" she challenged. "Could be even more fun."

On the late news, CBS straddled the fence between wind and rain. "So if it rains, it rains," he conceded. "We can still go."

"It won't rain."

At midnight, Geegee was making potato salad. Ron was out in the front yard, feeling the first bursts of unseasonable hot wind. The sky was heavy with gray, weighted clouds.

"Wind'll blow 'em all away," she predicted. "You'll see. Tomorrow's going to be a lovely day."

They were up at six. Through cornflakes and coffee, taken on the run, he kidded her that she should get a job as weatherman. The sky was cloudless. Temperature, 72.

"Geegee, you are going to have to step on it." He filled the thermos and tucked it into the tote bag she had only half finished packing.

"We've got plenty of time."

"Check your clock."

"Seven twelve."

"You see, your clock's slow. It's seven sixteen."

"Can't be. I set this clock yesterday with the news."

"The power goes off, you know, now and then." He set the clock for her, verifying with the telephone time. "The power company does that. You have to keep checking your appliances. Especially the freezer. If the freezer goes off and you lose all the food. . . ."

She threw a cataloguing glance at his blue jeans, banlon shirt and bedroom slippers, interrupting him. "You're not dressed either."

"All but my shoes. . . . Where are they?" he called back from his bedroom. "They were here last night."

"In the dryer."

"The dryer?"

"Sure, I washed yours and mine both when I got up. Don't worry, they should be done. Did you feed Aubie?" she asked as they passed in the gallery, he bound for the service porch and his sneakers, she for her bedroom to finish dressing.

"I fed him."

"And give him water?" Her voice drifted back to him.

"Geegee," he called back, "I've been feeding and giving that dog water for seven years. I never forget. Where are you?"

"In here."

He brought her sneakers and tote bag to her dressing room. She had on white bell-bottom pants and was adjusting a striped basque sweater as she put a roller into her hair.

"You're not going to set your hair now?"

51

"Just the front, hon."

"We have to leave the house in less than six minutes."

"I'll take the roller out before we get to the bus."

"Let's go." He thrust the tote bag at her.

"Where's your blazer?" she asked.

"It's going to be hot."

"What if it gets cold?"

"Why should it get cold?"

"Go on, get your blazer."

They met in the living room, both heading for the front door. "You have got to be kidding with that beach hat," he said.

She looked out from under a foot-wide brim. "Why? It looks good on me."

"What about that little yachting cap I bought you? You never wear that."

"Yachting cap on the bus?"

"Why not?"

"Okay, I'm game. Why not?"

"Come on, let's go, Geegee. Please, come on—"

"I can't find it," her voice came from somewhere in her closet.

"Forget it then, wear something else."

"No, I want to wear that."

"Hey," he said appreciatively when she came out with the cap jaunty over one eye. "See, I was right. That's cute."

They were outside the house and he was dead-bolting the front door when she thought about the gas under the coffee.

"Didn't you turn it off?"

"No, didn't you?"

"I think I did."

"Aren't you sure?"

"I know I did."

"Do you know, or do you just think?"

"Go check."

While he ran to turn off the gas which wasn't on, she rushed to turn off the light in her dressing room which was. They were in the car, backing out the driveway. "Wait—the tickets."

He had them.

The Vegas-bound bus was revving to pull out. Geegee had to run to get on, cajoling the driver into waiting a tiny minute while Ron parked and locked their car on a side street just off Lankershim. He boarded in a dead run. Together, they made their way, breathless and laughing, back through the bus.

"Oh, damn!" The pleasure left her face. The last seat, stretching from window to window, had appeared empty as they started toward it. Now that they could see past the height of the seats in front, they discovered the right window seat was occupied by an old man.

"I told you, Geej, we should have gotten started earlier."

Not only did the old man occupy a seat, but his string-wrapped parcel took up its share of the six spaces. "Now it won't be any fun." Geegee, spreading out tote bag, food basket, sweater, like staking a claim to the Cimmaron, so clearly indicated to the old man that he was the usurper that he drew himself flat to the window, trying to diminish the size of his parcel by pressing it between his knees.

"Of course we'll have fun." The bus, in sweeping turn onto the freeway, rocked like a foundering ship. "See? Your yachting cap isn't out of place. We're on a boat," he announced.

"I'm not in the mood."

"Come on, Geej, we're going to have a good day, let's not spoil it."

"All right," she conceded flatly, "it's a boat."

"Going where? Go on. Your turn. You choose first. Ocean liner or freighter?"

She wasn't sharing his game but peering around him to the interloper at the other window. High cheekbones, skin that seemed an extension of the wrinkled brown paper covering his parcel. She concluded the obvious. He was Mexican.

"Okay, we're on a bus," Ron announced with annoyance, "going to Yermo." He fell silent. Her attention remained on the old man, her mouth pursed with indecision.

They had chosen Yermo with a pin. It had all the qualifications. Close to Los Angeles, yet far enough away so you felt you'd been somewhere. With round-trip tickets within the resources of the Fun Pot (eleven dollars round trip each). Making Sunday unique was getting to be a chore; Ron had felt blank when the subject came up. The pin idea had been Geegee's. "Close your eyes, Geegee, you're cheating." "Well, how do I find Los Angeles with my eyes shut?" "I'll put your finger on Los Angeles. There now, no more than two inches away." The pin had gone through the map in the o of Yermo. He, happily, had then come up with the bus idea.

"Buenas dias."

The old man turned from his window, eyes uncertain, to find Geegee smiling beguilingly at him. "Señora?" With a touch of gallantry, his bent fingers touched his forehead as though doffing a sombrero. "Buenas dias."

"Yermo, si? No?" she asked the old man. He did not comprehend. "Yermo?"

"It doesn't matter, Geegee," Ron insisted. "We can change seats."

"Las-Ve-gas?" she accented carefully.

"No, no, señora, no Las Vegas, no *dinero*." His rueful smile shared with her assorted tobacco stained teeth. "Sahn Bairrrnadino." The fluid elegance of the Latin tongue was wasted on Geegee's ears. All it told her was that he was going to share *their* seat a good part of the trip.

She pulled a small neck-yoke cushion from her tote, put her feet up and slept.

I can't sleep. Too dangerous for me to sleep. Anyone notices this bulge around my waist, there'll be a knife in my gut. Keep awake. Awake. Let her sleep, poor kid, she's exhausted, three days and three nights making the desperate run for the border. The diamonds? If they kill me, who'll get them? He wondered if they'd really lost the fat man and his little round assassin. The remembrance of his accented, soft, oily voice sent a shudder. Poor Bogie, lifetime buddy, bleeding back there in an alley. I'll just keep my gun butt warm, keep it warm and ready. Wait, that isn't the conductor. That's Peter Lorre. What happened to the conductor? Have they killed him, too? Is his crumpled body back there somewhere on the lonely tracks? I can feel that million dollars worth of cold ice wrapped around me getting hotter by the minute. Once we get into Istanbul we'll lose ourselves in the market crowd . . .

"San Bernardino, ten minute stop . . ."

His eyes opened and the Orient Express evaporated down memory's track. He had been eight years old again, sitting up on an all-night, window-rattling, soot-smelling local, while Geegee converted the tedious miles into adventure. Then (as she told it on their way to a summer job in Sparks, Nevada) Leslie Howard (or was it Boyer?) had been the *agent provocateur* posing as the conductor: Mortally wounded, he had passed the secret papers to Marlene Dietrich, who wrapped them in her hat veil and entrusted them to Ron. . . .

Geegee stirred and saw him looking at her through tender eyes. "Way you're smiling right now reminds me when you were a little boy."

He patted her hand. "I'm going to *that* room. How about you?"

"No." She stretched. "I can't stand public toilets."

"Going to be a long day."

"I'm a camel."

His laugh went up the aisle with him. With the old man gone, Geegee marked off the entire back seat as theirs,

55

and was contentedly reading the Home section of the Sunday paper when Ron returned. He settled at the other window with the financial page.

The last new passenger boarding was young, barefoot, in a gray-white sexless garment, with limp reddish hair and beard. He came down the aisle, intent on the back of the bus. Geegee felt a moment's concern that the Christ-with-tattooed-arms was going to mooch in on them, but when he saw they were in residence he raised his hand in the peace sign, put his scarred guitar on the rack above, and took a seat two ahead of them. Their private compartment was assured for the rest of the trip.

They climbed. Their backs to city, smog, pressure. The narcotic of the engine drone pulled him from the Dow Jones to look out the rear window. Houses grew fewer and less important until finally there was only an occasional cabin. And growing, ascending space.

"I feel good."

She looked up from the paper. "You look good. You know, you're very handsome today."

"I am?" His slow grin loosened the muscles of his cheeks. "Feel good. Really feel good." Geegee looked good, too, now that he thought about it.

They didn't talk much. Nibbled. Shared mountains with each other. Passed the thermos of coffee back and forth, saving their appetite for the picnic basket later. The railroad tracks, miniature in size far below, wound their way into the mouth of a mountain and disappeared.

He felt free. Felt it in his body. A letting go. And he began to see color in the colorless high desert. Purples and pinks . . .

"Bet I beat you today."

"Bet."

"How much?"

"Penny a point." He dealt the cards, four to her, four open, four to himself.

"Let's make it interesting. A nickel."

"You can't afford that."

"I've got a rich son."

"Oh, well, in that case. . . . As long as I know you're good for the money. . . ."

As she studied her hand, she reminded him who won last time. El Cajon Pass achieved forty-two-hundred-foot elevation. The bus picked up speed and Geegee picked up Little and Big Casino giving her a total of nine out of eleven points. "You ten, me forty-five; that's thirty-five cents you owe me and the deal's mine. Go on, write it down."

"My books are always open to audit." He laughed.

The bus, its burden lessened now that it was on level ground, embraced the 70-mile-per-hour speed limit with abandon, relieved that the tortuous climb was over. Ron applied the metaphor to himself. It had been an uphill week. But now his rotten mood, his confusion of the past days, no longer mattered. *Guess I just never realized how important she was to me, how much I cared . . .* Thinking about it again, he still couldn't understand his indifference at the grave. But it really didn't matter. *I must have loved her . . .*

"You didn't pick up your seven."

"Wha—?"

"With your seven, pick up the other one. This jack gives me last, that gives me cards. That's eight to three, write it down."

He was down two dollars and forty-five cents when they came to the end of their ticket.

The Christus Itinerus was stretched out across their seat before the bus door jackknifed and disgorged them into the alkali silt of the highway shoulder. Hot air hit them like a blast furnace. The bus belched a black cloud and disappeared down the road to Vegas.

Their eyes, squinting in the glare of scorching sun, searched the seared, withered, thirsting land that even Joshua trees found unfriendly, and located the body of the town. A few dozen dusty, aging buildings straggled in a broken parallel line a mile or so from the road, its suburbs touching the highway with only a gas station and a roadside EATS. A sign said drinking water could be bought for two bits a quart.

"So this is Yermo," she gasped in the heat.

"What do you expect from a pin?" They checked their watches. "Eight minutes," she said. "No, you're slow. Less than four. We're barely going to make it." He grabbed basket, tote bag and her elbow, maneuvering all out into the river of traffic. The gas station attendant, mopping sweat from a face as cracked as the soil, watched them in their reckless dash, thinking them damn fools to run in this heat and wondered what the hell they found so funny about crossin' a highway.

Ron and Geegee, laughing and sweating, had but one point of focus: the shaded concrete bench across the road. Had they looked beyond it they would have seen a distant, blotched mountain where the word CALICO stood out in relief, promising a journey back into time in its ghost town.

"I'm thirsty."

"There won't be time." But he bought them each a Coke from the machine. And, while he was at it, took a pamphlet from a rack nailed to a post since it said Free, Take One.

The bus bound for L.A. was right on schedule. They dropped their coke bottles, barely tasted, into a wastecan, hurrying past, without seeing, a historical marker that told of oppressed Mormons fleeing Nevada for California on this very trail.

"So that was Yermo."

They boarded the L.A. bus, laughing. Their own private joke at the insignificance of a flyspeck on a map.

There weren't two together, but they got aisle seats, she a row ahead of him. Geegee scanned the passengers, pegging most of them as losers having to come home from Vegas the hard way, and willed some of them to get off so she and Sonny could sit together.

Ron wasn't thinking about anything as he put a piece

58

of sugarless gum into his mouth. With it, he brought from his pocket the pamphlet he'd picked up. And took the time to read it. *Historic, Heroic Yermo*, in spare, simple prose telling of history, of hardship, of failure and survival. He looked out the window in frantic attempt to capture the essence he had missed, but the landscape gave him back only 20th-century high tension wires and the ugly pockmarks of gravel pits.

Had the abrasive hot wind he'd felt on his face carried the dust of bleached bones of miners, of pioneers, of long dead Borax-hauling mules, of a legendary dog named Dorsey who had carried the mail to and from a town destined to die called Calico?

He felt vaguely unfulfilled; fictitious. Then he dozed.

"Sonny . . . Sonny . . ."

"Wha—?"

She leaned across the aisle and shook him. "Hurry, those people in back, they're getting off—"

Geegee and Ron picnicked from San Bernardino to West Covina, and Geegee racked up another dollar-eighty in wins.

6

THE gates waited, as they had for more than forty years. Indifferent to those who entered or left. Shedding no paint at escrows that gave them from one human being to another as though they had no purpose, no meaning. Whatever their wounds or scars, never repaired, outlasting the craftsmen who created them, they never failed to open or close at the touch of any who put a hand to them.

From halfway down the block, Geegee could see that they were open. One pushed back, the other staggered forward. "You didn't lock them," she accused as she flung them wider for Ron to drive through.

"Me?" he called back as he made the semicircle, "I was in the car."

"In all the years we've lived here," she said, latching them, "all the years, *I've* never failed to close the gates. Not once."

They met midway on the lawn for the skirmish.

"I drove out, Geegee, how could I have closed them?"

"That's what I said. You didn't."

"No, no, *you* were last—you locked the front door."

"No, *you* did."

"Geegee, *I* was in the car. *You* were behind. . . . What's the matter?" he asked as he saw her face go lax.

"Aubie . . ." Her mouth seemed afraid to complete the rest of the thought. "Dear God, where's Aubie?"

On one thing they both agreed: He had been in the yard when they left. He should have been there to greet them, as he always did when they returned from a Sunday's outing.

Abandoning reason, Ron raced through one wing of the house, Geegee the other, their voices sounding as hollow as they felt—"Aubie"—"Here boy"—delaying the acceptance of the dreadful reality that he was gone. Run away. Geegee knew it as she stood, opening the gates for the car to back out. She could see the brake lights go on and off, hear him calling at the top of his lungs as he drove haltingly toward Oxnard and turned the corner.

"Aubie . . . baby . . ." She stood in the street, eyes closed, trying to eliminate all sound, concentrating on hearing Aubie's voice which she would know a mile away. Listened hard. "Au-bee—Ba-bee . . ." elongating the vowels, holding her breath, conjuring him to be Right There. When she opened her eyes, instead of the errant dog, there was a young woman, wearing the briefest tank top and jeans, standing at the rear of the moving van, shouldering a carton of toys. Geegee had been aware of the van when they turned onto Keefee, but what did it matter to her if the house across the street was occupied or not so long as they didn't bother them.

"You see our dog?" she asked. "So big—short hair, mink color and white, his whole muzzle's white, wears a collar and tag—j'see him?" In the finger-snap instant it took for a reply, Geegee sized up the new neighbor as too thin, she could sure use some makeup, and this no-bra fad—a year and she'd be sagging, although she wasn't risking a hell of a lot.

"Brown dog?" the young woman puzzled. "No, I don't think so. How about you fellas?" The two muscled, long-haired, cocoa-butter-tanned draymen listened as Geegee repeated the query, then shrugged indifference and carried a mattress and stereo into the house.

61

"Mommy . . ." The knee-high voice came from a shaggy towhead clinging to its mother's skin-tight faded pants.

"Understand," Geegee said, "I'm not accusing, but do you think your little—"

The young mother crisply filled the pause. "Boy." Geegee nodded tolerantly; these days it was so difficult to tell. "Could he have been in our yard? Somebody opened the gates . . ." The new neighbor didn't think this possible, but you could never be certain with kids, their motors were always running. "We're just moving in, he's been with me most of the time."

To Geegee's eye, there didn't seem to be much furniture. And the moving van wasn't much, either, with its high rear end and oversized tires. Sand, stuck to the sidewalls, suggested beach bums one day, furniture moving the next. Takes all kinds, Geegee thought. "Well, if you should see our dog, *Miss* . . ." she said pointedly, and the new neighbor let it pass, "his name's Aubie. Come right across the street, dear, and tell us. We live right over there behind the gates. Tell him he's a bad bad boy and to go right home."

"What'd you say his name was?"

"Aubie," Geegee called back from two houses away. "Aubrey Beardsley," thinking *that's some kind a' mother with her navel hanging out in the middle of the street.*

"Au-beee . . ."

The new neighbor was left with a definite impression of Geegee as well. As she watched her moving in and out of view, calling into each yard for the dog, she pegged her a real fox. Lotta sex. But a big ass. "Come on, Ace," she said to her kid with a friendly toe at his behind, "let's get crackin'." They traded grins and headed into the house with the box of toys. Geegee could still be heard plaintively begging her baby to come home.

Dulcie Carpenter had not planned to move from Venice. At least not so abruptly, and certainly not in the middle of the night. Her last day there (although she

62

hadn't known it would be her last when she and Kevin awakened on Saturday morning) was as perfect as any since they'd lived there.

Every day the same. The morning haze burned off by nine, nine thirty, a gentle, steady breeze; not the wild wind that bent trees into twisted shapes and brought to the land the constant story of turbulent seas and ship-threatening rocks that she'd known all of her life on the Monterey Peninsula, and missed, would always miss; but breeze, salty enough to tell you there was an ocean just past the Speedway, the Walkway, and the bland, wide, sandy beach.

The sun found its way around the corner of the two-storied apartment building they called home, along with four other tenants. It had a new facade of bricks and was stylishly fenced with cuts of telephone poles and anchor chain, which was like putting eyeshadow and a blond wig on an old crone: The orthopedic stockings were still a necessity.

With all its creaks, the building wasn't anywhere near as old as some others in the block, built back when the century was in its teens and the developers who put in the canals (and the gondolas) had visions of creating a little bit of Italy on the Pacific Ocean. That dream had turned to dust, along with some of those developers, but the Pacific Ocean was still there, and the canals were home, mainly for beer cans and debris and a few lonely ducks.

Venice, caught between past and future. Like Dulcie.

After a long interval, boom was following bust, evident in the activity of the building trades' union halls, and in the real estate offices that had sprung up all over, like toadstools. High-rise apartments had begun to thrust up from the sand like stalagmites. That's how they looked to Dulcie, a thought she shared with Kevin who grasped it immediately in his four-year-old's imagination, and from then on called every building over three stories, *lagmites*.

They stowed their beach gear at a lifeguard station and walked back the alley Speedway, Dulcie jogging, mostly, to keep up with Kevin who was doing a running count of the *NO PARKING, Violators will be towed away* signs.

Their morning routine. A walk to Washington Boulevard, where she always bought the *Times* in front of the Bait and Tackle, reading it with her third cup of coffee at the Sandy Sandwich while Kevin devoured a second breakfast: always a wonderment to Dulcie where he put it. The door of a battered VW camper parked at the curb opened and a muttonchopped young man with tied-back long hair yawned, smiled good morning, brought out his Coleman stove and prepared his breakfast on the sidewalk. The macrame lady was opening her boutique, the swim store owner was stacking surf boards in front of his shop. It was warming, sitting there at the sidewalk cafe. Almost every time Dulcie glanced up from the paper there was someone to nod to.

She dug old Venice. Easy people, doing their own thing and letting you do yours. There were problems sometimes. An occasional narc bust, and in the next block there had been a knifing. But that could happen anyplace.

The talk of the beach was of a baby seal that had washed up during the night. By the time Kevin and Dulcie got there, the Animal Regulation truck was backing to the water's edge to rescue the frightened, bawling thing. Kevin patted its head and told it not to cry.

They walked for a while—it was as yet too cold for the surf—past some of the original houses that still stood, dark brown, green, some as weathered as the hulls of old derelict ships and as mildewed, stopping to admire the cactus as they always did. Thirty-five feet high, its spiny base wider than both Dulcie's and Kevin's reach combined. At Christmastime, one of the longtime residents had told them, it was always hung with decorations. They were both looking forward to seeing that.

Kevin plopped himself into a sagging, weather-stained, overstuffed chair in front of a house that could, in another setting, have been a sharecropper's cabin. The chair must once have been red. It was now a bedraggled bluish pink with streaks of cerise in the corners and a broken spring spiraled from it. But the chair had a mission that gave it a dignity, in spite of its decrepitude, as did the man who sometimes sat in it. They hadn't seen him in several days, but his works of art were prominently displayed: flower pots of sunbaked red clay that all wore elongated, stylized African faces. Dulcie had said, the day she bought one from the old man, that they looked Haitian but he'd said, Lord, no, he was born in Leavenworth, Kansas, in sight of the penitentiary and spent his whole life as a porter on the Southern Pacific lookin' out at all that open land and made up his mind, when it was time, he'd just sit out his days in the California sun.

Kevin wondered if the old man was sick.

They were about to go on when they saw him coming out of his house—a tall, spare man, steadying himself on a stout cane.

"How do you feel today, Mr. Claypool?" Dulcie called, loud enough for him to hear.

"Hmm . . ." He turned eyes that had almost lost the power of sight, reaching out a trembling hand to find and touch Kevin's head. "How you today, li'l man? How you, young mothah?"

"We missed you, didn't we, Kevin?"

"Well now, ain't that nice . . . old Simeon just had to take hisself some rest." He lowered himself into the chair, saying it wasn't all that bad, getting old. "Howsoevah . . ." he said, settling into the familiar stuffing, "was I young today—lots more a black man can do—I think I'd turn mahself into a lawyah . . ." adding that he wasn't complainin', mind you. He'd been lucky, for his time, since he was born just the right shade of color for the

65

railroad. "See y'all tomorrow." With gnarled fingers he began fashioning another of his primitive faces.

They jogged back to the beach, to snooze on the sand until the sun lured them out of their shirts and sandals. Then, running to meet the rolling waves, being lifted, tossed, hurled back to shore like driftwood, Dulcie giving Kevin his freedom to fight the sea, but always close enough to reach out and grab him.

Lazing, just letting your mind blow away like the feathered clouds.

The old Jewish ladies were out on the sand now, taking the sun on their faces and hands, and sometimes, their bare feet that told an immigrant's story of hand-me-down shoes, resulting in disfiguring bunions. But they had little vanity about such things. Mrs. Leopold, who always brought along her wicker chair, had said to Dulcie one day, "What's to worry, I'm alive. You tell me, how old am I? Don't be bashful, how many birthdays you think I passed, go on, I got no shame. . . ."

Dulcie had ventured a gentle, seventy-four?

"Seventy-nine," Mrs. Leopold had said. "That shows it's not how you look, it's how you live that counts." Dulcie couldn't have agreed more.

The sun, starting its downward arc, poured intense rays onto the broad expanse of toasted skin between the scraps of material that were her bikini. *Peace*, Dulcie thought as she wiped a bead of salty sweat from her eye. Two months of peace. She pulled on her shirt, rolled over on her stomach, and through a curtain of sun-streaked hair watched him at play. Brown as a little nut, a beachful of friends. And he sleeps nights. No more screaming tantrums, no nightmares. What she would do next, she'd figure out when the time came. If they found her . . .

Kevin zipped down the slide, shrieking joy and terror. Waited his turn, ran up again to slide down again. Up. Down. To land each time in a tumble of arms and legs with all the other kids. Suddenly abandoning the game,

66

he ran to her and she knew the alarm clock had gone off in his stomach.

But Mrs. Leopold wouldn't hear of it. "Don't go eat that *chazarei*, dolly, look, I brought plenty . . ." producing from her ample shopping bag gefilte fish, cold. Chicken soup, hot, from a thermos. And hot tea which she served in thick jelly glasses. Fried chicken. And *chale*, a bread Dulcie and Kevin had never tasted. Or the gefilte fish, for that matter. "Go on eat, eat, I just got to throw it out . . ." explaining, as she disbursed staggering portions, that her daughter and son-in-law had been over for Friday night, but of course they couldn't stay. "He's very busy, important man, a business dinner he got, but they didn't want they should disappoint me . . . so they stood twenty minutes. . . ." her loneliness punctuating the transparent loyalty. "So this way, dolly . . ." she was spooning a touch of horseradish onto the fish, "you'll eat, it's good for the baby, and I don't have to carry it back, and I got compn'y, like a pitnic."

They shared her feast and enjoyed it.

On a rental bike, with Kevin on the kid's seat behind her, Dulcie worked off the meal. The breeze was at their backs most of the way. At Windward Avenue, pedaling over to Pacific Boulevard, they stopped for a while at the purple-painted Flea Market and sat on a bench to watch the admixture of population that was Venice, then rode on to Kevin's favorite destination, the bus yard, where dozens of yellow school buses took their weekend siesta.

Washington Boulevard that continued out over the water to become a pier was taking on its night garb when they returned the bicycle. The swollen sun, a smoldering ball, hung so low it looked as though it would drop into the sea from sheer weight.

"I don't want any trouble," was the first thing her landlord told her when she stopped into his delicatessen to buy baklava for dessert.

"Why should there be trouble?" But Dulcie knew even before he told her.

"There's been somebody around askin' questions about you . . ." He moved away to package an order of rice and grape leaves to go.

"Who? What kind of questions?"

He shushed her, motioning her to the back of the store out of earshot of the customers. "A cop," he said as he joined her. "That's what my boy Diamond thinks; he talked to him. I didn't, I was down at Central Market; you can't count on the grapes today with all that labor trouble in the fields . . ."

"Where is Diamond?"

"Out, making deliveries, he'll be back." Now that the deli was momentarily empty of customers he talked freer. "My boy is smart, he hasn't got a big mouth, so when this guy shows him a picture of you and the kid, he just shakes his head, he don't know nothin', wouldn't even tell him where the apartment is. Look . . . your rent's paid till Tuesday, you're a good tenant, I like you, your boy, but I'm a hard-working man. That building is my life investment. I don't want trouble. Diamond thinks this cop's maybe from Narcotics . . ."

"No, no, nothing like that . . ." Dulcie's assurance was echoed by the black curly-haired great-great-grandson of Aegean fishermen who came through the back door. "No, Pop, why do you say that? I didn't say he was a narc, I don't even know he's fuzz. I don't know what this cat is."

Mr. Raffides grabbed his leonine head with both hands. "You send a boy to college and look what language he talks—fuzz, narc . . ."

"What did he look like?" Dulcie asked of Diamond.

"Big guy, thirty, thirty-two, ordinary lookin'."

"Blond?"

"No."

Then it wasn't Peter. Of course it wouldn't be Peter. He'd never do his own dirty work.

"I was outside cleanin' off our window, I saw this cat

68

go into the Head Shop. Later, I talked to the guy over there. He said he showed him your picture, and picture of the kid, and asked the same questions he asked me."

"Like what?"

Diamond shrugged. "Like, are you shacked up with some guy—or some broad."

Mr. Raffides' bellow filled the shop, his negligible accent thickened. "Dia-mon'—sham-n you—wha kina talk is that. . . ?"

"Pop, come on, she's hip." Diamond helped himself to a handful of ripe olives as blue-black as his eyes.

"What else did he ask?" Dulcie had to know.

"Wondered if you were on anything—grass, hard stuff —or if you get, you know, juiced . . ."

"Look, please, please . . ." Mr. Raffides was having an advanced case of heartburn. "Diamon' didn't tell him nothin', but that man knows I'm the landlord, he told Diamon' he knows, he's comin' back, he said he'd be back tomorrow. I tell you somethin', I don't want you to feel bad, you're a nice lady, but your rent is up in two days, it could be better—"

She spared him the need to ask.

"I'll leave, Mr. Raffides. I know how you feel, I understand. If he comes around again, just say I disappeared, you don't know anything else . . . you're a nice man . . ."

Kevin was cranky, wanting to go home.

The pleasure of the day was dimmed. The breeze was heavier and damp and Kevin, slung over her shoulder, began to weigh a ton as she hurried across the street to buy an early edition of the Sunday *Times*. To find a place and be gone by morning before the detective showed up again seemed a horrendous task. The distressing thought that he might be waiting for her when she turned the corner to the apartment got her off the Speedway, crossing through an empty lot and several private walkways until she came to the back door of two neighbors who lived across the street from her. Eugene was home alone, had dinner ready to put on the table, and was waiting for Lamont to close their plant boutique in Westwood.

"I'm being hassled," was the only explanation she gave him.

"Honey, sit down, have a drink." He brought her a Bloody Mary and Kevin milk in a champagne glass. To keep the child from picking up Dulcie's tension, Eugene kept him busy talking to the plants.

"Hello, plant," Kevin said to a struggling fern.

"His name's Christopher."

"He don't talk."

"They don't talk, Kevin, they listen." The logic of this seemed proper to Kevin, and for the next while he regaled the greenery that cluttered the small Victorian sitting room with his day. Dulcie worried at the window, watching night descend on her apartment, wondering if other eyes had it under surveillance.

There would be no way to get a moving van on a Saturday night; still she made several calls to transport companies that listed emergency numbers, all unsuccessful.

It was just as well, Eugene pointed out. A moving van could be traced.

When Lamont came home, bringing an armload of plants in need of therapy, he offered a solution. "I know these two Muscles," he said, as Dulcie ate the lambchops they insisted she share with them, Kevin having long since fallen asleep. "They've got a van and they can always use the loot . . . if I can just find them. Trouble is, they've got no phone and I don't know where their pad is." But he did know where they hung out, and who their chums were.

"I shouldn't bring you my troubles."

"Honey, it's so damned dull around here, putting on a hairpiece is a big event." Urging her to stay put, that they'd work everything out, the two slender, graying men put on identical Irish hand-knit sweaters and set out to find the help she needed. With a sense of madcap, she

70

felt. And thought warmly of them. Neighbors for less than two months, aware a detective was looking for her, and they hadn't asked why.

Fatigue dulled her drive to escape. She gave up going through the rental ads, adjusted the afghan over Kevin on one sofa, and curled up on the other. It was almost two in the morning when Lamont awakened her. "They're here." Beyond him, in the stabs of refracted light from a Tiffany lamp, loomed two devotees of Narcissus with biceps bigger than any ordinary man's thigh. There was a short discussion, half whispered so as not to disturb the child, Dulcie handed over fifty dollars in cash, and by five A.M. every bit of her stuff had been stowed in the van. The overflow filled the back of her VW.

Just minutes to dawn the caravan pulled out. On South Venice Boulevard they drove across the narrow bridge over the canal, past the little row houses that looked like cribs, and for all she knew or cared, might be. For several blocks, the driver of the van led a zigzag course down alleys and side streets to verify that they were not being tailed. Assured, they cut back to Pacific Avenue, following it until it blended into Neilsen Way with its luxurious condominiums.

Dulcie looked back at fading, garish Venice and hoped they wouldn't change it too much. But she knew it was inevitable. It had to disappear. The signs that were everywhere stayed in her mind: *Save Our Canal* . . .

At a remodeled railroad car that was a diner called Lands' End, they ate breakfast. While her moving men body-surfed and Kevin played in and out of the van, Dulcie tried to coordinate the real estate section of the Sunday paper with a street map. *Rentals, Houses* filled page after page. A city with which she was almost totally unfamiliar. When first she'd fled, Cambria had been haven for awhile. It felt good there, since in many ways it resembled the Peninsula, then it began to depress her because it wasn't the Peninsula. Venice, she had never asked to be anything but what it was. Now where?

Outflank and out-guess the enemy. Where wouldn't they look for her? Somewhere, so far from the sea they wouldn't think it likely she would go. The map gave her the answer.

The San Fernando Valley.

Marvin Hinckley Associates' sign had been in front of the house on Keefee Avenue so long the spike that stuck in the ground had rusted. He'd tried to tell the owners they'd put too high a price on the property, it was just a tract house, no pool, no built-ins, no carpeting, just two bedrooms, what could you expect? But these divorce sales, one side always trying to get the best of the other, and by the time they agreed on a realistic price it was winter and the house market was dead. Now they were yelling for him to at least get it rented.

A nothing-special neighborhood, in Hinckley's opinion. The only house of any distinction was that one across the street behind the iron gates. It had struck Hinckley as good for business to go over there one day when he was changing the sign from For Sale to For Rent, just to let the owners know he'd like the listing if they ever decided to sell. But that red-headed shrew that lived there had almost taken his head off.

"Yes. . . ?" All he could see of her were her eyes through the small square of iron grillwork in the front door. "What do you want?" He'd tried to shove his card through but the grill was too small.

"Sell. . . ?" she shrilled when he explained his purpose. Her beautiful hacienda? She would never sell it, never, and what the hell did he mean coming into their yard uninvited, nobody was ever allowed in their yard, Go on, get out . . . "And close the gates. . . ." she yelled after him.

He had latched them carefully, but even so she was out

72

there at the gates herself, wearing something like a striped awning, double checking the latch, before he had crossed the street.

"Up your hacienda, Lady."

Tillie Frees had an ingrained habit of muttering to herself, and Marvin Hinckley had given up trying to break her of it . . . "Goddam insult . . . asking anybody who's passed the real estate board and got her license to make the coffee. Who's 'Associates' in that sign out there anyway? Me. Just me, Tillie Frees. Bring as much business in as he does. If he wants a slave, why doesn't he buy one? Tillie do this, Tillie do that, Tillie isn't that desk over there dusty, let's wipe it, shall we? We . . . when did he ever get off his duff?"

"How's the coffee coming, Tillie?" Hinckley's voice reached her in the closet-sized storeroom.

Tillie was fifty-seven, a widow, a grandmother, a Notary Public, and if that old poop didn't change his arrogant attitude she'd start looking around for someplace else to hang her license.

"Tillie . . ."

"Coming . . ." To him, handling a silex and opening a box of doughnuts required ovaries. She poured two mugsful and went back into the wormwood paneled office they shared, her outrage punctuated by the clack of platforms that brought her up to five three. What a wasted Sunday. They might as well have kept the office closed. The whole morning had been an exercise in futility, showing six houses to a client who didn't know what he wanted, and now the afternoon was almost shot and she'd forgotten to bring the Sunday paper.

Before she put the cups down he was saying, "Tillie, as long as you're not doing anything, we might as well get a letter off to Harris about that land he's subdividing—"

"There's that We again."

"Tillie, stop talking to yourself. Dear George."

"Marvin, I don't carry a pencil in my teeth, and when are you going to hire a secretary?"

"What do you mean? Why do I need a sec—?"

They both looked up as the door opened. Dulcie, in spite of no makeup and hair badly in need of combing, had borne up better than Kevin. The child showed the effect of having been dragged from one real estate office to another. The draymen, it turned out, knew the San Fernando Valley no better than she did, and they'd lost precious time going in wrong directions, waiting for one landlord to show up only to find the house already rented, and another prospect took them twenty miles of driving and turned out to be a dud.

"I saw your ad. I'm looking for a house to rent," she said.

Hinckley, who was near the window, while viewing Dulcie in her tight, faded jeans and brief top, peripherally saw the van and the men who drove it. Having spent an unaccustomed length of time cramped up in the seat, they were loosening up their muscles by doing body presses on the sidewalk while they waited.

"It's been rented," he told Dulcie.

"Thanks anyway," she said and turned to go.

"Wait a minute," said Tillie. "What about Keefee Avenue. . . ?" ignoring the glare he threw at her. "How much do you want to pay, dear?"

"Two hundred. . . ?" Dulcie proposed.

"There, you see?"

Hinckley balked. "Hold it. How many of you want to move in; it's only got two bedrooms."

"Just the two of us, my son and myself." She answered his look out the window. "They're friends, moving me."

"Just the two of you, huh . . . no pets, huh?"

"No pets."

"Just the two of you."

"That's right. Just the two of us."

Hinckley reluctantly drove her over to look at the

74

house. She walked in the front door and said, "I'll take it." They went back to the real estate office to draw up the lease.

"Six months?"

"Fine."

Tillie rolled original and copy into the typewriter. "Name?"

"Dulcie Carpenter."

"Is that Mrs.?" Hinckley quickly interjected, "or Miss?"

"Just Dulcie Carpenter will do. That's first and last month's rent, right?"

"And cleaning fee of fifty dollars," Tillie said.

Dulcie sat down to write the check.

"Look," Hinckley said, "the lease to be legal has to say your name, a married woman, or your name, a single woman—"

"What do you do," Dulcie asked, "if two boys move in together? Or two girls?"

"My kind of people," Tillie told her.

"You're not moving in with somebody else?" he asked, worried. "You said it was just you and your son."

"That's right. Who do I make it out to?"

"Hinckley Associates."

Hinckley worried it like a bone. "You have a job?"

"Not at the moment."

"You mean you're unemployed. You're not on welfare?"

"Mr. Hinckley, I have more than adequate means to pay the rent."

"What is your husband's occupation?"

"I'm renting the place. Just me."

"Well somebody has to be responsible . . ."

"I am. Look, Mr. Hinckley," Dulcie spoke quietly, "you want to be unpleasant, okay, you're being unpleasant. You don't have to like me, I certainly don't like you. I want to rent the house, that's all. I'll pay the six months' rent; does that do it?"

The onslaught surprised and cowed him, and discretion told him this rental would get the owner, who was a terrible nag, off his back for six months. He backed off. "When do you want to move in? Tomorrow?"

"Now." She was figuring on the back of her checkbook and when she had the total, voided the first check, rewrote one for the six months' sum, tore it out and handed it to him. "Now, if you'll just give me the key I'll move in."

"Now just a minute . . . this check—"

"Did I figure it wrong?"

"Well, the bank's not open today."

"You don't have much to lose, do you? Tomorrow's Monday. You can call my bank. I'm not going to skip; I'm too tired, my baby's tired. I just want to move in so we can get some sleep."

Tillie filled out the details of the lease. In the brief moment that Dulcie had her drivers' license out of her wallet, Hinckley tried like mad to see if it said M or S in the place marked Married.

"Marvin," Tillie ordered, "go heat the water, get us some fresh coffee." The minute they were alone, Tillie proposed collusion. "I've got to put down something to please him. Shall I make it Mrs. or Miss?"

"Just put Dulcie Carpenter."

"If you want, dear, I'll make it Mrs. for you."

"Would you believe six bridesmaids in yellow *peau de soie* and a maid of honor and a ring bearer and flower girl, and a mother of the bride, and a six week honeymoon cruise to Tahiti, and I walked down the aisle with such a sunburn the only thing we could do for three nights was play chess, and on the fourth night I discovered that chess wasn't the only dull game in town . . ."

Ms. Tillie wrote on the lease in front of Dulcie Carpenter, with feeling of pride in her sex.

"That little bitchaballoo . . ." she said to herself as Dulcie and her moving men drove off. "One of the best goddam liars I ever had the pleasure to come across."

From the moment Dulcie started to bring things into the house she had very definite ideas on what to put where. The white interior had a sense of clean and fresh. Kevin rode her foot the last few steps. She put down the box of toys and they both flopped onto the mattress in the living room. It became a trampoline for Kevin.

As she lay there for the moment's respite she could still hear that woman from across the street calling for her dog.

7

I did not leave the gates open she has got to know I didn't how could I we came outside I locked the door she said what about the gas I went back to check she turned off the light in her closet she locked—no, he had locked—yes, *I locked the door got in the car backed out she closed the gates.* . . .

His breathing stabilized.

"Sonny . . ."

"Be right there."

"Sonnnnnny . . ."

He took the ice tray from under the faucet. Now the cubes were small enough to squeeze into the mouth of the ice bag. "I heard you, I'm coming . . ." She should know he had to refill the tray. She knew how hard it was to get the ice out with the release lever broken. He'd told her half a dozen times the damn thing didn't work. Every time they had drinks she was the one who put it under the faucet and complained. He pressed out air, screwed the top on the bulging bag and hurried across the living room to the study where Geegee, cigarette smoldering, was dialing the phone.

"Who now?"

"The police." Her finger, poised uncertainly above the dial, questioned who else there was to turn to.

"No, Geegee, no, they can't help." He broke the connection, gently slid the cigarette from between her teeth and snuffed it out. "We just have to be patient, dear. Wait . . ." He eased her back onto the sofa, pillow at her neck, icebag over her eyes and slipped off her shoes, assuring her the dog would come home, and if he didn't, in the morning he would go to the animal shelter to see if he had been picked up.

"He's in a gutter someplace—dead—I know it."

"If he's dead, wouldn't I have found him? I crisscrossed every block for a square mile."

"And we were off having fun and all the time the gates were open . . ." Her tone fitted him for the hair shirt. Well, he wasn't about to wear it. He wouldn't even dignify that with an answer. His eyes played over the room, realizing he hadn't sat in here and read for months and suddenly missed it: the fireplace, almost big enough for a man to walk into, the huge oak desk that had passed with the house from one owner to another since it couldn't be moved through an ordinary door. A room where novels should have been written, brandy sniffed after dinner. And what was it to him—? A room where he kept the household checkbook and the Sears' service policies on the washing machine and TV set.

"Everything I love . . . first Duchess, now Aubie . . ." The whimper begun under the icebag graduated to a full sob. Her hand tore at the air, grasping for him. "Sonny, Sonny—"

"I'm here, Geegee, I'm here." He listened for pity in his voice, heard only resignation. *I'm here mother I'm here anybody comes around to hurt you mother you just tell me I'll chop 'em to pieces. . . .*

"Don't leave me, Sonny."

"I won't leave you."

"Aubie'll come back?"

"Aubie'll come back." He released her hands and looked out to the front garden; the iron bars on the window grill, the tangle of hibiscus encroaching on the house, fishpond slimy with fallen leaves. The high wall,

79

hemming all in. The sky, low now, the color of solder. A lid.

"Where's he gonna go?" he questioned himself. Where did Aubie know to go, any more than Ron would know if he suddenly decided one day to open the gates, drive out, not close them, and not come back. Looking out the window, he remembered being on the observation platform of the last car on a train, years back, where everything he saw disappeared and there was nothing to hold onto.

Aubie would come back.

Ron sighed. The private joke of *To Yermo and Back* seemed hollow. A waste.

"That woman!" Clapping the icebag onto her head with both hands, Geegee sat up like a joke-store snake coming out of a can. "Go right over there—"

"What woman? Where?"

"Across the street. The one that's moving in. She doesn't know about our bell."

Dulcie Carpenter and her son were looking for faces in the clouds.

"That's a lion—"

"No, that's a rabbit."

"Not that one, mommy—that one."

"Wow," she said, "that is a lion. A ferocious boy lion."

"No, it's a mommy lion, and she's gonna eat everybody." Dulcie took the cue, pushed his sweater sleeve up, and began nibbling the delicately boned arm while he giggled and ran from her in mock horror.

It was turning cold. She dug into one of the cartons the movers had left in the garage and found her shapeless "Mahler Grooves" sweat shirt wrapped around the alarm clock. Pulled it over her head, rolled up the cuffs and felt at home. Keefee Avenue, North Hollywood. A far cry from Venice. Could be weeks before they found her. Let 'em. Her door was locked, bolted, sealed. Trying to get her back would be as futile as a buck tracking spoor out of season. . . .

"Catch . . ."

The beach ball came at Ron, thrown eight feet short. He picked it up at the curb and tossed it back to waiting, four-year-old arms. Overanxious, the child dropped it; eager for more play, ran to retrieve it.

"Don't let Kevin trap you." Dulcie's voice came to him from the garage where she was on her knees, putting toys back into a carton that had spilled.

"Excuse me," Ron said, adding a racing car to the box, "I live across the street."

"We haven't seen your dog." She flicked long dark-blond hair out of her eyes and shoved the carton into the corner with others, wiping her face on the arm of the sweat shirt.

"I came over to tell you our gate bell doesn't work. So if you do see him, just come through and knock on our front door."

Her direct gray eyes met his like a firm handshake. "Sure."

"Thanks." The way Geegee had said "woman across the street," he had expected forty-five and overfed. What he saw was less than thirty, sinewy, sensual and without guile. "Thanks again," he said.

"Are you strong?" Kevin was at his heels as he started away.

"Well, yes, I suppose so."

"Could you pick me up?"

Ron's hands, fit under the little boy's armpits, lifted him until their faces were level, and stepped into the mirror of the child's gleeful eyes.

Sonnnnny, where is Sonnnnnny . . . where are yoooooo . . . His favorite game when Geegee came looking like that, knowing where he was all the time, hiding behind that big old chair, the one that scraped when you moved it because it had no wheels,

81

or under the staircase in the front hall, or upstairs on the roof behind that big, rusted whirring ventilator. Geegee knew all the good places but always pretended. Where is Sonnnnnny. . . ?

Where was he?

"He means way up," Dulcie interpolated.

"Okay, Sonny, way up . . ." What perversity made him call the child that? He quickly put him down.

"Again, again . . ."

"Cool it, Kevin, the man's busy looking for his dog."

"Well, if you do see him, just knock on our front door."

"I will." Dulcie, watching him cross the street, thought warm eyes, nice man. From the other curb, he paused to call back, "Oh, his name is—"

"Aubrey Beardsley. I know. Your wife told me."

"My wife? Oh, no. She's my mother."

"You're putting me on."

He leaned against the gate, finding her easy to talk to. "I know what you mean. Sometimes I feel that way about her myself."

"She doesn't look old enough—"

"I'll tell her you said that. It'll make her day." Ron's wave was for the child. The smile that was for Dulcie stripped years from his face but still didn't broaden the gap enough for her to believe that woman could be his mother.

She watched through her garage window as he latched the gates and moved back down his driveway, calling his dog's name.

"Aubie . . ." A perfunctory call, without conviction. There was no possible way the dog could be on the property. Still, the hedges were overgrown, the ground cover so deep, he might have encountered a poisoned snail; a lot of people fed snails strychnine. . . . "Here, boy." He moved, ankle-deep in ivy, along the matted Texas privet that screened the entire side of the property, peering and poking into it. Midway to the back yard he noticed the screen that covered the crawl-hole had been partially torn away. He squatted to study it, ripped the remains clear, and lay on the ground, easing his head underneath the house. "Aubie—? You in there?" As his eyes adjusted to the minimal light of the narrow, dank space, a pair of eyes looked back at him.

"Geegee . . . I found him!"

Headache and icebag abandoned, Geegee negotiated the distance from study to kitchen to crawl-hole with the celerity of a sprinter, balancing in her hands a dish of horse meat with which to welcome home the dog.

Only Aubie's eyes and nose were visible. Geegee understood completely why he resisted the bait. "Poor baby," she said. "Don't you see? He's depressed. His mother dies and we go away and leave him behind; he thinks he's got nothing to live for."

"Don't shove the dish at him, Geegee, make him come out for it."

"He could starve under there. Num-num-num-num, baby."

Ron took the dish from her and moved it a distance away. "He's hungry, he'll come out."

"I read," she went on resolutely, "about a dog committed suicide when he was left alone, threw himself under a truck."

"How come I never read these things in the paper?" adding that apparently Aubie hadn't read the item either, since he was belly-crawling out to the food. They stood by, pleased at the prodigal's return, and watched him eat. "We've got to keep an eye on him, Sonny," she said, careful that Aubie shouldn't hear. "Every minute. His frame of mind, there's no telling what he'll do. I mean, he must be desperate, tearing the screen out like that and—"

Like Lot's wife, Geegee turned her head and became fixed.

The crawl-hole was disgorging a second occupant. A medium-sized, yellow-matted-haired, long-tailed, undistinguished, limpid-eyed mutt. A snort of admiration

escaped Ron. "Son of a gun . . ." Geegee's eyes flared
with disgust. Her voice ripped like a hacksaw.

"Get that bitch out of here!"

It had all been too easy. So unlike her. She had said,
"Get her out I won't have her." He had said, "No, Aubie
needs someone; hell, Geegee, we're no answer for him,
he needs someone to be with. . . ." And she'd given in.
Just like that.

He didn't feel he'd been that forceful; to be truthful,
he didn't really care if Aubie had a companion or not.
Most dogs live alone in a house. Why was he suddenly
a champion for Aubie's cause? And what made Geegee
give in so readily? Somewhere there was an answer. His
head ached in the search of it, but no flash of light turned
itself on.

He propped his pillow against the headboard and
looked across at the peacefully sleeping dogs on the other
twin bed. Aubie and his girl. He wondered what they
should name her.

Ronnie's got a girl, Ronnie's got a girl. . . . June Wonder-
man, Crenshaw Avenue, and he—fourteen? thirteen? He
had touched her breast; that's all he remembered, all that
came back to him. There was no person there. Just fumbling under a blouse for hooks and cupping a breast in
his hand.

He found he was sweating. Raising up on one elbow,
he reached, without looking, into the back of the third
drawer of the dresser for the almost dried up half pack
of Kools that he kept hidden for himself for the rare
occasion when he needed one. In the bathroom, window
open, door closed, he lit it. Sat in the darkness through
a few puffs that filled his lungs but brought no satisfaction. The clandestine smoking of a stale cigarette could
in no way satisfy his need.

Soundlessly, his fingers turned the door knob. Pain-
fully slowly, he slid through the corridor that separated
their rooms, stopping just short of her bed. In sleep, she

84

had thrown the blanket back; one long leg extended bare from the twistings of her nightgown. Voluptuous full breasts rising and falling with each sonorous breath. He held there, silent, then backed carefully into his own room, closing the doors between Geegee and himself. Aubie stretched and his female slid into the arch of his legs.

In ten minutes, Ron was in front of the pink building. Before he rang 301 he glanced across the street, wondering if she might be in Mac's bar, which was still open. His finger held long on the bell. He was about to turn away when her voice came through the speaker.

"Yes?" Impatient? Sleepy? "Who is it?"

He identified himself, reminding he was the one in Mac's place, the one whose dog died.

"Oh, sure, come on up." The security door clicked him in. When he got out of the elevator on the third floor, Edna Trumble was standing in the corridor just outside her apartment, monogrammed flannel robe hanging open. Her hair, tightly rolled against her scalp, created a skullcap of metal doughnuts. As he came closer he could see her low breasts through the nightgown. She moved flat against him in the doorway and smiled a welcome.

"Took you long enough to get a hard-on."

The streets were wet with the light rain that had fallen in the early hours. He had the world to himself. Freshly bathed shrubs and ivy greeted Ron as he drove through the gray morning. The faintest flush of pink began to appear in the sky as he pulled up to open the gates. He reached through the garlands of iron to unlatch them, and saw her—crawling out from beneath the thick overgrown oleander of the parkway that served as inadequate shelter—body wet, yellow fur matted, ears and tail drooping.

If Geegee had engraved the message to him it couldn't have been clearer. She knew—but hadn't he known she would know?—that he was gone, for how long and why. And he'd been so agonizingly careful handling the gates so they wouldn't betray him. She'd never really given in about the dog, he realized. She'd just waited her time.

He clanged the gates open and closed without giving a damn that they trumpeted his arrival.

The dog sat on the parkway, patiently waiting to be invited back in. "Sorry, old girl." He left her out there and turned away, feeling squandered, as though Geegee had been in the room with Edna and him and watched from the foot of the bed.

Where are you spying from, Geegee? He wanted to thumb his nose at each window he passed.

Smart ass, she thought, watching through her bedroom drapes, as he moved toward the back of the house, passing not three feet from her; suit jacket slung over his shoulder, carrying his necktie like some kid come home from a street game, dirty and mucked up.

He sensed—hoped—she was watching. But as he rounded the bedroom wing to the back plaza where all the dark-stained doors waited for him in the U of the house, fatigue and despair overrode the temporary release the night had brought.

Doesn't this plaza put you in mind of Warner Baxter and Lupe Velez? Geegee had asked when they first moved in.

Not particularly, not a fucking bit, he said to the warped lock that resisted his key. He was certain he'd left his bedroom door unlatched so he could slip in easily—as he had on other occasions when the acuity of his need overwhelmed—and now the door was locked from the inside by Guess Who. Well, he was damned if he'd go around to the front door, or the kitchen door where he'd have to walk by her room to get to his. The key would either let him in or he'd go through the bathroom window.

With persistent maneuvering, the aged lock obliged. Aubie barely looked up when he came in and flung his clothes onto the chair and fell into the bed.

"Aubie . . . we've both been screwed."

At five of six he heard her bath water go on, level with his head on the opposite side of the wall where he slept. She knew how it irritated him to hear the rush of water in his ear. She, who always bathed at four in the afternoon, suddenly to get an immaculate urge at dawn?

Keep it up, Geegee, keep it up and you're going to be so sorry. . . .

Sometime between six and six fifteen sleep hit him. At six thirty Aubie's whining had him stumbling out of bed, eyes burning, mouth rancid, reaching the door by instinct, to let the dog out. The routine of the morning made its demands and he packed bowling bag with sweat sox, shoes, towel, remembering to wear a T-shirt underneath his white on white. Monday's suit hung to the left where it belonged. He put it on.

"Breakfast . . ." her voice trilled from the gallery like a fingernail on a blackboard. The odor of the peace offering—or was it victory celebration?—bacon, eggs, coffee, French toast, overpowered by her perfume, drifted into his room.

"Morning, sweetheart . . ." With one hand Geegee held the skirt of her voluminous brocade housecoat to keep it from sweeping the floor. With the other, she was pouring coffee.

"Morning." All he wanted was to get out, avoid any possible discussion, but his thudding head brought him to the table. He drank his orange juice and took his vitamins, standing.

"Sit down, sweetie—everything's hot and beautiful."

"I'm not hungry."

"Not even one little bite for Geegee?" She cut a sliver of French toast, touching it with syrup, and held it temptingly to him. "It's a sin to waste . . ."

Ghastly Monday, the longest day with a bowling ball at the end of it, loomed ahead. Lessened his resistance to the chair being pulled back for him. "But just coffee," he insisted, shaking his head to bacon, eggs. Unheeding, she piled his plate: She knew her customers; he'd eat.

"My baby's grouchy. Didn't sleep well—?"

God, was she going to play the whole fraudulent charade? "I bounced around . . . quite a bit."

"Well, you'll make up for it tonight." She smiled at him and syruped her toast. He cut his into inch-squares, arranged all the pieces symmetrically on his plate, and finally said it.

"She's still out there."

"She'll go away."

That was all that was said till all the little soldiers on his plate were finished and he was in the car. They exchanged wishes for a good day, she said have fun bowling, he said don't smoke and for God's sake eat, and backed out. Holding the gates for him, Geegee felt satisfaction that, as she had prophesized, the bitch was gone from the parkway. It was with a feeling of things set right that she stretched both arms expansively to bring the gates together. And felt the nails driven into her hands.

His car had blocked her view, but now that he'd completed the full arc of backing out, she could see them both. Sonny, nodding, smiling, grinning like an idiot at that new woman across the street. *Slut*, to come out barefoot with nothing on but a man's shirt . . .

"Bye . . ." Geegee's voice cut between them. "Getting late, better go . . ." The smile she wore to wave him down the street dropped like a hot rock as she closed the gates. "We found our dog, dear," she called, concluding the relationship with the new neighbor. "Thank you." And swept back into the house.

Dulcie read the Keep Out, This Means You message in the hard clang of the latch.

Involuntarily, she said it aloud, "Ooooooh, Mother . . ."

Ron hooked into the conveyor belt of Monday. Tuesday preceded Wednesday, and both blew away like the storm cloud that had gone east to plague the rest of the nation. Scarlet berries began to appear on the pyracantha bush, Thanksgiving turkeys in the food market ads, there was only light eye irritation in the basin, and Geegee said, "Isn't it lovely to have things back to normal again?"

"You can only mourn so long, Sonny. Face it. It's over, we can't bring her back."

He'd said that. When they were his words, she'd been implacable. "That's what I—

"That's what you what, dear?"

"Nothing."

With surgical precision she trimmed the fat off her lambchop until all that remained was the eye. "Are you sure nothing?"

"My mind wandered . . ."

"Well, pay attention because there are so many things we put aside with our tragedy. Now the first thing I want —Do we have an album?"

"Album? Whose?" he asked, thinking she meant music.

"Picture, picture. Eat your beansprouts, sweetie."

"They're dull."

"They're full of protein. We owe it to Duchess, we can't just pretend she never existed . . ."

"That'd be pretty hard to do," he said dryly, "we've got Aubie."

Geegee went on talking, vigorously enthusing about doing a full photo album of Duchess. "We took so many wonderful pictures during the years. Now where'd we put them. . . ?" As she puzzled over where the pictures might be stored, Ron glanced at the impassive animal underneath the table and surprised himself by nudging the dog sharply with the toe of his shoe, disturbing his peace. Aubie walked away and lay over by the door but his eyes stayed on Ron, reproaching him.

I'm not treating him any differently, Ron told himself. *Don't I feed him, same as always?*

The image of Aubie lifting his leg over the grave was becoming less frequent now. At first, every time he saw him outside, smelling around a tree or a bush, it reoccurred. And his dreams . . . One still broke a sweat from him. He was sitting on a tiny swing that hung from the ceiling of Geegee's bathroom, spider-sized, unnoticed, watching her, naked, showering. Only one needle of water coming out, then the showerhead became Aubie and he was urinating on Geegee. Ron felt the same chill now that awakened him that night as he was starting to wet the bed. He'd barely made it in to the bathroom, rationalizing the chill that engulfed him as prologue to a virus. But it passed. He had rinsed the sheet in the washbowl, hung it over a chair to dry, and lay awake waiting for daylight so he could remake the bed.

He pushed his plate away.

"How many asparagus did you eat?" she wanted to know. "Five, six?"

He swallowed bile. "I don't know . . . six."

"Six." She marked it down on a little pad at her elbow. "That's twenty-one, and two lamb chops—" informing him with a smile that she was counting calories. "I've put us on a diet. Like you wanted."

Like *he* wanted? He'd never said that. Not once. Not out loud.

"After the funeral," she answered his thought, "that's all you talked about. And how you could even think a thing like my putting on a pound or two when Duchess was just fresh in the ground . . ." For her to move so freely through the crevasses of his mind left him feeling exposed.

"And you're hardly the one to talk when it comes to fat," she prodded. "You can barely make the zipper close on your pants."

Under cover of the napkin, he checked his fly. "I never said you were fat, Geegee, never even thought it . . ."

She held up her hand to stay the conversation while she added the column. "That's four hundred eighty-five calories. That's wonderful; now you can't have another bite till morning; how much did you have for lunch?"

He told her never mind his lunch, he'd buy her an

album in the morning. Was it his turn to do the dishes? No, hers, but just put 'em in the sink. She wanted to spend the evening looking for the pictures.

They didn't find any that night, but in one of the back bedrooms (originally intended for live-in help, but which they used for storage and which neither had entered in at least a year) they rediscovered some long forgotten whims: fishing boots and poles—his and hers—skis, easels, dried brushes and paints, modeling clay, rock hard. And the tandem bicycle, dust-covered and flat-tired. Geegee's disappointment at not finding any snapshots was leavened by the prospect of reactivating all those wonderful hobbies. The bicycle especially pleased her. Since they were on a diet they ought to exercise.

Her enthusiasm was infectious. They laughed together as they retrieved some of their past indulgences from oblivion, carrying them out to the gallery like little sins taken to confession. Both went to bed feeling a sense of clarity, of organization, about their life. Nothing was ever wasted, Geegee pronounced—and what wonderful Sundays they could look forward to, fishing, painting! Ron promised he'd put the bike in perfect shape first chance he had. Looked forward to it.

Sleep came to him easily that night.

Ruth crossed Wilshire at the caution of the light, one of the vast army of secretaries on the lunch hour dash. Navy-blue-suited to the top of the knee, comfortably shod; if not a recipient of the fifteen-year pin, at least the ten. She was somewhat out of breath from walking so fast, but the exertion heightened her color. A couple of male heads turned to appreciate a flash of leg, knee to thigh, as her pleated skirt fanned out and up to accommodate the sprint she burst into as she saw Ron's car.

He was just backing out of his parking spot.

"Mr. G."

He braked and watched the slim, delicately structured woman, one hand struggling with her skirt's decorum, the other burdened with a bulky package. How pleasantly windblown she looked, he thought, eyes shining as though just come from an adventure.

"I got your albums—" She caught her breath and joined him at the driver's side. "I thought you might want to put them in your car."

"Very thoughtful of you, Ruth, but you didn't have to run."

"Well this way you won't have to come back. You know how the Commissioner is. He'll keep you there all afternoon."

"I'm afraid I put you to a lot of trouble, Ruth."

"Please, Mr. G., I was glad to do it."

"Oh," he reminded himself. "Did you have enough money?"

"I forgot, there's change . . ." and she counted forty-two cents into his hand from her jacket pocket.

"Thanks, thanks again, Ruth, very nice of you—"

"I just hope you like them." She smoothed her hair and waited. He pulled one of the photo albums free of the wrappings, and gave his approval. "You surely didn't get these in the drugstore?"

"No. Ohrbachs."

"You walked all the way to Ohrbachs?"

"Oh, you wouldn't have liked the ones in the drugstore. They were cheap. Cardboard. Now these—" she leaned slightly into the car as she touched the album, "they're vinyl, you could almost take them for leather . . ."

"I bet you missed lunch, Ruth."

"I don't mind, Mr. G. I know how you appreciate quality. And I know these will please your mother . . ."

Just "thank you" didn't seem adequate, but he said it again, "Thank you, Ruth. Very much. What would I do without you?"

"Well, that's one thing we don't have to worry about, do we, because I'm always in there, solid, nine to five—" She backed off, as though she'd said more than she meant to. "Well, have a nice weekend."

"Weekend?" He was surprised.

"Yes, tomorrow's Saturday."

"Oh . . . yes . . . well, you too."

Moving into traffic, he caught a glimpse of her through his rearview mirror. He reached out the window and waved his hand above the car. She saw it, smiled, and waved back.

He thought about her off and on during the long, dull, chart-heavy discussion with the Insurance Commissioner.

Ron sat on a ladder in the dark, narrow, airless storage closet that flanked the living room fireplace. Waiting. And a story that Bill Hoffman had told him one day at the catering wagon about a little old Jewish man in Russia came alive in his mind. *This little old man,* as Hoffman told it, *no more'n a hundred five pounds dripping wet, is walking along the street in Zhitomir, bent over double with this enormous, heavy, burlap sack on his back, barely making it. Now this little kid across the street is looking out the window and he sees the old man and he calls his father over and he says, Tata, why is that old man—such an old man—why is he carrying such a heavy sack, What's in it to make it so heavy?* The father (how Ron envied Hoffman his accents and wished he could do stuff like that) *the father says to the kid, Mein tierehr zun—that means my dearest son—in that sack that old man is carrying on his back all the things that it's a sin to throw away.*

Ron hadn't laughed then. The story made him vaguely sad—he hadn't been sure what it really meant, and Hoffman had been perturbed. "Don't you get it? It's talmudic, it's beautiful. I love you, Gohdiener, but you're a goyishe kopf."

Ron could tell Hoffman now he understood it. What little light filtered into this dusty storage space where spiders lived serene showed him the sated, overfed, glutted closet filled with things they had never thrown away. And he felt the weight on his back. Incomplete chess sets. Slant board. Attachment for the barbeque to

93

smoke your own hams, never once plugged in. Badminton with birds missing and a torn net. So much, he brooded; obscured, confused. *Wasted, wasted, wasted.*

He would miss Hoffman, when he transferred to the new branch office after the merger. He seemed to have a little old Jewish man for every condition. Ron wondered if he had one for what he was feeling now. "Dammit, Geegee, what am I, an idiot, hung up here in the dark? I can't see, can't breathe—" His irritation came around corners to the kitchen where she was trying to remember what he'd sent her in to get. "Flashlight, Geegee, flashlight!"

When his message penetrated, she was concentrating on a recipe for moussaka torn from a 1967 magazine. She stuffed it back into a drawer filled with other yellowing newsprint and found the flashlight, as he directed, in the middle drawer on the left.

"Coming . . ."

Aubie lay impassively across the threshold in her way. "Does baby want a num-num?" His raised eyebrow, which she took for consent, turned her back into the kitchen, trying to determine where the num-nums were. Ron stepped over Aubie a moment later and found the flashlight on the sink. He could hear Geegee foraging around in the pantry. "Wherever you are," he called with resignation, "I've got it."

"What'd you say?" Emerging with the treat, and noting both Ron and the flashlight gone, she gave her full attention to the dog. "Here, baby, here's your goodie . . . num-num, num-num . . ." She touched his nose with it. He turned his head away.

"Okay, you want to pout over that bitch," she told him, "pout—" To punish Aubie, she ground the biscuit up in the garbage disposal.

"Geegee, there's no blue suitcase up here . . ." Ron's voice came, muffled, from the upper reaches of the closet. She leaned in, directing the beam of the flashlight.

94

"The small one with the stripe. See? The little one in the corner, the overnight bag, that's the one."

"It's brown." He was sweating, uncomfortable, needing air.

"Brown, blue, it's a suitcase."

Adjusting his precarious position on the ladder, one arm tense against the packed shelf, he slowly withdrew the small bag as though defusing a bomb. For an instant, his light played on her eager face as he handed it down to her, then followed her out of the closet. "Well. . . ?" he asked from the red velvet depths of the sofa. "The pictures in there?"

"Oh, Sonny, Sonny, Sonny, you won't believe what's in here . . ." He raised up on one elbow to see what had mellowed her voice. She and the suitcase were on the floor where she had anticipated uncovering a trove of photos. The few snapshots that were in the case she pushed aside as she mined the greater vein of treasure. Baby clothes. His.

Her eyes glistened with tears as she clutched to her a faded, shrunken, moth-chewed, 40-year-old sweater.

"My God, Geegee, don't you ever throw anything away?"

"Throw it away?" Her eyes threatened to burst from their sockets. Italics sprang from her mouth. "This is Us, Sonny. You. Me. This is our Life." *And his asthma inhaler all the way in the other room.* "If it makes you happy, Geegee," he urged, gentling, "keep 'em, keep 'em."

"Oh, Sonny . . ." she held the little sweater out to his chest, like a postage stamp on a packing crate. "You wore this." His lips worked into a smile that did not involve his eyes. "I don't think it'll fit, Geegee." He stood up, subtly out of reach of sweater and hand. "Let's find the pictures, hmm? I'm dog tired."

Sunday was their shortest excursion ever: Olvera Street for two quick tacos at a sidewalk stand, some new candles purchased from the basement shop that had been there as long as he could remember, and back home to the quest.

It crossed his mind several times in the next days that the search had begun to possess Geegee. That she only found a few random snapshots, tucked here and there, didn't seem to bother her. The motherlode of pictures was *somewhere in this house* and she was confident that ultimately they would be found *in a blue suitcase!* but meantime, wasn't it fun looking? All the things they'd put aside and forgotten—it was like a rerun of your life. *Rerun.* More than once she used these words.

He moved through the days with a yeasting detachment not unlike what he'd felt at the grave. The gallery took on the appearance of a Flea Market. Each new recovery, and she was calling him at the office. "The tango records, remember? The Valentino album I bought? I found 'em."

"Geegee, they're seventy-eights . . ."

"They play. Wanna hear?" The scratchy strains of "La Cumparsita" came through to him, augmented by Geegee's *te-tum-TUM-tum-tum.* "Not now. I'm going into a meeting. Haven't time . . ." The next day, her first call —URGENT—had him running back from the men's room. "Guess what else? The rug."

"What rug?"

"On the top shelf of the pantry—"

"What're you climbing up there for? You'll break your neck. I told you when I got home I'd do all the climbing."

"It's gorgeous, I don't know why we never finished it . . ." With the phone cradled against her shoulder she crawled across the rug, tracing a river of yellow that ended abruptly on the coarse canvas backing. "It's fate, I was thinking of buying a throw rug for the side of my bed, now we'll just finish this and it won't cost a cent 'cause I found all the yarns. And I found your first little football helmet . . ."

96

You'll eat the cake, it's your party. You've got to eat it; I had it decorated special, cost three dollars and thirty-nine cents.

Yes, Geegee—wanting to eat the cake, just to please her, but knowing if he did he'd throw up. And he didn't want Geegee to see him throw up. He didn't care about the kids, he hardly knew them, one new school after another. But for Geegee to see him—smell him—like that.

You eat the cake or you'll never have another party.

"Two weeks, we'll have it done, I mean if we really spend every evening on it. And if we haven't forgotten how to hook—" There was that little yarn shop on Fairfax, she reminded him, where they had all those fabulous colors—

I threw up all that night. And never had another party. I was nine. Why did you have to wake it all up, Geegee?

8

BONJOUR, maman chérie. He could have sworn as he turned onto Keefee Avenue that the words rolled down the block to greet him. *Good morning, Mother dear.* From the moment she'd found the French lessons album, it was *Leve-toi, Jacques, il est tard . . .* Get up, Jack, it's late, assaulting his ears through breakfast, putting him to bed at night.

Il est tard? Quelle heure est-il?

The point that they couldn't get to France this year, might never be able to afford it, couldn't penetrate the Gallic wall of sound that engulfed the house, decibels turned up to reach them no matter in which room they were.

"Il est déjà neuf heures?" Geegee questioned along with the booming record as Ron applied Gypsy Auburn to her roots in the kitchen. "It's nine o'clock already?" the flat, instructing voice articulated. *"Oui, il est déjà neuf heures . . . "* they said in concert.

"Can't go to Paris," Geegee's voice reverberated in the sink as her natural red went down the drain, "without learning the language. It would be an insult."

"Geegee, if you want to learn French, that's fine." The sand funneled through the egg timer, and he rinsed off

98

the hair conditioner. "But get it out of your head that we're going to get there."

"*Embrasse-moi, Jacques . . .*" She came up, smiling, from under dripping hair, and pursed a kiss at him. And the needle stayed in the groove. He could look forward to it all day Saturday.

Bonjour, Charlie. Comment vas-tu, petit frère?

The sheet billowed out over her kingsized bed. He caught the ends and stretched the corners to contour and let his mind play with the idea of a vacation. Alone.

"Hospital corner." He corrected the lapse she pointed out and ventured a trial balloon. "Look, Geegee, with the merger I may not get any time off this year. Why don't you go someplace by yourself?"

"Who'd take care of you?"

"You love Palm Springs. . . ."

Oui, maman, je me leve. Toute de suite.

"I could take you there, pick you up."

Yes, mother dear, I'm getting up right away.

"Do you good to get away from me, Geej . . ."

She wasn't hearing him. Her concentration was on the lesson, echoing slightly behind the tutorial Voice. "*A tout à l'heure, maman . . .*"

The bicycle was ready at eleven o'clock as promised. In the six-block walk from the house to the cycle shop he found himself startled by changes taking place in the neighborhood. The two huge empty lots—he remembered sunflowers blooming and kids playing baseball —now the same lots had spawned behemoth apartment buildings. Landscaped and almost totally occupied.

All this going on, while he drove by, twice a day, in a vacuum. He felt subverted: When had he stopped looking?

"What'n hell's the matter with me?"

"What'd you say?" a voice called.

Ron's head jerked upward, embarrassed at having spoken his disquiet aloud, but the voice—an elderly man watering a rubber plant on a second-floor balcony—was answering his wife's summons to brunch, which she repeated loudly enough for Ron to hear.

He walked on, asking his senses to feed him whatever else he had missed. The second Gorgon in stucco, crystalline in the sun, was bright pink and Edna Trumble ran through his mind.

What would he have, he remembered her asking, booze or coffee? Bourbon was his preference. With a little goose, she'd headed him toward the portable bar. "Just let me get these curlers out of my hair, don't want to put a permanent dimple in your ass. The bed's in there," she directed. "Mattress is firm but not too firm, lotta bounce in it; get your drink and get your clothes off . . ." and she was in the bathroom, pulling off the curlers behind a half-closed door. As he folded his clothes neatly on the chair, carefully buttoning the rear pocket of his trousers that held his wallet, he could hear her gargling. He finished off his double after he was in bed and covered with the sheet. He could feel the alcohol reaching his fingers.

Lying there alone, he tried, but failed, to distinguish whether this was a furnished apartment or the result of one quick lunch hour at a department store. His eye searched, but could not find one curve, spiral, or personal signature, and the room began to feel clinical, as though he were waiting for a doctor.

She came from the bathroom, bringing with her the mixed odors of Tabu and Lavoris. The curlers, he noted, were gone, but the hair remained a skullcap of tight, graying swirls. Her body looked firm, with skin, very white, that should be hard and cool to the touch. Her breasts were smaller than they'd first appeared through the sheer nightgown. Low and wide spaced, flushed nipples thrust up in relief against flat, dull-pink aureoles. As she threw back the sheet and surveyed the weaponry, her exploring hands descended her own body. "Well? How do you want it? Fuck or make love."

100

Never had it been presented to him quite like that. She didn't expect or wait for an answer but headed straight for the groining point. He lay, passive, letting the warmth swallow him, then he thrust up to reverse their positions. But her arm was steel. "Take it easy, baby, we'll get there, just do what Edna says . . . you're doin' great, baby, doin' great, let's get the peg up . . ."

He could have walked, but didn't, taking the satisfaction for what it offered. His need was to summit, to conquer. "I know you're strong, baby, you don't have to prove it." She fed him a breast as pacifier. "Just be good, baby, Edna'll do it all. . . ."

His arms pained in resentment. He flexed his fingers, releasing his tight grasp of the handlebars and blood came back into his knuckles. He'd have to get used to riding a bike again. His leg muscles were sending up protest at being disturbed from indolence. Still, he felt strong, riding, pumping away. He had stayed beside Edna Trumble, watching her sleep, her belly muscles spasming in aftershock. When daylight edged through the curtains, he got up and dressed; thinking how ironic was his concern for his wallet. He left, feeling if anyone was to have been paid, it should have been he.

"Miss Edna Trumble of Security Trust . . ." He took the call with the door closed. Was he alone in his office, Edna wanted to know, because she was alone in hers. "Know where my hand is. . . ? Go on, baby, you know . . . tell Edna where she's got her hand . . ."

A raucous horn shocked him back to the moment. He laboriously pedaled the long-framed bicycle home through the rest of the memory: the sweat he'd broken into, fearful someone else might be on his line; the effort of avoiding her, finally having Ruth tell her, with secretarial pre-emption, that Mr. Gohdiener was always in and out and was there anything she could do?

"Gorgeous, just gorgeous, I wouldn't believe it, only seventeen dollars and forty-eight cents, it looks brand new—" Geegee tucked the receipt into the pocket of her Saturday jeans and was ready to go.

"Look, I just walked a mile, rode half a mile, I'd like to get a cup of coffee or something."

"When we get back." She carefully closed the gates, settled onto the rear seat of the tandem, and they pedaled away.

"You're not giving me any help—"

"I am, too," she replied, "I'm pumping as hard as you."

"You're coasting, you're letting me do it all—" Who did she think she was kidding? He'd been on this bike often enough in the past to know whether she was putting forth effort or not. And if she had any illusions about reducing the size of that can of hers, she'd have to work. Under the pretext of glancing back to check for cars, he caught her with her feet barely touching the pedals.

"I slipped, my foot slipped—"

For a block, it was easier. Her pedaling was equal to his. Then he could feel the change of pressure and decided to irritate her a little.

"I saw her," he said, "in back of the market. Eating garbage."

"Well, if she comes around our place," Geegee took her feet completely off the pedals and rested them on the frame, "I'll just call the dog pound."

"*You* want to be up front?"

She let his sarcasm blow past. *Oh no, little boy* . . . she wasn't stepping into that trap. Before she'd answer that kind of crack, she'd wait until the muscles of his neck relaxed. The hunch of his back and the fury with which his legs pumped told her he was far from finished with the subject. In breathy soprano she sang an inaccurately remembered phrase from "A Bicycle Built for Two."

"It's a natural instinct," he finally volleyed as they made the third right turn back onto their own street. But his anger seemed flat. Spent.

She smiled to herself. She'd outwaited him. "Well, he never had that instinct when his mother was alive."

102

"He never had the chance," he countered.

"Okay, Sonnnnny!" Her thigh muscles cried for relief and the seat was too small and bit into her cheeks. "You had the last word. Drop it."

Dulcie had seen the tandem go up the block when she came out to wash her VW. It was the first glimpse she'd had of him all week. Must leave early, she thought, before the bus picked Kevin up for nursery school. The mother she'd seen three or four times, coming out to get the mail or pick up throwaways in those flowered tents she wore. Cold broad. Either nearsighted as hell and can't see across the street, or she's erasing us from the landscape. The nearsighted theory Dulcie didn't buy for one minute. How could anyone overlook a Comanche like Kevin?

"You stay put," she told him. "Don't ride your trike out into the street."

Sandals kicked off, warm suds running back down her arms, water squeezing between toes, the metal of the car hot beneath the thick terry cloth . . . it all felt good. *My God, Peter, don't you understand there's more to sex than getting on and off?* The terry cloth rag made her think of him. When it had been a full robe, she'd dropped it beside the swimming pool and dived in, naked, urging him to do the same. *Come on, Peter, come on in. . . . What're you afraid of, that I'll jerk you off in the water? Oh, Peter-Peter-Peter, you're the last in the world who should have a name like that.*

She hosed the soap, restoring the whiteness of the tire wall. Her distorted image looked back at her from the chromed convex of the hubcap. Bulging eyes, bulbous nose, lantern jaw. *That's not me. That's not Dulcie. I know me now.* She laughed. If she'd restring her guitar she could put that to music. *I Dig Bein' Alone* . . . or how about *My Screamin's All Behind Me* . . . or one dedicated to Peter, *If You Won't Screw, Baby, Screw You.* . . .

Not funny, she decided. Aloneness got to you. Not out

103

here, with the air and sun. But in there. In the bed. In the night.

The only male she'd been near in weeks, aside from those two who moved her and the ones at the market and gas station was this half-pint at her knees. And that man across the street. In the brief moment in the garage, she'd felt he wanted to stay and rap. Or maybe she'd read that into him. She remembered his eyes turned slightly downward at the outer edges. Gave him a sweet, sad look. But his hair was too short. Longer hair and sideburns, he'd look better.

As the heavy spray drove the suds off the hood, the tandem reappeared, with him doubled over the handlebars doing all the pumping. She really rides his back, Dulcie thought. As they came closer, she smiled and raised a hand, Hello.

He responded. Breathing heavily, chest heaving with the exertion, he braked the long bicycle and called out "Hi" loud enough for Kevin to hear it, who Hi'd back at him. But not loud enough, obviously, for his mother, who had to be deaf as well as myopic.

Dulcie went on about her work, unaffected by the obliterating stare, noting that it was the man who flung open the gates, the mother who closed and latched them.

Myopic as a hawk sighting on a field mouse, Geegee's eye had recorded every stitch, muscle and fiber of Dulcie all the way from the corner. Long bronzed legs stretching, body arched over the rounded roof of the car, every full swipe of her supple arm lifting the skimpy, frayed-edged, cut-off jeans to show a slice of white ass. Another inch and she'd be serving it all up. I know your kind, baby, Geegee thought as the gates settled into their scabby latch. You'd crawl under the house with anybody. Had Sonny really seen her eating garbage? No . . . no dog hangs around in one place that long. Sonny was just being snotty, she decided, and dismissed it.

Wheeling back to the kitchen door with him, she

thought of several places they hadn't yet looked for the pictures: under the bookcases in the study, and they hadn't yet tried the bottom of the hutch in the dining room. . . .

Bonjour, maman chérie . . . Good morning, mother dear. . . .

"You left the damned thing playing—"

"I knew we'd be right back, we're not ready for the Olympics yet." He opened and closed the refrigerator door and sat down at the kitchen table with a carton of skim milk. She spread crackers with peanut butter and strawberry jam and opened a Diet Pepsi.

Leve-toi, Jacques, il est tard.

"Yeah, Jack," he yelled back at the cannonading voice, "get your French ass outa bed."

Geegee's tongue worked a lump of peanut butter off a tooth before rebuking him. "Nothing like having a little refinement in the house."

"Please, Geegee, at least turn the volume down." His lower lip smarted and he realized he was biting it.

"I couldn't hear if I turned it down." *Natural instinct, huh?* She'd remember that crack about Aubie not having a chance when his mother was alive.

"You talk diet," he accused, "and make me starve—look what you're eating." *He was stronger than Edna Trumble. She could have been forced under him, spread, held through it all—*

"Use a glass, Sonny. It's disgusting to see a grown man drinking out of a bottle."

"Carton."

"Bottle."

Her body, slippery with sweat, as elusive as a threshing seal in heat, had demanded supremacy and he'd given in to her, ending up with her astride and he the one looking up. . . . The thought soured the milk in his mouth. "I'm going to take a shower."

"Use the one on this side, I wanna take a bath myself and you never leave enough hot water."

105

"You go first then." The spring that lifted him from the chair uncoiled at the door. "Go ahead, Geegee. I can wait. I don't know what's the matter with me today. Not your fault, it's me. . . . Go on, take your bath. . . ." A boy's apologetic smile softened his face, and she saw him as nineteen years old, in the apartment on Cherokee, opening the box. Saw it clear as anything.

"That hat!" It was Columbus sighting land. "Sonny . . . the hat!"

"What hat?"

"*What* hat?" Her offense bridged two octaves. "*The* hat—the Borsalino—thirty-two dollars I paid for that for your graduation and you say what hat?"

"Oh, Geej . . ." he laughed patiently, "so long ago, we got rid of that."

"Oh, no . . ." She was out of the chair. "No, no, if there's one thing I remember where it is, it's that hat—" She was trying to wriggle past him, but he was squarely in the doorway, arms extended wide, octopus loose. "It's gotta be in your room, in a chest or closet; that's where you put it last time you wore it when we drove down to the Coronado Hotel for dinner. . . ."

His arms encircled her. "You've done enough, Mother. I'll look for it." Firmly, he edged her back to the chair, sat her down to the temptation of the remaining food. "Now you stay. If it's around, I'll find it."

"Right now? Because I'm dying to see what you look like—"

"Right now." His smile didn't change, but panic sweat burst from his palms. He had to rein the impulse to run across the gallery. The back of his neck told him she was watching through the grillwork. Her eyes stayed with him after he turned the corner of the tiled dogleg to his room. *Embrasse-moi, Jacques*, the hi-fi propositioned. Give me a kiss, Jack, it insisted even through the door which he closed, regretting there was no lock, but it was too late for locks now.

He should have prepared for this, should have known

106

—anticipated—that this corrosive digging for the past would uncover the hat. Standing on a chair that put him a head above the door frame, his hand moved in the darkness of the closet with the certainty of a blind man at his own table. His fingers felt it, knew it, and brought the soft package forward from the far corner of the top-most shelf. Pulling off the rubber band that was stretched with age, he unrolled the old T-shirt and felt the soft hairs of the dark green Borsalino between his moist, trembling fingers.

The closet light shocked on. "You found it! Wonderful, I knew I was right."

"Yes, Geegee, you were right." It surprised him to hear how calm he sounded, as his hand slid into the hat and gripped the money.

"Gimme, gimme . . ." She was reaching up, grasping like a child for candy from a smashed piñata. He held the rolled, soft hat immobile on the shelf with his left hand, shifting his body as though to maintain his balance, and blocked her view. His right hand slid the money out of the hat and to the back of the high shelf.

She neither smelled his guilt nor heard the thudding of blood in his ears. She was caressing the creases out of the long-crushed hat.

"That's one thing about a Borsalino—smooth it, put a little steam to it and it's forever. Go on, Sonny, put it on, try it on. . . ."

"Never really fit me." With the closet door closed on his secret and the chair back in place, the beads of perspiration that had oppressed him a moment before now felt cool on his skin. He moved to his bathroom for a towel. "So hot up there."

"It'll fit now, you're older—" The hat followed him, in her insistent hands. "Go on, Sonny, put it on." He attempted to back from it but she was reaching up, placing it on his head.

"I look like a gangster," he asked for release.

"No, you don't." Flaring the broad brim, tilting one

side up, one side down, she stepped back and surveyed him. "Raise your eyebrow."

He stood rooted, feeling ridiculous.

"Please . . . for Geegee. . . ?"

The long untested muscles performed, furrowing his right eyebrow toward his nose, elevating the left one. His mirrored image mocked him from both doors.

"You know, Sonny," she said with pride, "you're really beginning to look like him. Especially with that eyebrow up."

"I don't look like him—don't want to look like him!" He felt maligned. Slapped the hat into her hand and left the room.

Bon soir, Maman. . . .

Good-bye, Mother. . . .

"You should be grateful to look like him," her reprimand pursued him. "He was a beautiful man. Beautiful . . ." As she swept past on her way to the kitchen, his impulse was to grab the hat from her, shove his knee through it. Shred it. He'd get rid of it, he promised himself. First chance. Wouldn't be easy, now that she knew it was still around. Get rid of it. Burn it or something. But he wouldn't wear it.

Through the door he could see her turning the flame high under the teakettle, bathing the neglected hat tenderly in the soothing steam.

Au revoir, Jacques. The groove gave out.

Good-bye Jack Good-bye Jack Good-bye Jack Good-bye. . . .

9

BRUSHED, contoured, glistening, the hat was waiting on his pillow when he came out of the shower. He picked it up as though expecting to find somebody under it. And felt a vague sense of displacement when all that appeared beneath the wide brim was the jacquard of the bedspread. *Little fly upon the wall, ain't you got no home at all?*

"Get the hell out of here, Aubie. Go on, get out." The dog gave him a look like Caesar must have given Brutus. Ron closed the door, shutting out the injury in the agate eyes. Through the house, silence announced itself. Apparently, to Ron's relief, Jack had taken the *au revoir* to heart and turned off.

Geegee, rolled in a bath sheet on her bed, was napping. He closed the doors between them, spread his towel and sat naked on his bed, studying the hat. *I ought to pee in it, that's what I ought to do.* Then he felt ashamed. Geegee had worked so hard to buy it, saving, putting nickels and pennies away in a jar. He could remember her sitting at the kitchenette table on Cherokee, rolling them up in bank wrappers and saying, "Are you ever going to be surprised."

She loved the game of it, the waiting.

"Guess."

"Morocco leather wallet?"

"I'm not gonna tell you."

"Wristwatch?" Since he had a job, he could use one.

"You're cold." And she kept adding change to the jar.

"A cardigan. Mohair."

"Warmer. But not really."

The day of graduation, when she brought out the hat-box, he was sure it was one of her games—something very small—a box in a box, figuring it to be a ring, probably a ring with his birthstone. . . .

"Unwrap it. Go on, Sonny." Her hands reached out in anticipation, touching the elaborate bow, barely able to resist opening it herself, her eyes darting back and forth from the box to his face not to miss the moment of revelation.

"Cryin' out loud," was all he could manage, and was grateful that she mistook his antipathy for awe.

"Really knocked you off your pins, huh? Just like the hat *he wore*. Go on, Sonny. *He wore.* Go on, put it on. . . ." He did, and felt as sick green as the color of the hat. And wore it to graduation, positive everyone around thought he was an oddball, wearing a hat when no one else did. But who really knew him anyway? At a series of similar ceremonies in different schools, all he'd ever come away with were the names of two or three people whom he wouldn't recognize on the street. Strangers he knew less well than he knew Dorothy and Snookie on the *Lucky Strike Hit Parade*, his companions on sixteen-inch Saturday nights as he killed time waiting to go down to the bus stop and pick Geegee up from work. With them, he'd seen the harbor lights and the shrimp boats a comin', and gone onna their house.

The sixteen-inch set had been a big improvement over the first TV he'd seen. And so had the apartment. The twelve-inch box, viewed through the skylight of two inside rooms they'd rented near Echo Park because Geegee worked downtown the whole year he was sixteen, gave off a perpetual snowstorm. But Mrs. Ploven, the landlady, was very nice about sharing it. Since his mother and her husband worked evenings and Sonny was alone so much, wouldn't it be selfish of her not to?

At first, she just made certain her shade was up so he could view from his open window across the airshaft. Along with Kukla, Fran and Ollie, serving up generous portions of Mrs. Ploven. With robe. Without robe. With bra and pants. Without bra. Without pants.

"Wouldn't you like some cookies and milk? Or a glass o' beer?" she smiled across the open space, lifting one pendulous breast to pat away perspiration with a handful of tissues. "You're a big boy now; you can have a little something. . . ." He was embarrassed, when she opened her door to him, by the dark wet spot appearing in the crotch of his tan trousers. But she understood and was very nice about drying them and showing him how not to waste this precious fluid. He could be perfectly free with her, she said, and explained all about her hysterectomy scar.

Geegee was thankful to the landlady for permitting Sonny to share her set.

Ron removed the hat and lay down, damping his erection and the memory with the cool moist bath towel.

It would pass. He knew. The pulsating blood would recede.

He looked over at the despised Borsalino. At graduation he'd gotten Geegee to hold it in her lap and he'd carried it from the stadium to the bus stop. He'd had it on for a little while one Sunday when Geegee was toying with the idea of joining the Catholic Church. He remembered wearing it to the door of St. Cyril's, but it was raining when they came out so he rolled it up and stuck it inside his jacket. She never went back to the church, she said, because what did she have to confess to? That she'd worked her butt off to raise her kid? That's all she ever said about it. For himself, he couldn't have cared less, but he always felt she kind of wanted it.

There was one other time. The one Geegee had spoken

111

of. The Mother's Day they drove down to San Diego to eat at the Coronado Hotel and he'd explained that wearing the hat while he drove blocked his rear view. She'd insisted he at least put it on from the car to the hotel, analyzing him from every angle as they walked, making sure it had just the right slant. He checked it the minute they got to the dining room, and later on carried it in his hand back to the car.

That was '53, as he thought back. The year they bought their first car. Fifty Chevy. Green and white. Two door, clean, one owner, low mileage. Rough mileage, the sign should have said, and that's how Geegee played it with the used car dealer who sold it to them; so glad to get her off his back he refunded sixty-five bucks. The waxy perfume of her gardenia corsage could not completely mask the burnt-oil stench of the engine.

"Butter on silver plates . . . this's the way we're gonna live, Sonny." She ate with her pinky in the air, nibbling like a rabbit. The Coronado really flipped her that day: vaulted ceilings, venerable woods. "When we get our house, it's gonna have style, like this hotel. Not a crackerbox, but a house, a real house, an honest t'God house with a dining room table so long you have to roller skate. . . ."

Their dining table wasn't quite that long, but on the rare occasions they used it—she at one end, he at the other—he always felt alone, small, far away; like seeing himself through the wrong end of a telescope. Geegee said it made her feel like the movie *Citizen Kane*.

It was the gates that sold the house to her. "We can be alone here. Do you realize we don't ever have to let anybody in we don't want to?" It went right by her that they couldn't afford it, not on his salary, not with her working so rarely anymore. He'd cut his molars hearing they were saving for a house of their own, but . . . *seventeen thousand dollars.* . . .

Ron lay on the bed, looking at the handhewn beams

held in place by carved corbels, the massive adobe fireplace bordered with earth-red tiles from Spain, and thought bitterly of all the rabbit warrens they'd lived in through the years, the cheese-paring life they'd led. And all the time she was socking enough away to make a substantial down payment, bargain for most of the original furniture, with a nest egg left over. *Seventeen thousand dollars. . . .*

He wondered if he would have to move his money or if it was safe where it was hidden.

The corner of the closet was high and deep. Even if Geegee stood on the chair, as he was doing now, she'd never be able to reach all the way back. But you never could tell about Geegee. . . .

(The shower had been too hot, and he had stayed under it too long). Thirsty and debilitated he started for the kitchen and the spring water, tying on his robe. And realized he'd left the hat exposed on the shelf, the chair there, and the door to the closet open.

"Zat you, Sonny?"

He seesawed from the ball of one foot to the ball of the other. Go on to the kitchen? Go back to his room? He'd read about the point of no return in flight, and here he was—in just that predicament.

"Son-neee . . ." The ascending scale caught him like a choke collar. "What're you doing out there?"

He stammered, "Uh . . . getting a screwdriver."

"Screwdriver? Why a screwdriver?" It was a lying-down voice, a contented voice. A voice that would stay put. The maelstrom within him settled. "For a hook for the door," he called through the leaded glass pane, "so I'll see the hat all the time and won't forget it's there."

She responded to the salve like a muscle toned by massage. "Wond'ful, baby, it's right in style again, bring me a diet drink, hon, I'm glad you're gonna wear it."

Like hell he'd wear it. He'd dump it one of these days. In an alley. Trashcan. Humiliate it. But meantime, with it visible on the hook every time the closet was opened she'd be less tempted to look further.

He came unglued from the gallery floor, moved quickly to the butler's pantry and rummaged for the screwdriver and hook he'd manufactured out of thin air, knowing all the time that until they found the pictures no hiding place was sacrosanct.

Behind a large roll of white butcher paper, which he could never remember their reason for buying, there was a breadbox labeled Nails and Screws. That's where he found his reprieve.

"I told you it was blue!"

"You said suitcase."

"What's the dif?" She tightened the bathsheet securely over the shelf of her bosom and sank her hands exultantly into the depths of the blue bread box filled with old snapshots as into a cache of jewels. "We found our num-nums. . . ."

The familiar word set Aubie's nails clicking on the floor tiles of the gallery in frenzied flamenco. Ron brought out the dog biscuits and poured some wine. There was a feeling of celebration in the room.

And relief. Because now he knew the obsessive search was over. His money would be safe where it was.

In the second glass of wine he found the promised sauvignon bouquet lacking. In the third, it didn't seem to matter. He moved two sets of skiis and a Coleman camping stove from the banquette so he could sit down, and ran a tab in his mind of all the useless stuff they'd collected that now cluttered the room, but he thought, What the hell, let her have fun.

She was glowing over pictures from the year one. "Lookit this—Oh, Sonny, were you ever cute then—You won't believe this one!—And Duchess, just a puppy—!"

The evening was as pleasant as any they'd ever spent together. Ron prepared his famous lobster bisque which they took on trays, so as not to disturb the work on the big table.

"Hey, lady, that's some caftan you got on." The sheer batwing float of huge roses she'd changed into tinged her skin to the texture of coral velvet.

"That ain't no caftan," she countered without looking up, "that's a jellaba."

"I bought a jellaba once, from a used car lot."

"No, that's a jalopy."

"No, a jalopy's an old tango you used to dance to."

"No, that's Jalousie."

"Ja-lousy," he triumphed, "that's when you have bugs."

"My own flesh and blood," she groaned. "I'll just pretend I didn't hear that."

"Well . . ." he feigned injury, "I'm outa practice." As his glass filled again he was looking at her over the rim and laughing in silly bursts. What was so funny, she had to know.

His last birthday. Something she'd said.

"What'd I say? Come on, what'd I say funny, Sonny? Ha-ha, funny-sonny, huh? What'd I say?"

"You were cutting the cake . . ." His tongue tingled. "And you shaid—"

"You're high! Oh, Sonny, you're high, that's cute—"

"No'm not—"

"Yes y'are—"

"Y'wanna shut up an' hear the story?"

"I'm shut."

"Well you said—and I give it right back to you, Madam—" His glass raised to her. "You said it isn't every boy of forty who's got a mother of thirty-nine."

"You're a doll." Her finger beckoned. He came to her and bent over to be brushed with a kiss. "Who's that?" he asked of the snapshot in her hand. Vaguely out of focus, vaguely calling to memory.

"Why, that's Mrs. Ploven and her husband. You remember Mrs. Ploven."

He didn't, he told her.

"Sure you do, hon. Echo Park? Mrs. Ploven and her TV?" He stubbornly shook his head and moved to safer ground, pulling a picture of Duchess from the pile, but Geegee was busy trying to place an Aubie picture in sequence. "Go way, go way," she said. "Don't touch anything, you'll mix me up. . . ."

She had barely sampled her first drink. His fourth tasted bitter. Harsh. *He had not lied to her.* Mrs. Ploven did not look like that. She was younger, buxom, with firm, round belly. Not tired, sagging, sallow. That could not be Mrs. Ploven in that picture.

He sat opposite Geegee, taking positives and negatives out of drugstore envelopes that bore dates thirty or more years back. Who were these faces? This infant, puffy, in a cocoon of blankets, thrust at the lens so that he was all nose, by a headless mother in formless raincoat and boots . . . this cipher of a boy, skinny-legged, apologetic, with eyes that seemed to be asking *Who, me?* The same uncertain face appearing over and over in the admixture as the body beneath it grew taller.

"Ugly," he said aloud.

"Don't talk that way about my baby."

Foregrounds, backgrounds, none of it awakened anything. It was like watching someone else's home movies.

"Put 'em by years, Sonny. I want a whole album of Duchess, then I want one starting with that darling little snap of you when you were six weeks old. . . ."

He stirred the pile idly like in preparation of morning oatmeal. "When was this?" passing an overexposed square across to her.

"Lessee . . ." The recall he hoped for, tried for, she supplied. "Oh, sure—you're fourteen and a half here, that was Big Bear, first time we had a real vacation, remember? I took a week off, you learned to swim? Oh, that lying brochure—first class cabin with an outhouse yet—" The erupting laughter threw back her head, closed

116

her eyes. She didn't see the picture he found at that moment that pierced his jugular of memory.

"Oh, that outhouse . . . real class. . . ."

The rectangle of anguish in his hand disappeared into his pocket. Her laughter hopscotched into small coughs.

"Sonny . . . what'll we do tomorrow?"

His mind was struggling back over fourteen years. "Wha—?"

"Tomorrow, sweetie. It's Sunday."

Anything, he said. Anything she wanted to do was okay with him.

When she tired of arranging the Kodak of their lives into neat little stacks, he brought the portable TV into the kitchen for the late movie, but all he viewed was the lacerating memory in his pocket. She fried chicken for a picnic.

Scattered leaves on the ground were tobacco yellow and dry. The deep-rooted fir, taller than the coupled sycamores at either end of the green carpet, filtered early winter sunlight, deceptively warm, masquerading as spring. Occasionally the flash of a fish jumping out of the water at a foolhardy moth added a gracenote to the sound of waterfall. Except for an occasional car and the now and then whine of an airplane rising in sharp defiance of gravity from the Burbank airport, the quiet, Geegee said, was like religion.

"You haven't tasted your potato salad."

"Don't want any."

A teasing wind that came and went on impulse lifted a corner of the blanket. Geegee weighted it down with the wicker basket and opened a plastic container of hard boiled eggs. Would he like one? No. She foraged in the basket. "I don't think I brought salt. No, no, sweetie, don't move—" (which he had no intention of doing). "I'll go."

117

She popped up from the blanket and ran happily across the driveway and in through the front door.

He lay there on the park bench they'd bought from the L.A. Department of Parks and Recreation salvage sale and studied the front of the house. It could be a mission. Or monastery. He saw himself walking about in saffron robes. No . . . that was Buddhist. Brown. Coarse-loomed, with rope belt, sandals, shaved head, a staff in his hand, walking from sunup to sundown on the Camino Real. A solitary figure. A speck, plodding across an arid landscape. . . .

Geegee came out of the house, waving the salt shaker, announcing, again, that when you had a front yard like a park it was crazy to go anywhere else for a picnic. Aubie gave up his hypnotic stare at a squirrel in an acacia and ran to meet her, wagging his tail for alms.

"You're not eating," she admonished sweetly as she vigorously salted her egg, fed a tidbit to the dog, and deposited a sizable portion into her mouth.

"Not hungry." Ron's eyes were open to slits, tangled eyelashes diffusing the sun's rays into rainbow colors. Like looking at her through a barely opened Venetian blind, he watched her shift the food from one cheek to the other, and wished her his pain. Then sank deeper into his depression at the futility of such thinking. Why had she kept the picture? It would have been so simple to throw it away. . . . But then, why had he kept the hat?

"Please eat something, sweetheart; Geegee fixed all the goodies just for you."

He shook his head and closed his eyes again.

Moody, she accepted. Some children were happy-go-lucky. Not Sonny. He'd still be in bed if she hadn't tried to take his temperature. Letting her lug all the heavy stuff, basket, cooler, out to the front yard. Had she complained about that? No. She knew the night he snuck out he was smelling after some cheap hooker. Had she thrown that in his face? He'd done it before. She always knew when. Did she ever bring it up to him? She looked at him with concern. Could he be anemic? It was too soon for him to be tense again. Just one of his funks, she decided. It was her fault, she had to take the blame. He was spoiled. Her baby, and she'd spoiled him.

She peeled and ate another egg.

"Chicken?" she said in a wisp of let's-play-games voice.

"Hmm?" he questioned from somewhere remote.

"Chick-kennnn—" she telegraphed her meaning. "Come on, Sonny . . . chicken."

"Okay," he gave in. "Wing."

"Wing? Wing?" she rolled it in her sinuses. "Hewwo . . ." He sat up like a rocket taking off. "*Hewwo—?* Christ, Geegee, I'm two times twenty, what kind of games are you playing?"

"All right, you're so smart, you start one."

All right. He would. "Obscene," he said.

She looked at him sharply. Was this a word? Or some kind of insult crack? "Uh . . . police," she said.

"Club," he answered quickly.

"House," was her bright answer.

"House," he repeated. And shot one in. "Whore."

Geegee, pouring beer in the pilsner glasses since only slobs drank out of cans, handed him his and drew the battle lines. "It seems your Royal Highness has a flea up his—" She never got to the destination of that flea. Aubie was at the gate, barking hysterically enough to justify the Beware of Dog sign.

Dulcie had told Kevin a dozen times, Watch the ball, don't let it get away from you. "Stay here," she yelled back at him as she chased it into the street. "Look, dog, I'm a friend . . ." She reached for the ball that had lodged against their fence and became aware of the *intime* front-yard pastoral beyond the gates. Mother and son. Tête-à-tête on a blanket. In the instant that her mind photographed the still life and she thought, All that's missing is the croquet, Ron was on his feet, apologizing for Aubie's behavior.

119

"Sorry, my fault," Dulcie called and picked up the ball. "Aubie, quiet."

Geegee saw the slow smile forming on his face and a like smile on the face of that cooze from across the street, and she acted out of pure instinct, thrusting the large wicker basket in front of him, short-circuiting his forward motion toward the gates. "Take this in the house."

When he regained his balance, Aubie was still barking. But Dulcie was gone.

There was nothing left of Sunday for Geegee except to go for a ride.

Wind from the sea was sharp and penetrating. It whipped his pants around his legs and made her hair stand up in a way that reminded him of the *Bride of Frankenstein*.

They walked in the same leaded silence that had ridden with them down the San Diego Freeway and past the one-story sameness of Pico Boulevard. Attempts at conversation—It's windy. . . . I'm glad I brought my rebozo. . . . Sure you'll be warm enough with just your sportshirt on?—all were from her, all unanswered by him.

She kept ahead of him, aware he was deliberately walking the off beat of her footsteps just to annoy her.

Ron focused on the wooden planks of the pier underfoot. It became a game—what he could see, in the brief instant passing over open knotholes and spaces between planks, of the ocean below. He stopped once, intent on a dead anemone floating on the surface, its billowing parachute body formless in death. Without looking up, he knew she had stopped, waiting for confrontation, and he wasn't ready for it. Leaning against the rail, he looked back on Santa Monica and then to the curve of the malibu diminishing in the haze. Closer, on the beach below, his eye was drawn to a man who seemed to be alone, lying on his stomach. The man rolled over and there was a girl under him. Ron moved from the rail.

Geegee was not to be further denied. Feet firmly

120

planted, she waited in his path. "All right, Sonny, you might as well spill it. What's eating you?"

He drew the answer from his pocket, held it out to her. What was left of the snapshot in his hand was a younger Ron—fourteen years younger—standing in profile, smiling at someone or something, his extended arm severed at the elbow.

"Why did you cut her off? I didn't marry her. . . ." His hoarse tense whisper could barely be heard above the circling wind. "Why couldn't you let her alone? All that was left was this picture. . . ."

The wind was her ally, keeping color in her cheeks in spite of the draining blood. "I don't remember cutting it; it was so long ago, Sonny . . . I don't even remember what she looked like—"

"I'm not with you, y'hear me? You're here alone," he yelled, not caring who heard. "I don't want you near me. Just do what you want—" He turned and walked away. She wanted to go after him, tell him she felt rudderless when he left her like this. But she didn't. Then she saw him slow up and stop, and felt secure that he'd never walk off and leave her stranded. She went into the souvenir shop to give him a chance to cool off.

As he walked along he slowly tore the half picture into bits, faintly aware of chili peppers immortalized in grease, generations of mildew, fish entrails heel-ground into rough-hewn wood by long-gone anglers, a hint of somebody's last night's vomit, residue of too much beer and probably not enough years of practice to hold it down. He clenched the scraps of the picture in his fist for a moment, then opened it to drop them into an available trashcan. A gust of wind carried the confetti of his memory out over the ocean. He felt cold and stepped into the shelter of Soldier's Place.

"Dog? Burger?"

At first Ron didn't hear, he was so intent on looking back at the shop where Geegee had disappeared.

"Wanna shoot?" the man behind the counter said, a lit-

121

tle louder. "Ten for a buck? Fifteen for a buck. . . ?"
Ron realized he was trying to interest him in the shuttered shooting gallery that was Siamese twin to the hot
dog stand.

"No thanks."

"I'll open it for you. It's my place. I'm Soldier." He
adjusted the black patch that covered his left eye, revealing the deep ridge the elastic that held it in place had
cut into his forehead.

"Coffee." Ron slid onto the cracked vinyl cushioned
stool. The man swabbed at the counter with a sour rag.
"You ain't never been 'round here. I can tell. I remember
faces."

"Black." Ron closed the conversation. As the man who
called himself Soldier shuffled to the back wall and
poured coffee into a thick, white, chipped mug, Ron
noticed he was wearing bedroom slippers, no sox, and
the ancient overseas cap that covered his wispy hair was
sweat-stained all the way around. A relic among relics,
Ron thought as his eyes traversed the memorabilia. Fly-
specked American flags crossed on the back wall, framed,
grease-dulled pictures of a young soldier in World War
II uniform, hung crookedly. On top of the pie stand,
glass-cased to protect them from the elements, were medals. And guns. German, they looked like, to Ron's limited
knowledge. And shell casings.

Soldier put the coffee in front of his only customer,
spilling some, wiping it up with his greasy apron.

"Thanks."

He didn't read the dismissal and go back to scraping
his grill but leaned in, confidentially imparting an inside
secret. "How 'bout it?"

"How about what?" In Ron's view, although he wasn't
focusing on it, was a sign in the shape of an arrow point-
ing toward the rear: Live Model. With a wink of his one
watery eye, Soldier called attention to it.

"She's got nothin' on. I supply camera, film—enny way
you like it." He laid the inference on thick and patted

Ron's arm paternally. "Nothin' to worry about. I got a permit. It's all legal. You know, you read the papers. You can have naked entertainment if you don't serve booze, only soft drinks. Go on, take a crack. Don't cost much, a fin. Unless you want somethin' special . . ."

Ron shook his head and withdrew his arm from the heavily veined, yellowing hand. Soldier bothered him. Not the eye patch so much, but the moldering face. The only link to that young man in uniform on the wall was the old suntan overseas cap. It depressed him, made him think of the picture of himself that had blown off on the wind, the younger, hopeful Ron that was gone. Would he—could he—one day look like this man? Hairs on ear-lobes and growing out of the nose, an accordioned upper lip, a face like a much-played-on page of tic-tac-toe?

The coffee lost its invigorating warmth. Ron turned to leave, but Geegee was nowhere in sight on the pier and the wind was stronger, biting.

"Not even a bear claw, huh?"

"Just coffee."

Soldier figured this guy for a deadhead, but at least coffee was pure profit. Maybe he'd drink a second. And a third. Soldier treated himself to a cup and reached into the faded, scratched, plastic display case for the one remaining tired bear claw, dipped it into the coffee to soften it. Holding it above his mouth for the drippings, he confided to Ron, "I'm goin' down a' drain, right down a' sewer." He adjusted the overseas cap and leaned on the counter. "Nobody wants to shoot no more. Used to be the kids alone was good for fifty, sixty bucks a Sad-diday, but now this Veet-nam thing, they don't wanna go near a gun. I say, love it or leave it," Soldier went on without stopping. "That's what I say. My old man put a twenny-two in my hands when I was six, y'know? We went to hunt jack. You do your bit?" he challenged.

Ron's mind pulled itself away from the gun case. "What'd you say?"

"Looks to me you could'a made Korea."

123

"I—would've gone," Ron wished it hadn't sounded so defensive. "But I had to take care of my mother."

Soldier hung a stare on him that made him feel inadequate. "Army makes a man." Ron sat up straighter, pulling in his gut. Stretched, so that the short sleeves of his sport shirt rose to show flexed muscles.

"My father was with Patton," he said, returning Soldier's penetrating look. "Regular army. Didn't make it back."

"Old blood and guts?" It was pure reverence. "Hey, that's somethin'. Your old man, huh? With Patton."

"That's right."

"Never made it back, whaddya know . . ." The admiration on Soldier's face crisscrossed the creases. "Coffee's on me, buddy." Soldier pulled up a companionable stool. "D'ja see that movie? When the general said, God I love war, that really got t'me. I know what he was talkin' . . ."

"Excuse me . . ."

"Call me Soldier, buddy."

"Soldier . . . I think you got it wrong. What the General said was God help me, I love war."

"Oh yeah, yeah, 'at's right, you're right." Soldier didn't get the subtle difference and Ron didn't point it out. Or move his arm away from Soldier's intense grip this time. He was feeling better. Less cold.

"I'll take one of those doughnuts."

"On me. All on me, buddy. So your old man was with Patton . . ."

"Yeah. Third Army. He was gunner in a Sherman, and they would've finished the war earlier if Montgomery had come down sooner and closed the neck of the trap on Von Kluge. That's where he got it, my father, in Brittany. . . ."

Let Geegee take her time, Ron thought.

"Hey, you two, y'wanna shoot?"

The young, long-haired, sandaled couple who had paused to discuss the camp art on the shooting gallery waved their peace medallions in answer to Soldier like a thumb to the nose, and walked on. Soldier watched them with disgust: couldn't tell the he from the she anymore.

Abruptly, the he whirled, drawing a pair of imaginary six shooters and wiped Soldier out. "Bang, bang—man, you blew it, you're dead." They walked away, laughing, arms around each other. Ron's eyes went seesawing with the belt on the girls' supple hips.

"They're all Commies." Soldier tapped Ron's arm to regain his attention. "Queers. Just look at 'em. Whole fuckin' country's gonna be without balls. End up singin' soprano." He brought down his case of medals and gave the glass a swipe with the rag, which only smeared the grease. "See this'n? Bizerte. Got me six that day, seven, I don't know—twenty yards—could see 'em just like I'm lookin' at you—flip, flop— but, fuck it, six-ten-twenny, I don't pay my rent here, good-bye Joe, I'm down a'sewer."

"Seven—and you saw their faces?"

"Never was sure o' one of 'em. Bastard kraut crawled away. I hit 'im, I know I hit 'im . . ." Soldier's eye gleamed and all the lines in his face seemed to turn up. He looked strangely, briefly, young as he brought the mordant scent of death between them. "But I wasn't smart." The vitality that had come so abruptly with the necrophilic moment was gone. "I should'a done like your old man—stayed regular." Soldier was sure he would have had it made by now. Thirty years, he was saying . . . "Tell ya straight, buddy, I'd do anything to lay my hands on a few bucks. Yes, sir, if I had me a bankroll I'd pack in and get my ass outa here. . . ."

The image of six or seven blood-saturated bodies, stacked like a cord of wood, filled Ron's mind and he wanted to get away. But Soldier held tight to his arm, intent on sharing his stupidity. "I quit the army to screw a dame. You never screw a dame, right? They screw you, right? Hmm, right. . . ?"

"Sonnnnny . . ."

She was there. Waiting. Stronger than the wind. Ron pulled change from his pocket, dropped two quarters on the counter and left without good-bye. Soldier let the quarters lay. Watched the man fall in behind the woman. *"Sonny. . . ? Oh, shit. . . ."*

10

HE'D *asked her*—not once but a thousand times—*Not in public*—At home it didn't matter—but in public, use his name for God's sake—his name—! Not SONNY. . . .

Pier planks reverberated beneath his feet as he thudded across them in imperative strides, passing her as though they were strangers. In short, running steps she came up alongside. "I wasn't trying to leave you behind, sweetie," she appealed, "I'm just cold, I wanna get to the car. . . . Hon, you're going so fast I can't keep up with you. Don't you wanna see what I bought?" She tore open a small box and let the wind take it. "I thought you'd like 'em," she said, breathlessly, dangling a pair of gaudy earrings at him. "I bought 'em 'cause you always liked mother a' pearl."

"Even pearls have mothers?"

He was in the car, elbows curled around the steering wheel like a disgruntled ape, as she slid in beside him. Hostile silence hitchhiked with them to the Pico Boulevard on ramp heading north.

"That girl was no way right for you, Sonny . . ." When she finally spoke it was like cutting the ribbon of a new section of freeway. No Stop, Slow, Caution; Geegee was in high gear, "You were so young, Sonny—she didn't understand us—you could've married her, I could've kept on working—*you* were the one always said I'd worked long enough and hard enough—I can still remember exactly what you said—your exact words—you said I'm not going to let you kill yourself for me, Geegee—that's what you said."

"That what I said? You remember every word?"

"Don't you make fun of me! You know damn well that's what you said. *You* wanted me to have the house. I didn't say that you, the girl, me—I didn't say we couldn't all live together—God knows there's room enough—you're raising more fuss now than you did then, more fuss, my God. I should'a cut my arm off before I cut that picture, all this fuss—" Her words were overlapping one another as his indifference fueled her desperation. And he felt better. He was actually beginning to feel good. Like when he talked about Patton with Soldier.

"Remember what you said when *she* walked out on *you*—?"

"Not exactly, Geegee, but I'm sure you do."

"You said, Geegee, if she can't appreciate what we mean to each other, it's her loss. *You* said it. *Her* loss . . ." She played variations on the theme all the way to Oxnard Avenue. "And here you are—right now—the best time of your life—no responsibilities. Unsaddled. You're free. We can come and go as we please. . . . You do see that? You see it, don't you, Sonny?"

He saw. More than she did, and the brakes grabbed to the jam of his foot that threw Geegee against her seatbelt. "Why'ja stop? 'Smatter?"

He opened the door. Whistled. A streak of dirty yellow fur raced from behind the market, bounding across the empty parking lot, and up into the car. Panting happily, tongue lolling, Aubie's female settled onto the back seat like coming home.

"She stays." The calm injunction surprised even himself. Geegee turned her disgust from the slobbering dog with a hissing intake of breath. And collided with his eyes. They were different. Murky. Not her Sonny's eyes. She

128

couldn't find herself in them and felt uncoupled, derailed.

Her intended verbal onslaught spent itself like a slow leak in a tire. They rode the last block in galling silence.

The ocean and the valley were strangers. Once over the crest and into the saucer that was the San Fernando, the wind that fathered storm warning flags and kept the Sunday sailors in their slips was placid. Benign. Denying the angers on the periphery. The same atmosphere prevailed in the house on Keefee Avenue for several days. It took Geegee until Thursday at dinner to make the concession and apologize for cutting the picture. Said she had no right to do it; it was mean, petty, little and cheap of her. He said, "Fine, Geej, it's over," and went out into the backyard to watch the dogs.

The same every night. Home from work. Dinner. And out to sit on the cracked fountain wall with his coffee cup to watch them until dark. And when she'd asked him when was he ever going to put the fountain in working order, he'd said, "It's on the list, Geej; we don't have to talk about it."

He'd stopped helping with the dishes. The amount of conversation that flowed between them you could put in your eye, she thought as she cleared the table. Not in *his* eye. His were closed as though he'd hung a No Trespass sign over the pupils.

She smoothed the napkins carefully (they could be used again before laundering) and hesitated at the window. Through the invading darkness she could barely see the deep-brown Aubie, but the yellow bitch, reflecting the last of the day's light, was tearing around and she knew Aubie had to be hot on her tail. *Dirty*. . . .

But she smiled into the night beyond the window in case Sonny would look up and catch her there.

She would wait. See which way the tomcat jumped.

The City of Los Angeles has an agreement with all of

129

its householders. If you put out your trashcans on Wednesday night, their highly reliable organization, rain or shine, almost as good as the mail service if not better, comes and collects it sometime Thursday. Someone had written a treatise once about Beverly Hills garbage (Ron had read it in the magazine that came from the Auto Club). He wondered how the valley garbage compared, never having paid any attention to it before. As he finished stacking the cans out in front he felt tempted to wander up the street and do his own survey, but didn't. Instead, he just studied what was in the battered metal cans in front of his house (he'd have to buy the new polyurethane ones; they were lighter and held up better). After concentrating on it for the moment and shifting about some of the contents with a branch that was in one of the cans, he pronounced it dull. The garbage is dull. The people who live in this house leave dull garbage.

Across the street, there was nothing in front of the new neighbor's house. He wondered, should he go over and tell her collection day was tomorrow? Then realized she'd lived there for more than a week. Almost two weeks. Ridiculous to tell her that now, although he didn't recall ever seeing her trash on the street.

In the morning, going off to work, he was glad to see everything neatly organized in front of her house. Cartons used in moving. Trash cans. A formidable pile. And felt he should have obeyed the impulse and gone over to help her.

At the end of the day when he returned from work the empty cans, one looking like it had been run over by a truck, greeted him. Without changing clothes, he wheeled the dolly out to get them. The first trip back up the driveway relieved him of the damaged can and one other. When he wheeled back for the last can, Dulcie was at the curb on a similar errand.

"Hi," she said.

"Well, how do you like the neighborhood so far?"

"No complaints." She was stuffing one trash can into the other.

"Need some help with that?"

"I can handle it, thanks."

"Wait, that's too much for you"—as she easily lifted both cans.

"No, really—"

But he was across the street, nosing the iron lip of the dolly under the cans. "Where do you keep 'em?"

"By the kitchen door," she told him, preceding him down the narrow area alongside the house. The back-yard, fenced with grape stakes, was deeper than the smallness of the house would indicate. The lawn wore scattered patches of winter-brown devil grass and was bordered by a ragged collection of shrubs. But the yard was distinguished by one fine walnut tree, and the absence of color from any flowering plants was more than compensated by a yellow sandbox and paint-bright new set of swings with a short slide between them.

"Thanks a lot," Dulcie said as he put the cans in place.

"Say, this is really cozy back here. It's not a patio, it's a backyard. That's what I like, a real backyard. When I was a little kid we moved a lot—I always wanted to have a yard with a tree like that to climb . . ."

"It is nice," she said. "Thanks, thanks again."

"You must get a lot of sun."

She agreed.

"And shade. You'll get great shade in the summer from that tree."

"Excuse me, I've got something on the stove." She had tried, in her thank you's to him, to indicate there were limits placed on their relationship, like a dolly ride for her garbage cans. Not that it wouldn't have been pleasant to stay and rap with him about backyards, or anything else he had in mind, and take the inevitable step to "How about a cup of coffee?" and they would both be at the kitchen table, savoring this quicksilver moment between day and dusk, watching Kevin get an eagle's view of the earth by hanging upside down on the bar of the swing set. Through the open service-porch window their voices came to her.

"What's your name?"

"Ron, what's yours?"

"Kevin, what's yours?"

"Ron."

"No, you're supposed to say Ron what's yours."

While they repeated the roundelay of names, and Kevin pointed out exactly where among the branches his mother was going to build him the tree house, Dulcie thought of that cold-turkey mother across the street, and wished Ron would go home. She'd had enough of hassling and of one thing she was certain: She didn't want any part of that neurotic scene across the street.

Ron was lifting Kevin to the higher bar and catching him as he leaped from it, the action punctuated by the child's delighted laughter. It made her smile. Something very appealing about that man. . . .

"Kevin, dinner." And immediately realized she'd barked the order. God, she was getting to sound like a shrew herself.

Dulcie was not the only one viewing the outside world through a pane of glass. When he hadn't come right back with the dolly, Geegee knew in her bones Sonny had gone across the street. He never loitered out there at the curb, so what would make him do it this time? Geegee had to laugh, it was all so goddam obvious, that broad over there, no one else in the house but a kid. . . .

She put the stuffed pork chops and creamed peas on the table. Let 'em get cold.

Whether Ron noticed they weren't at peak heat, he didn't comment. As he had all week, he ate without conversation, although he did acknowledge someone else was in the room. "Hello, Mother . . ." and "please pass the ketchup." Ha-ha . . . big deal hello, Mother. . . . Well if he had a good, mediocre, or lousy day she wouldn't ask. If he wasn't going to talk, neither would she.

132

And yet he wasn't pouting. When he pouted, he kept his eyes on his plate and shoved the food around with his fork. He wasn't doing that. Just seemed to be someplace else.

As soon as he'd taken the last swallow of tapioca, he pushed back his chair, went outside with his coffee cup, and that's where he stayed all evening. Just looking at those damn dogs.

She stays. Those two words had made the last few days more palatable than any of recent time that Ron could remember. This street mongrel, ungainly, flop-eared, undisciplined—not a bad looking dog, now that he'd cleaned her up. But it was Aubie who commanded his attention night after night. Aubie, who never ran for a stick or a ball without a num-num at the end of it, had found the endurance of a cross-country runner. Chasing. Letting her chase him. And when she flopped to rest, barking, demanding her to her feet. Then the race again. He, streaking alongside, jaws open to the widest of their hinges, his fangs to her jugular until she lay on her back and permitted him the illusion of having conquered. Then, sudden twist of her supple body, and she parried his mock savagery with a powerful thrust of her flank against his, toppling him so that for the moment he seemed to be sitting on his head, contorted. Then he was on his back, spreading hind legs in ritual of total trust. And they would run again. The pursuit, begun millions of years back, repeated through the week. Through Sunday.

A wasted day, as Geegee saw it. Having to work on the picture album when all week he'd known she wanted to look at those condominiums that were for sale in Costa Mesa not three blocks from the marina. So what if they weren't in the market to buy? It was just having somewhere specific to go. A new place every time was getting harder to find. Yermo had been fun, but the truth of the matter, she hadn't enjoyed that bus ride as much as she'd pretended. It was for Sonny. Sonny liked those offbeat things.

And for him to repay her, killing a Sunday by staying in bed, faking a headache until it was too late to go anywhere . . .

He could never get away with lying to her. He couldn't keep track of a lie. But this time it seemed as if he didn't care if she knew.

She centered a picture of Duchess with her puppy on a page, and wondered what made Sonny lie. Look at him, out there in the backyard in just his shorts, head uncovered to full hot sun, watching those damned dogs. Headache, her behind.

"Oh, damn . . ." Her elbow sent a stack of pictures onto the floor. On her knees to gather them up, she was eye level with the sea of flotsam that had been salvaged back into their lives, and felt the pinch of obligation. It was his fault, their rediscovery. When she told him *blue* he should have remembered right away it was the breadbox, and not put them through all this.

The pictures on the floor, all of Duchess, initiated a wave of sadness. For a brief moment she gathered the illusive years into her lap. But they were just black-and-white prints.

Things hadn't been the same since Duchess died. Damn him, anyway. Out there, watching them smell and lick each other. . . .

At breakfast on Monday he said to her, "Aubie's changed. He's different since the lady came."

"Well sure," she answered, "course he's different; what'd you expect? He's jealous; you spring another dog on him, he's gotta be jealous."

"No . . ." Sonny, she was aware, was beginning to talk slow and deliberate. "Not jealous," he said. "You notice he doesn't yipe anymore?"

"What d'you mean, yipe?"

"Always yiped, like an infant. Doesn't yipe at all. Hasn't yiped—" he repeated, annoyingly, "not once all week, not

134

since she's been here. He's different. Excuse me, I'll be late for work."

She scraped the skin of the cantaloupe for the last ounce of flesh and followed him with her eyes as he headed back to his bedroom to dress. If he wasn't going to mention his upper lip, it'd be doomsday before she would.

He thought of it as an un-birthday birthday. The shirt that came out of the Magnin's sack, which he carefully unpinned and unbuttoned, was pale yellow with stripes of little blue flowers. The tie, wide and brighter than navy, caught and held the light in its opulent satiny depth. He did not avoid the mirror, as he had been doing, but stood in front of it, tucking the shirt into his trousers, Windsor-knotting the tie, and watched his image assemble itself.

Middle button of the jacket. Shoot the cuffs, just one inch showing. Thumb-roll the lapels. The closet door was almost closed when impulse reached in for the Borsalino. It turned him back to the mirror. Carefully, he set the hat on his head. Arms still upraised, he held, mannikin-like. A long moment. Then slowly he tilted one side of the hat down. Flared the other side up. His left hand sought his jacket pocket as, with his right, he finger-brushed the shadow on his upper lip. The eyebrow elevated of itself.

The hat had lost its malevolence. Always he'd expected to find someone else under it. Now he was that someone. He turned as gradually as on a revolving display window pedestal, and as slowly, a smile emerged. Aubie's changed, he thought, Aubie's changed.

He hung up the hat (because nobody wore hats to the office), gathered his bowling equipment, and moved determinedly through the gallery to avoid any possible comment from Geegee. Her "Don't forget to close the gates," hosted him through the door.

135

Who did he think he was kidding? she said to herself. How could you miss that shirt and tie? He's found a broad. Comes from watching those dogs all the time.

"Aubie, get in here."

She slammed the gallery door almost on his tail as he skidded through. Let the bitch stay out. "Hot or cold she stays outside," she told Aubie, but he didn't get the message. He was at the door, nose pressed against the glass, whining, whining.

"Just shut up and behave yourself."

"You look good, Mr. Gohdiener . . ."

"Very hip, Mr. Gohdiener . . ."

If he'd had any doubts about the shirt and tie, they were immediately dispelled. Even a couple of girls in the elevator had nodded a smile at his plumage.

The new girl (he'd have to learn her name) stood up as he came through the aisle of desks and complimented his appearance with *"Muy macho . . ."* which he knew from high-school Spanish to be a favorable comment on his masculinity. He smiled thank you.

"Where's Ruth? She isn't sick, is she?" he asked the new girl.

"Oh, no, Mr. Gohdiener. She went down the hall to the you know—"

"Oh, yes, of course."

"Anything I can do, Mr. Gohdiener, I'd be only too happy . . ." Her hands ran down her torso and brushed imaginary wrinkles from the abbreviated skirt. Now that he really looked at her he challenged Kemper's evaluation of 39-D cup. This girl's proportions—even her coloring—were much like Geegee's, and Geegee was 38-C. "No. Thank you," he refused her services. "Oh, Ruth—" he called, as he saw her returning, "would you come in, please?"

"Yes, sir."

He was standing behind his desk, setting out papers from his attache case when she came into his office.

"Good morning, Ruth."

"Morning, Mr. G.," the pleasantry as automatic as pulling the chair to the corner of his desk, poising pencil above the pad to catch his words. But none fell. She looked up to find him straightening his already straight tie, adjusting his collar.

"Why, Mr. G., I don't think I've ever seen you wear a colored shirt before."

"Oh? Haven't you?"

"And you're starting a moustache . . ."

"Well . . . just a couple day's growth."

"I think it will look good on you."

"You do, Ruth?"

She studied him earnestly. "Very good, yes, very good, Mr. G."

"Why, thanks . . ." He touched his upper lip with just a hint of twirl. "New dress?"

"This?" She tugged, but the skirt wouldn't cover her fine-boned knees. "I've had it for ages . . . you've seen it before."

"No . . ." he said, "I don't think I have."

"Oh, I've worn it a lot. I bought it in the July sales. I'll bet I've worn it twenty times."

"I don't believe you, Ruth."

"Oh, yes, I have—" Then she realized that behind his solemn eyes there was laughter.

"You make it look new." He felt high, like he'd had a drink or two.

"Why, thank you." The sudden flush in her cheeks, and he realized she was self-conscious, that he hadn't given her much preparation for the unfamiliar intimacy of their conversation, and decided he was pushing too hard.

"Cashews?" He offered from his pocket.

She shook her head gently, refusing. "They're fresh roasted," he urged. "I bought them on the way in." She took a few and held them in her hand. And he understood why he'd bought the shirt and tie in the first place.

For Ruth. He'd been planning all along without knowing it.

"Ruth?"

She poised notebook and pencil. He took a deep breath and eagerness tumbled the words. "Will you go out with me?" The smile on her face fled, taking the blush with it. *She doesn't want to go. . . . She doesn't like me.* "Some night? Like—tomorrow? Or, if you're busy, any night would do—" In her stark silence he heard himself diminishing but couldn't stop. "Any night at all. Look, you don't have to tell me right away—Think it over—Tell me—tell me tomorrow. . . ."

It was like hanging onto a phone gone dead. She got up from the chair, her eyes looking for a place to hide.

"I'm married, Mr. Gohdiener. . . . Don't you remember? Over a year now—you contributed to the present —the silver sugar bowl and creamer?"

Married . . . a year. . . . Then he remembered the buildings near his house that went up in the sunflower field. Built in his daily path and *they* had slipped by him. . . .

"I don't wear my ring because I'm allergic, you know—acid in my system. . . ." She was pulling a chain from inside her neckline and showed him the gold wedding band on it, trying to help and making it worse. "My finger turns green from gold. Some people have that problem, you know."

"I apologize, Ruth—didn't mean to come on so strong. Sorry."

"So am I." Their eyes touched. "Truth is, I wish you'd asked me before."

He tore the answer from himself. "I thought about it, Ruth."

"You did. . . ?"

"A number of times."

"I thought about it, too."

When her hand released the knob on the other side

138

of the door and the bolt clicked into place, the need to scream left him. He dropped the bag of cashews into the waste basket and, with the transistor razor he kept in his drawer, shaved off the three day's growth.

Then he started his day.

Mid-morning, Kemper stuck his head in to tell a bad joke. When it came time for the fellowship lunch, Ron locked his office, turned off the lights and his mind, and sat in the dark. And, for no reason, Aubie was there with him, wetting the grave. He wanted to escape, but couldn't. He'd imprisoned himself. At three o'clock, Kemper was back wondering where he'd been, deposing Ron's alibi about an emergency trip to the Commissioner's office with his own enthusiasm for the great new lyrics the boss wrote to "Pop Goes the Weasel." The group sing was a helluva good time, he said, and before Ron could usher him out, he treated him to the first verse:

> All around Los Angeles Town
> We all sell life insurance
> T'make the million d-hollar club
> You gotta have endurance . . .

Ron could hear Kemper bellowing team spirit clear across the outer office as he went away:

> Renewals are our mainstay here
> That's how we'll all re-tire
> So if you wanna make it big
> You gotta keep on fi-yer. . . !

Bowling hung like a guillotine. Mr. Meader might overlook his not having been at the sing, but Monday night's bowling was high mass. And Kemper would be the choir, brown-nosing with the new lyrics. If only he could get away. Get in the car and drive. Sit alone, stare at the ocean with nothing but the monotony of waves coming in without end, receding over and over and over again. No way, he faced the truth. No possible way.

It was just five o'clock when Ruth rapped on his door. He could see the outline of her slender body through the opaque glass and willed her to go away.

"Come in." Standing where he was at the file, checking out his day's work, he could avoid looking directly at her. Would he ever be able to look at her again? He hadn't known his awareness, but now he realized he knew everything about her. Without looking, he could see that the top of her head came to the bridge of his nose; her eyes were grayer than blue; when she walked there was a brightness to the sound of her step.

"I'm leaving now, Mr. Gohdiener . . ." She hesitated in the doorway.

And there was never a jagged edge in her voice. "Good night, Ruth."

"The forms in this envelope have to be filled out."

"Just put them on my desk, please."

She did, explaining that everyone had to complete the forms by the fifth, since the whole organization was going computer. He told her he knew.

"After the merger," she volunteered, "you know some of us will be moving to the new office."

He turned his head. "You?"

"I put in," she said. "Today."

He nodded that he understood, but still she didn't leave.

"Mr. Gohdiener . . . you know Arlene?"

"Who?"

"The new girl. She said you had a nice conversation at the water cooler once, and today—"

"Oh," he said. "Why? Is there a problem or something?"

"Well . . . she doesn't know many people. I hope you won't be angry at me. She has two tickets to a play—"

Ron began shaking his head. "She's very nice, Mr. Gohdiener, and you're alone so much. She asked me to go, but I had the idea that maybe you—"

"No—"

"She's always saying what an interesting looking man you are, the tickets are for tomorrow night—"

"No, Ruth—no—no—thank you—thank her—but no, no—"

His tension made her apprehensive, locked her out. "The forms," she indicated on the desk, "by the fifth. I'm sorry, Mr. Gohdiener . . ." Her eyes asked him to understand. "I was just trying—trying to help . . . good night."

His breathing was shallow, painful. It was over and it hadn't ever begun. He thought he was going to strangle.

The nine-to-five occupants began to desert the steel-and-glass battlements of Wilshire Boulevard as if fleeing a city under seige. Ron felt safe as part of the mass exodus where he could nod answers, to the impersonal *good-nights* without involvement, since all were as anxious to get away as he was.

He stepped back to let the Riviera parked next to him pull out and found he was only a space away from Arlene. Like two actors left on a stage in a miscue.

He no longer could cloak her in the anonymity of the new girl. Now she had a name and had burgeoned into his life without being asked. He moved quickly, hoping her preoccupation with putting packages into her car would allow him to go unnoticed.

"Good night, Mr. Gohdiener."

"Oh . . . good night, Arlene . . ." He felt obligated, moved toward her a little so he could keep his voice down. "I hope you understand about tomorrow night —that Ruth explained—"

Under her makeup was five o'clock pallor. There were lines in her face that the fluorescence of the ninth floor had not revealed. "Ruth explained," she said, and then informed him she wasn't a charity case; nobody had to make dates for her. "Who needs that jazz? I've got plenty

141

of friends . . ." Her noontime shopping was in a shoe box and dress box. Theater wear? he wondered, that she'd planned to inaugurate with him? "Plenty of friends," she repeated. The shoe box broke apart as she tossed it onto the seat, revealing slim heels and straps, not to be dashed out in for tunafish on rye.

"I'm sure you have lots of friends," he said. "I'm sorry, really sorry I couldn't make it. Good night."

"From what I hear you can't make it period."

The vitriol stunned him, pulled him back but he wanted to run. "What's that mean?"

"Kemper told you, didn't he? The sonofabitch . . ."

"What you said just now—" Ron had to know. "What did you mean—can't make it. . . ?"

"That bastard, that supply-room groper; his face almost fell off when he made a grab and it wasn't there!" Her cumulation of anguish left Ron no cover. "He tell you which one?" she shrieked a whisper. "He tell you?"—thrusting first one breast then the other hard against Ron's chest. "Will the real Arlene please stand up? What's your problem, Gohdiener, haven't you got any curiosity? Don't you want to grab a feel and find out for yourself?"

It was like being on a runaway carousel. When he spun loose she had already started her car.

"I didn't know, Arlene . . ." he leaned in through the open window on the passenger side, urgent for her to understand. "Believe me, I didn't—honest—Kemper never—Look, I'll take you out anytime—I'll be glad to. . . ."

"What for? Whole office knows you fly—" The racing engine lent a grotesque vibration to her voice. "Well, I've got news for you. With or without a tit I get all the head I need!"

The key was in the lock where he'd left it. Panic bricked on panic till he found it there and managed himself part way into his car, but one foot seemed anchored to the pavement. Unable to make the effort, he just sat, long after she had gone, half in, half out. He heard Kemper call his name, heard him ask if he wanted to chow before they bowled.

"You all right, Ron?" He was leaning in close, so close Ron could see the large pores on his nose. "What's the matter?" The concerned deep-blue eyes seemed an opening gateway and Ron swung onto them for reassurance.

"You're a friend of mine, right, Kemp?"

"You know it. You got trouble, man? Lay it on me."

"You'll tell me the truth?"

Kemper studied Ron's clutching hand that dug into his forearm. "What d'ya want, a loyalty oath?"

"You won't say anything to anybody. . . ."

"Come on, Ron, we're friends. If you trust me, you trust me."

"I just want to know one thing . . ." Ron's stomach had a knot he could feel in his throat, and he was grateful that the parking lot had almost emptied, "Who in the office says I'm a fag?"

The question teetered in Kemper's eyes, then he laughed. "You—a fruit? Queer? Hell, everybody knows you're a stud."

Ron searched the craggy face. "They do, Kemp? They say that?"

"Sure. . . ." Kemper slapped Ron's extended leg. "You know, I even think my wife's got the hots for you. All that polite thing you do. Where'd you get that crappy fag idea anyway?"

"Then nobody says that about me—nobody?"

"My word to Jesus—nobody. And believe me, *I* know what goes on in the office."

"Nobody ever says anything?" Ron worried it.

"Nobody. Nothin'. Never. Well . . ." he qualified, "sometimes people do pass a crack about livin' with your mother, but screw them, right?" And Kemper played back the theme Ron had heard so many times before. "You really got it made, everything taken care of, free to do what you want . . ."

143

He did. He did have it made. Geegee did take care of him. And he thought of the Borsalino. It was the same color as Kemper's suit. He began to relax a bit, nodding acceptance of Kemper's oil on the water. Poor Arlene, he thought. She was just hurt. Sick. You couldn't blame her.

"You know how people shoot off, Ron. Do it myself even." Kemper leaned against the car. It was man to man. Truth, whole truth, nothin' but. "Everybody gets a flappin' lip, once in awhile. We're friends, right? Know what I said—*me*—first time I saw your mother—before I knew she was your mother—? I turned to one of the guys and I said, Now there is a real piece o' tail. . . ."

Nothing changed in Ron's face for the eternity of a second. Then he came out of the car like a brahmah out of a shoot, grabbing fistsful of green plaid lapels, slamming this two-hundred-ten-pound animal against the car, intent on smashing its skull.

His victim, shocked, frightened, half choked in the maniacal crossed-arms grasp, managed to pull free enough to plead, "You're crazy—'matter with you —y'nuts—"

Sanity reclaimed him. His fists unclenched and he let Kemper go.

"Stay 'way from me . . ." Kemper was backing, gingerly touching his bruised neck. "What're ya, nuts? Do a guy a favor, what d'ya get . . . just keep away—you're crazy—don't talk to me—keep away. . . ."

Kemper powered his Cadillac out of the lot. And Ron was left alone with the horror he'd found in his own hands.

II

NIGHT mothered the occupant of the single automobile in the parking lot. The bowling ball on the passenger seat forgotten, the ignition key still unturned, Ron sat, not knowing or caring what time it was, staring at the tall, empty, checkerboard-lighted office building across wide, almost deserted Wilshire Boulevard. Towers tenanted now only by the machinery of service—typewriters, water coolers, computers, photocopy machines—and the people who brought the vacuum cleaners and would carry them away.

He couldn't erase Kemper, who loomed as large now as when he had held him spread-eagled against the car.

With the blink of an eyelid, one of the windows across the street went dark. *What was he doing here?*

Ron was lost from the first turn. Left, was the pattern. Right ultimately brought him to the neighboring country he so seldom visited at night it seemed foreign. Downtown L.A. A stranger, he wandered through it, forced to circle by one-way streets, the signs changing with ethnic islands from Anglo, to Chinese, to Japanese, to Spanish, until the open jaws of the freeway sucked him in. There, at high speed, windows open, wind blowing, he felt unidentified. Unseen.

The freeway was a haven. A world apart. A river, flowing forward, backward, cloverleaf. Destination, unknown. The Pasadena to the Golden State to the San Diego, eventually back to the Hollywood and the off ramp his Plymouth took like a horse returning to its barn.

He touched the brakes as he neared his house, red tail lights ghostly on the unlighted street. Then they went off as his car picked up speed. He knew now where he was going.

"Ron," he said into the perforated brass that covered the intercom. "Ron Gohdiener."

"Oh, sure," Edna's voice welcomed. "Come on up, Bob."

"Ron," he corrected. "Sure it isn't too late?"

"Hell, no, baby, never too late. You must have ESP. I'm ready to climb the walls. I mean, how much Ovaltine can you drink. . . ?" The buzzer, reflecting her eagerness, came on while she was still talking.

It was twenty of eleven. Plenty of time for Edna. Only this time, his way. After tonight, she'd remember his name. She'd be begging him to quit. And begging him to come back. When he got through she'd know who was the fuckor and who the fuckee. And he was ready. His shorts felt tight, constricting, by the time the elevator door closed behind him.

She was waiting. As he rounded the corner, he saw her, standing just outside her door, wrapped in the same flannel robe, smiling, extending her hand in greeting. In it was the Borsalino. Then Kemper and Arlene were there. They had Edna sandwiched between them. All talking at once. A discordant trio.

Put it on, put the hat on, you'll really look like Somebody . . .

What a piece a'tail . . . Kemper kept repeating.

You really fly, Fag. Fly. . . .

Then Aubie lifted his leg.

He felt himself losing touch and he was sobbing. Through tears, he saw Edna, standing alone, but couldn't

146

walk any closer. He turned and went out through the door marked Exit and started down the stairs.

"What's the matter, baby. . . ?" She followed quickly, distressed; in anxious whisper she called down after him, "Did I say something? Edna needs you, baby. . . . I didn't mean . . . whatever—"

He didn't look back, just kept following the spiral of the stairs. All she had of him were his footsteps on the metal tread, mocking her. Who did he think he was? Her name was on the door in gold leaf. If he came into her bank to do business with her, he'd be kissing her feet. Who the hell was he? Just a warm body. No Steve McQueen. "You bastard," she shrieked down the impersonal concrete silo. "Dirty bastard . . ." Her loneliness bounced off the walls and died. He was gone.

Ron knew he wasn't crazy. He knew Kemper and Arlene and the Borsalino weren't in the hall with Edna. It was all Geegee's fault. It was as if he'd been slit open with a knife when he found the cut picture. The girl, he'd wanted to marry her, why couldn't he remember her name and what she looked like? How would Geegee feel if she lost a breast? Poor Geegee . . .

"Dirty bastard . . ." came down on his head from the third floor. It didn't matter. Edna wasn't a very good lay anyway, he told himself as he crossed the street to his car. The numerals on the dashboard clock glowed green. Bowling nights he never got home till after one. If he walked in now Geegee would take one look at him and start asking questions. Did he go to the bathroom today? Before he could answer, she'd be there with the Milk of Magnesia and a thermometer.

He was back on the freeway, arguing with Geegee. *I'm fine. . . . Let me look at your tongue. . . . I'm okay. . . . And that slop you eat all the time, when you could take your lunch. . . . She's been married a year—A YEAR—and I forgot. . . .*

It's no disgrace to carry a lunch; I could fix you a nice little basket. . . .

"Leave me alone!" His yell wiped Geegee out of the car.

It had been a lousy day for Soldier. The register had played a breadline tune. Eleven dollars, eighty-two cents. Hell t'Christ, that ain't no way to live. The pier was goin' to hell. Usta be a time, six, seven years back when it was kinda enjoyable. Once in a great while even a broad from over the counter took a shine to him. What did he have now? The hustle in back wasn't workin'. Cost more to feed that cunt than she was worth. And skin pictures? Who wants to take skin pictures when they're screwin' right out on the open beach? Every kid layin' every kid. The goddam pill. Kids walkin' around with their tits showin' through their shirts. Couldn't even sell rubbers any more like he usta. All sweat, no money. Where the hell was he headin'? Zero. Zero to nowhere. . . .

He pressed the button and the targets started moving. Maybe he'd pick up a few bucks shootin'—a little bet on the side, here and there. Most of the assholes that came around nowadays couldn't hold a gun anyways.

The Donald Ducks moved by and splashed into the little pail of water at the end of the long track. The hot white light from the target area reflected on his creased face as he laid the stock of the .22 against his shoulder and rapid-fired. Three outa four ducks. Not bad. The guns on the counter weren't too accurate anyway. With his good piece, he'd hit a bull's-eye every time. He set himself to fire the rest of the clip. The pad of his thick forefinger pressed against the trigger, but held. It wasn't anything he heard, but he knew someone was behind him. Watching. A rip-off? These junkies today would take you for a nickel. Crummy as things were, he wasn't buckin' for a coffin.

He turned slowly, holding the gun at rest. His finger was still on the trigger.

148

There was no wind. The air was still, filled with the weight of moisture and the taste of salt. Ron's thigh pressed against the chain drawn across the pier to keep out late-night intruders. The pieces of the picture that had blown away . . . had any of them blown back? Were they lying on the pier, mixed with empty bags and discarded paper cups?

He stepped over the chain and started up the narrow boardwalk paralleled by stalls that were shuttered for the night. Their gaudy colors and noises stilled, they seemed lonely. Unfrocked. In a pool of light ahead he saw the figure of Soldier and curbed the impulse to call out to this gross man whose touch brought with it the smell of stale sweat.

Soldier was raising the gun in his hands, the stock against his shoulder. What was he sighting on, Ron wondered? The German who crawled away? And he felt an elation at the sudden, frightening explosion, a rush of blood not unlike the sensation in the elevator on the way up to Edna.

Ron hadn't moved. He couldn't have been heard. It must have been the sharp, excited intake of breath that gave him away. Soldier shifted from one foot to the other as he turned. "Yeah . . ." he called into the dark perimeter, "I'm closed. Whaddya want. . . ?"

What did he want? He was a sleepwalker, awakened in the street.

"Hey . . ." Two eyes that could see turned fully on Ron. "Ain't you been here before?"

The surprise of Soldier without the eyepatch brought back to Ron the confusion that had been tranquilized by his arrival at the ocean. He took several uncertain steps backward, then bolted. Running up the pier, he tried to figure out what brought him here in the first place. If he'd come to the ocean for some peace, why go to Soldier? He remembered how they'd talked of his father, and Patton, and he'd felt Somebody. Was it that? Was it that Soldier made him feel important? Then why did he set up such a curtain of fear? Idiocy, sheer idiocy. "Crazy," he muttered to himself, "crazy."

It took him three keys, even though the car door was open and there was plenty of light, to find the one for the ignition.

Soldier stood and watched him run away and felt relieved. Trouble was getting harder to handle these days. As he sighted on the moving rabbits he wondered, When had that guy been around?

Whenever Geegee got frightened she went to the bathroom a lot. The piss of fear, she always called it, but only to herself. Ogden Avenue, that was the first time when she peed scared. And again when her mother and father left her alone in County Hospital. She didn't want to think about that and pressed the handle to flush the memory away. The pipes rumbled within the wall and under the house, but still she heard. Any sound from the gates plugged directly into Geegee's central nervous system.

When she opened the front door, Ron was bent over about to insert his key. He wore an apologetic smile, a T-shirt and his bowling jacket.

"I'm sorry I'm so late, I hung around after bowling."

She closed and double-locked the door, not trusting herself to speak yet. He moved quickly past her, snapping his fingers for Aubie to follow.

"Good night, Geegee, I'm tired."

"That's all you have to say? 'I'm tired, Geegee, good night'?" Her bare feet padded after him through her room into his. " 'I'm sorry,' " she parroted his tone. " 'It's late, I hung around after bowling. . . .' And me ready to come apart at the seams?"

"I know, I should have called," he said, hoping to end it. He was under control and wanted to keep it that way. "I'm sorry, dear, that you worried," he called from the closet as he hung up his suit jacket and the new shirt he'd never wear again.

150

"You're a liar. You—are—a—liar!" she enunciated, bitingly. "You are a damned liar."

"Why would I lie to you?" The hat on the closet hook loomed at him with its former menace.

"I'm going out of my mind—and you—God knows what's happening to you. When they called from the bowling alley to ask where you were, I was ashamed—ashamed—to say I didn't know. . . ."

Back in the bedroom, he was aware the dogs' bed was unmade. "DID YOU LOCK HER UP AGAIN?" He didn't wait for or need an answer but went straight across the gallery, through the kitchen, to the service porch, grateful for the diversion that took him away from the guilt that he had lied to her. Geegee had built up a full head of steam.

"You have any idea what I've been through? What do I have in the world? All I have is you—" Her voice took on the sound of a whining saw that penetrated his bone marrow. "Now I don't even have you—What's happening to us, Sonny?"

He could hear the dog scratching on the service-porch door and let her out. She was ecstatic and raced away with Aubie.

"Why the hell can't we name this dog?" he yelled to the house at large on the way back to his room.

"When you were a little boy," she said on his heels, "you used to say Talk to me, talk to me, Geegee, when you don't talk to me I get a bad feeling. . . ."

"Lady. That's a good name."

"Now you're out with some cheap tramp all night without even thinking of me. You could've been dead. On the freeway someplace. I called the hospitals, the police—"

Ron's head nodded automatically as he threw the old sleeping bag across the bed and both dogs settled on it.

"I didn't know where to turn, baby. What else have I got in life besides you?"

This was the cord that packaged him always, and he

tried to stay free of it by insisting every dog should have a name.

"The hell with naming her, you had no right to do this to me . . ."

Through a mouthful of toothpaste he told her he never asked her. Did he ask her? "More than once I said, get married. Get yourself a guy. Excuse me," he said, "I have to go to the bathroom."

"Who?" she yelled through the closed door. "Someone like your wonderful father?"

He took his time. Zipped up his trousers. Washed his hands. Decided his hair needed brushing.

"We'll call her Lady," he announced as he came out of the bathroom and sat on the bed to remove his shoes and socks.

"I was on the streetcar . . ."

"I've heard that story, Geegee."

"Well, I go crazy when I don't know where you are—It's like when my father dropped dead and I didn't have a chance to tell him I was sorry . . ."

"Geegee . . . I know the story."

"I was on the streetcar," she persisted.

"Lady. We'll call her Lady."

"If I'd had money for a cab I would a' got there. He was going to forgive me—but he was dead. . . ."

He wiped off his shoes with his socks. She'd leave soon, then he could rest. Maybe sleep.

"When I think something's wrong, Sonny—you're hurt —I could lose you—I just run . . ."

"It's settled, y'hear me?" His voice submerged hers. "We'll call her Lady."

"Call her Bum," she fired back, "like that hungry looker across the street—Nobody understands—She talked to me like I was crazy. . . ."

"Who?" he said. "What do you mean—across the street?" And began to feel lost again.

"And she should understand," Geegee ripped on. "She's got a kid—wait'll he grows up, tears her apart—"

152

"You went over there. . . ? Over there?" he screamed from the edge of a precipice.

"I saw how she looked at you. I can tell a bree-a-zoad a mile away—And there's no guy over there—"

"Oh, God—Christ—I don't even know her—What the hell did you do—?" His feet jammed into his slippers and he ran from the room, stuffing his T-shirt into his pants.

"Son-neee—" Her voice reached him in the gallery as his arm viciously swept all the pictures from the table.

"Don't follow me!" His fury stopped her, but only for the moment.

"Close the gates," she called after him.

He had rung the bell at the house across the street before shame reversed his direction to send him back. Through the convex peephole, Dulcie saw his Tom Thumb image. What's he come for? To hide from his Mommy and smoke a cigarette? Or maybe even grass, if he's a bad, bad boy.

"Yes? What do you want?"

He was down the three brick steps when the door opened on the chain. He couldn't look at her, regretted he'd come, felt caught. "I'm sorry. . . . I know it's late."

"Your mother said it for both of you. Good night."

"Please—" He reached to hold the door open. "Just let me apologize . . ." He was pressing his forehead as though to hold it together, hiding his eyes. "All I want to do . . . apologize . . ."

"Okay, fine. You apologized." She eased the pressure on the door.

"You've got to try to understand my mother—"

"That's your hang-up. Just keep it across the street."

"She's really a very good person . . ."

"Cool. Send her a Mother's Day card."

"It's just she gets nervous when she's left alone—If you really knew her—"

Dulcie felt if she slammed the door the man would shatter.

153

Ron wished she had slammed it. It would have made things easier. Easing it closed, as she did, made him feel he'd been stepped on. Erased. The passion that impelled him across the street was spent. He closed the gates. Geegee was standing outside, under the night light, framed in the doorway bordered by a profusion of bougainvillaea. He raised the rifle until she was in the cross hairs of the scope. He fired. He killed her.

"Want a nice hot cup of cocoa, sweetheart?"

He smiled his refusal, patted her on the cheek and walked past her into the house where he got bombed on Jack Daniels and went to sleep.

12

GEEGEE got off the streetcar at Cahuenga and Hollywood and started up the street feeling lucky to have
caught the last car. She hated to think what would happen if ever she missed it. That was the worst part of the
job, getting off so late. Hollywood, in the daytime, made
you feel good, like you had a lot of friends even though
nobody ever talked to you on the street. At night, you
wondered where'd they all go? Were they all asleep in
their houses or were they in the alleys, just waiting for
you to come along?

She walked fast, near the curb because you could
always get pulled into a doorway. As long as she was on
Cahuenga where it was lighted, it wasn't so bad. The
block of stores, the nice looking apartment houses . . .
the night was trying to make up its mind whether to rain
or not. Just a kind of mist, chill, like a blade, cutting
through the thin cloth coat. She wrapped it tightly
around her body, but it didn't stop her shivering. For a
while, she thought there was somebody following her, but
it was just the echo of her spike heels on the pavement.
For companionship, she sought her own face in the glass
window of a printing shop. The dark-red lipstick looked
black, the phony eyelashes hung like tired fringe around

her eyes. How could she look so young, she thought, and feel so old. Skinny, skinny, skinny . . .

There were big fat oranges in the window of the Triangle Market on the corner of Franklin. She'd stopped to look at them last night and planned on buying a whole sackful come payday. She wanted to stop again and look, but there was a wino there, drinking his fantasy in the liquor display.

Always—every night—she hated to make the turn at the gas station because there she left the lights behind and had to fight the urge, all the way home, to go to the bathroom. By moving fast enough and making herself think of other things, she could get through the long double block without panic.

On Dix, she walked up the middle of the street.

There were some nice old houses there, big houses set almost like in a park. Once, when she'd had Sonny out for a walk, they'd prowled back through a vacant lot and found a little stream. The people had yelled for them to get out, it was private property. She'd made up her mind then and there that some day she and Sonny'd have a place fancier than that, bigger, better, good enough for a movie star, and walled off so nobody'd ever tell them to get out again.

The high heels had begun to jar. Her calf muscles ached. She took off her pumps and walked barefoot. The pavement was wet and cold. Approaching the bend in the street where enveloping bushes took on ominous shapes, she whistled her courage past one threatening bush that, on moonless nights, always looked just like King Kong.

She could see the rooming house now, under the street light at the intersection of Dix and Primrose, and ran the last few feet with the same terrible relief she felt every night to have made it home. It wasn't the worst place to live. The porch was crawling with termites and the whole building smelled from dust and mildew, but one of the roomers said Fatty Arbuckle's stand-in used to live there.

Going up the uncarpeted stairs, she put her shoes back

on to avoid the splinters that were hell to get out. At the top, she reached to unlatch the small folding gate and found it open. A dozen times she'd told them, he's a baby, two years old, he could fall down, but did any of them care? When she unlocked her door, Mrs. Wessel was asleep in the sagging overstuffed chair. They went through the nightly routine. She nudged Mrs. Wessel awake, gave her the seventy-five cents, Mrs. Wessel nodded, meaning Sonny was okay, and Geegee left the door open so she'd have light to find her own room. When the door closed down the hall, Geegee latched hers and started to undress. The 25-watt bulb in the bedside lamp muted the scars and stains left by too many tenants in the cold, damp room. The only fresh new thing here was her Sonny.

She hung up her coat on the back of the door, pulled off a threadbare woolen sweater. Before she put her arms through the sleeves of the flannelette nightgown, she took off her clothes underneath it. Brassiere. Too big tweed skirt she'd bought at the Salvation Army. As she sat on the bed to remove her shoes and eyelashes, she looked at him, thinking his face was like a church statue. She'd get him out of this cheesy joint.

She turned out the light and got into the lumpy bed, too tired to care about lipstick smearing the sheets. Then she remembered. Without getting up, she reached under her nightgown, pulled off the spangled G-string and tossed it onto the floor. Curled herself around her warm baby, and slept.

Primrose Avenue . . . what brought that ancient history to mind? Geegee looked at Sonny, sleeping, snoring from the booze, and searched his features for the lost, dimpled cherub, finding no resemblance in the slack-mouthed, sprawling body. She lifted the heavy arm that hung, limp, over the edge of the bed, and covered him with a blanket. High-strung boy. Getting so upset just over her going across the street to ask if a neighbor had seen her son.

She felt tired. Alone. The only one awake in the whole world. The heels of her mules clacked across the hardwood floor of the silent house. There was a carton in the hutch. Overhead lights snapped on to wipe out the shadows, until the cigarette was in her hand and the calming smoke filled her lungs.

But there was no way to stem the wave of featureless faces, their mouths foul with demands for *More—More—More* . . . fighting down the desire to throw up until your body could go through with it night after night while you were someplace else, away from the rotating tassels, the flesh-cutting G-strings, the dismembered voices that yelled from the darkness. Toilet Boy Scouts, trying for merit badges . . .

The beat of some distant, joyless drum moved her body into the remembered undulating patterns. A ritual of despair that led her away from the past and into the hollow of the hunger that was always in her. Her hands locked onto the hard, round finial of the Valentino sofa and pulled her rotating pelvis full against it. Pulsations raced through her body, once and again. After a bit, she dozed on the down-filled sofa. At four o'clock she went to bed, deciding not to say a word to Sonny about his getting drunk.

In the morning Ron went to look for his life and found nobody home. The Echo Park house had been torn down for urban renewal. The old neighborhood grocery man said he thought Mrs. Ploven had died a few years back. A sick old lady, he said. The apartment on Cherokee was now an office complex, housing a production company involved in making religious films. There was a tunnel on Dix Street with a six-lane freeway thundering overhead.

He wasn't missed, with so many people going back and forth between the old and new offices. Everybody being so busy, packing, moving, rearranging, made things easier, let a little grass grow before an encounter with Kemper, Arlene or Ruth. As it turned out, Mr. Meader had pulled a muscle and didn't know who'd been bowling and who hadn't on Monday night. Geegee called and said, don't be late for dinner, she had a surprise. He promised he'd be on time.

Dulcie figured a Hershey bar should last Kevin about a minute and a half, long enough to read the letter again. She bribed him with one and unfolded the embossed vellum:

Dulcie:

Really!—you don't have to keep moving since we always find you. It would save you money and us effort. And you surely ought to know that a rental agent would not only check with your bank but that, coincidentally, my bank supplies your bank, and, further, I also happen to be a stockholder with your bank. But the thing that most offends me is for you to sign a lease as Ms. Dulcie Carpenter, thereby giving total strangers the impression that Kevin was conceived out of wedlock. If you wish to lead this so-called free life, I won't object. A truce? At least you're out of that degenerate atmosphere of Venice. You can stop running. We have no intention of asking you back. [We? she questioned: the editorial we or the royal one?] I fully expect to be able to see Kevin on occasion. Am certain you will be amenable about arranging this. Or, as we say at the office, viable. My attorneys will be in touch.

Yours truly,
Peter

P.S. Had dinner Thursday with your parents.

We've arranged to go to the Open together. They
send regards.

The letter had his initials, his secretary's, with a c.c. to
his attorney. He should have married her parents, Dulcie
thought. The three of them, forever in formaldehyde:
quel ménage a'trois. She shredded the letter into the litter
bag. "Ace," she said to Kevin, "you've got a lot to live
down," and kissed chocolate off his cheek as they got out
of the car.

Ron came out of the stuttering door of the market,
wondering as always why the owners didn't put the electric eye a few feet farther in front. In all the years he
and Geegee had gone in to the "Welcome" sign and left
to "Thank You, Call Again" there was always the jarring
moment when the door hesitated, making them do a kind
of braking step so as not to run into it.

He stopped outside under the overhang and checked
the list Geegee had given him on her second phone call
of the day. The fresh-cut carnations and the bottle of
sparkling burgundy were his idea: to make up to her for
the terrible thing that had gone through his mind. And,
for the briefest instant, she was, again, in the cross hairs
of a rifle.

Geegee loved surprises, those she planned, those he
planned. *It's the thought, Sonny,* she told him when he gave
her the little vial of perfume. *What you think, not always
what you do, that's what counts.* She wore that perfume
every day and night until it was gone. Then she put the
empty bottle uncovered into her lingerie drawer and the
pungent fragrance remained. Always filling him with
shame and worry. What if Mrs. Ploven would smell
Geegee; she'd know it was hers.

Ron buried that old anxiety in the fragrance of the
bouquet he held. Things had turned out reasonably well
today. He felt finished with the past. What had he been
looking for anyway, in that trip back into time? His body

160

felt loose. He stretched his neck from side to side and nothing clicked. It had been a great idea to get smashed. Not the slightest sign of hangover, and all the guys he knew who couldn't hold their liquor. I feel good, he told himself, I feel good. And immediately felt rotten.

Nod hello. What else could he do? He couldn't act like he'd never seen her before. She nodded back, looked down at the pavement, and rushed by.

He had a painful idea of what Geegee must have said to her.

I've seen you shake your tail at my son, walking around with those tight pants that show every crack. . . . Dulcie, pulling Kevin along with her, ran a finger around the top of her jeans: They had shrunk some, she conceded. And she hadn't done too well last night in the cool department herself, yelling back and slamming the door. Why blame the poor guy for his mother, any more than she could blame Peter for his Calvinist cock.

The mechanical horse swallowed the quarter that would make Kevin stay put, and Dulcie was at Ron's elbow.

"If you've got any crow in that sack, I'll eat it—raw."

He turned from unlocking his car and looked into candid eyes that were devoid of anger.

"No, no, please, I'm the one who should apologize. I was walking on the ceiling last night."

"I'm in phase two of my thinking," she said.

"The truth is—" Their words were overlapping.

"Not just for your sake—"

"My mother had no right—"

"But for mine, I've got to tell you—"

"I'm sorry—"

"Sorry."

A draw. They were both sorry. She laughed and extended a tanned, ringless hand. "Dulcie Carpenter." He laid the flowers on top of the car with the sack that held the wine. "Gohdiener. Ron Gohdiener."

"And just so you know I won't cook up any witches'

brew," she said, "come try my coffee, or a Scotch— whatever—whenever—"

"Thanks," Ron said. "I might. You know, I just might. . . ."

The man, wine and flowers drove away. Dulcie wondered if they were a packaged peace offering. "More . . ." Kevin was demanding. She fed the greedy horse a second quarter and her buckaroo held on through another gallop while she mused, Would he really cross the street to see her?

The violin bow scraped a passion from the strings that penetrated even the thick cross-cut planks of the front door. All highs, no lows. The needle making a valiant but futile attempt to stay in the tired grooves of the outmoded seventy-eight as Carlos Molina and his orchestra delineated "El Choclo."

Ron unlocked the front door and left his ascending mood outside. Geegee was nowhere in sight, but her handiwork was. Crepe paper streamers—hot pink, orange, purple—draped from chandelier to wall sconces and back. Through the arch to the formal dining room he could see the baronial table set for sumptuous dinner, ceiling beams festooned with balloons in fiesta colors.

Like Pavlov's dog, he entered the game.

"Buenas dias, señorita," he called above the din of the music. "Ole!" and she was framed in the archway, Carmen, Spanish-shawled, hair pulled tight, enormous spit curls centered on her cheeks, hooped earrings dangling to bared shoulders. "Ole! Ole!" she repeated and glided to him on a long, shimmering, descending glissando.

He felt he had stepped into a wax museum, that he was on a track, being pulled along, like the ducks that moved across for Soldier.

"Last night didn't happen," she told him. He put the wine on the entrance table, the flowers into her extended arms. "Last night didn't happen," he agreed.

They came together in a deep, knee-dipping sweep and

tangoed in to dinner. Between *gazpacho* and *arroz con pollo*, they danced again. The *spañada* went from high tide to low in the cut glass pitcher and had to be replenished, but he gave it very little thought except that the end of his nose seemed to have gone to sleep. The carvings on the high, straight-backed chair dug into his back, but they kept him upright. The table was long and getting longer. One bulb of the chandelier was out, he noticed. He noticed many things as he sat through the courses. The amber of the light cast a glow of jaundice on Geegee's cheeks. A lacy spider web floated in the rising, heated air from the candles. He made a design in the tallow with the tine of his fork. A straight design. A squiggly design. The lemon slice, sinking again with the level of the wine, had a face in it.

Geegee, in the host chair with the lion's head arms, never seemed to stop talking. She seemed intent on starting from day one of his life and she could remember everything, which was something Ron couldn't understand since he could remember so little.

"You were twelve then—no, ten—you were big for your age . . ." Her voice came from her chair, then from the gallery, then from behind his chair as she put a plump album down in front of him. "See—? I'm sure ten, because I was still working at the Horseshoe. See the sign in back?" He saw. "This one's almost full, I'll need another album; get me another album?"

"I'll get you another album."

That pleased her. She kissed him on top of the head and took the wine pitcher back to the other end of the table and poured the last of it into her glass. Ron was sorry she did that; he liked the face on that lemon slice.

"That was the winter you had pneumonia. I didn't sleep for three nights. Remember that bastard landlord, kicking us out when he found out you were my kid, not my kid brother? I really told him—Some world, it's okay to sleep with your brother, huh. . . ?" The laugh she began deserted her. "What a rotten time."

163

"It's long gone now, Mother."

"Oh, Sonny, call me Geegee, please."

"Geegeegeegee."

"You're right, sweetie, you're right, hon, you're always right." She extended her hand, sending a wave of affection across the table. "It's happy times now, hmm?" She smiled into her wine glass before emptying it. "I love our house; don't you love our house?" He didn't answer. She didn't notice. "I know you love our house. . . . Lotta trips down a lotta runways. . . ." she told the room.

In measured diction he reminded her that he . . . had . . . helped . . . to . . . buy . . . this . . . house. "And I support it, right?"

"Of course, Dollface, we did it together. Geegee didn't mean anything. You're the man of the—" Whatever he was the man of got lost in a new concern. "I didn't hear you close the gates."

"I closed them."

They sat, smiling at each other. She pursed her lips and kissed into the air. He volleyed the kiss back. "We'll have brandy in the study," she announced and floated away. Both dogs got up and followed her.

Geegee felt satisfied. She could afford to be patient. From the moment she left the dinner table there was no question in her mind that Sonny would be easy to handle if she just let things ride for a while. Who knew him better than she did? No one. No one in the whole damned world. So sweet, the way he smiled at her all through dinner, and how his face lit up when he saw the decorations . . .

She replaced her treasured tango record with Mantovani.

Relieved to be alone, Ron rubbed his face with both hands to unfreeze the tense muscles from the smile that had set like cement.

He had fired a gun at her. Killed her. Saw her die.

"Sonny . . . Sonny—" her voice recalled him.

"I know. Brandy."

All during dinner, his back to the window, he had felt the pull from across the street. Through the narrow gap of the draperies he could see her house was lighted. Would she be alone, with just her little boy? Did she have company? Had she meant it about having a drink—?

"Son-neeee . . ."

As he came into the study with the bottle and two glasses it was all home and hearth. The dogs, stretched out in front of the crackling fire. Geegee, on the hassock, skeins of colorful yarn piled next to her.

He poured the Courvoisier, then surprised her by lighting a cigarette and handing it to her.

"I love a man who thinks of all the nice little things. . . ." Capturing his hand in both of hers, she caressed it with her cheek. He smiled at her, still wondering what Dulcie was doing, reached out and scratched Lady's belly, then pulled up the footstool and began working on the opposite end of the hooked rug.

Geegee smiled back at him, knowing she'd have to get rid of the bitch. But not just yet. Twice now, when she was in the dressing room, putting on pantyhose, Aubie had wrapped his front paws around her thigh and pumped away. He never did that when his mother was alive.

They hooked three rows before calling it a night.

13

THE culprit entered the forbidden territory unknowing, unaware, without fear, and stood at the edge of the great body of calm water, smiling as a massive fantail swam through his reflection, rippling it unrecognizable. He was prevented from following the fish by Ron's hands, and let out a yowl of protest.

"Easy, friend," Ron said to the child. "The water's cold, the pond's deep. What do you say I take you home?"

Geegee, voyeuring from the window, was certain now how Lady had gotten in the first time. It was the day that kid and his mother moved in, only the mother'd had her eyes on those two studs who carried in her furniture and not on keeping her kid out of other people's yards.

Dulcie came running across to collect her child and Geegee ran to the galleria for Sonny's attaché case. When she opened the front door, the kid was standing on his toes, illustrating with a stick how he managed to open the latch, and his mother and Sonny were laughing.

"You're gonna be late—" was all Geegee said, and waited until the invaders were gone.

"Don't wait up for me," Ron told her on the doorstep. "Staff meeting tonight, about the merger and stuff, could be very late. . . ." His lips touched her forehead. She held the gates for him to drive out. As he backed to her, he rolled down the window. "Lady'll be here when I get home, right? No tricks . . . no games. . . ?" The agitation she'd missed in his voice was in his eyes. She'd seen that look once before, that day on the pier when he had confronted her about the picture of the girl, and the chill of his look stayed with her even as she was cleaning up last night's fiesta and taking down the crepe paper. All the effort she'd given to their making-up party seemed so futile.

"Stop that, you animals!" She drove Lady out of the house, as she did every day, and kept Aubie in with her.

"What are you, scotch, vodka, beer?"

"Anything's fine—"

"In this house, everyone makes his own decision."

"In that case, vodka. On the rocks."

While he waited for her to come back, Ron tried to assess what there was in this room that was so comforting. Almost bare of furniture, not too large. About the size of his bedroom. The whole house could be lifted up and put into their living and dining room with some left over. He remembered the sign—*Knock on the wall, lathe and plaster*—when they were first building this house and five more exactly like it. He'd walked through it once when it was in the framing stage, never even thinking about what it would be like finished, never expecting to be sitting in it.

The room gave him the same feeling that he got from the girl. Both looked you right in the eye. No apology for having only one chair, for unframed Lautrecs, Warhols and original Kevins Scotch-taped to the walls. Colors from all directions as from a paintbox gone wild. Persian floor pillows, books, records. Lamps that sat on the floor because there were no tables. Even the long, white phone cord that snaked its way from under homespun drapes across the deep, earth-colored shag, seemed part of an innate design.

Ron stood up when Dulcie came back with their drinks.

167

She smiled at the formality and touched his shoulder to sit him down again.

"May all your trips be uppers," she offered.

"May your shadow never grow less." Their glasses touched.

"Hey, that's nice," Dulcie said, and sat cross-legged on the rug in front of the portable sewing machine, pressing her knee against the lever, running a vivid piece of printed fabric through. "I never heard that toast before."

"Irish," he said.

"You Irish?"

"No . . . I think I heard it in a bar once." Her expertise in rounding off a corner claimed his attention, and he realized she was making a pillow covering from the same cloth as what she was wearing: not a caftan exactly, it fit closer to her body. Sort of a long, skinny dress. As she reached to feed the machine the material, her small breasts pressed tight against the fabric, unblemished by any intruding brassiere strap. "No," he corrected. "Now that I think of it, I read it in the *Reader's Digest*."

She nodded and continued sewing and he fell silent. Unsure.

"If I've interrupted your work. . . ?"

"Oh, no. You don't mind if I sew?"

"No, no, go ahead."

"I've got to get these pillows covered so there's something to sit on in this house."

"Very pretty."

She smiled. "You hungry?"

"No, thanks, I had dinner."

"You want something, just go help yourself."

"Thank you." Sitting in the chair, above the glow of the lamps, he felt removed, an observer not a participant, and regretted not having accepted the floor pillow she offered when he first came in.

She seemed to read his mind. "You look like an Establishment Buddha up there."

"I'm very comfortable, thank you," and wondered why

168

the hell he said that. She answered his look at the closed hall door with, "Kevin's asleep," adding, "He sleeps like a rock."

"You know, he's welcome at our house—"

"I'll keep him home."

"It's just our pond's so deep, for him to be there alone—"

"I understand." The way Dulcie said it, he felt she did, that Geegee didn't stand between them. He watched Dulcie finish the seam, turn the casing right side out and lean over and pick up the pillow in her teeth. He laughed. "Here, I'll show you an easier way—" He was on the floor beside her, his hands dominating the procedure as he deftly turned the casing inside out and took the pillow from her teeth. "Now," he instructed, "put your hands inside—I'll hold the corners—You take them from me—That's it!" The covering slid over the pillow and fit like a stocking.

"Cool . . . where'd you learn that?"

The army . . . summer camp . . . a whore house. . . . He ran the multiple choice through his mind. Any answer but the truth. "Around . . ." he said and started to withdraw to the isolation of the chair.

"Stay. Just sit. Relax. . . ." Dulcie was inviting him out of his jacket, handing him his drink. "May *your* shadow never grow less. . . ." And he found himself accepted into the foam-rubber comfort of the Persian floor pillow.

"My grandfather was Irish." She was hand-stitching now, closing up the fourth side of the casing.

"I like this room," he told her. "It's—easy."

Dulcie made a wry face. "My family would throw up if they saw it. They're still all on the sixteenth hole at Pebble Beach. I'm the family sand trap." Her fingers were sure and moved quickly, making small stitches. She must have walked barefoot a lot in the sun, he thought, since there were hardly any sandal marks on her feet. Calves, slim but long-muscled, thighs hard against the soft material. "My father wanted a son," she related casu-

169

ally. "My mother wanted a nun. My husband was on her side—he's divorcing me because I talk dirty in bed." She looked over at him. "Shock you?"

"No, no, not at all."

"Good. You looked a little pale there."

"No, really," he insisted, "I wasn't shocked."

"You can use my name. It doesn't wear out."

"Dulcie . . ."

"Anyway," she went on, "I took a vow that Kevin's going to belong to nobody but himself. Took me four years to make that decision—I used to lie all the time, trying to please everybody—four years on the couch. That's why I like to sit on the floor. . . ."

Dulcie . . . it had texture, like heavy cream. "I was surprised when you invited me over."

"Why? I like you."

"I'm forty."

"You look forty, so what? That supposed to turn me off?" She leaned over and kissed him on the mouth then went back to her sewing. The taste of her lingered, his tongue reached for it again on his lips.

"Gohdiener . . . your father sure wasn't Irish."

"Rumanian."

She nodded, accepting his face. "That gypsy music, that's a gas."

"He had black hair . . ." Ron reached back over his head for the vodka bottle. "Always wore a moustache. . . . You should've heard him talk—brilliant—he was an engineer. . . ."

She listens, he realized, as she put down her sewing, really listens. And he wanted to tell her all of it. "You know, a trim moustache . . ." he described it with his fingers, "and had the habit of raising one eyebrow . . ." It made him feel good, the way she nodded, smiling, as he demonstrated. "Always wore a hat—turned up on one side, rolled down on the other—style, lot of style—Wasn't afraid of anything—he was killed, shooting the rapids in the Colorado River. . . ." His words broke and fell like

170

a rock that starts an avalanche. *Should he have said Patton?*
"How old were you?"

"What?" She'd pulled him back from Soldier.

"When he died. How old were you?"

"Uh . . . twelve—no, ten—so far back, it's hard to remember—my Mother—she's been great, I tell you it was rough for her—really took care of me—no help from anybody—she never left me—some of the jobs she took just to keep us together—" *Why had he said rapids? He'd never said that before.* The need to explain to her was like the current of a river, pulling, pushing him, and he couldn't seem to grab onto anything. Or take a deep breath. "You know—you know the night my mother came over here—that was my fault—she was so embarrassed —I'd told her we'd met and I liked you—she knows I've got a private life—whole thing my fault—should've told her I was going—out—late—"

The room was crowded with Geegee and Soldier and Edna and Aubie.

"Please—" he gasped.

The nebulizer from his jacket pocket gave him back the gift of breath. There was compassion in her touch as she loosened his tie, rubbed the taut, strained muscles at the back of his neck. And profound sadness in her question.

"Does your mother know where you are?"

"No she doesn't, Mrs. Wonderman, my mother's working—"
"Who the hell's 'at—?" the angry voice coming from some-where back in the flat.
"You better go 'fore June's father sees you—" Mrs. Wonder-man's bulk filling the kitchen doorway, blocking it.
"Please, I just came to apologize."
"Is 'at that kid whose mother's a stripper?"
Running. Getting caught. Mr. Wonderman nailing him, shoving him against the porch railing. "Listen, you little shit, you come around tryin' to cop a feel on my June again, I'll kill ya. . . ."

*   *   *

171

On a breath as tortured as the confession, Ron told Dulcie, "My car's parked around the corner. Block away. She thinks I'm tied up in a meeting at the office. . . ." He struggled to his feet. The floor pillow released him and returned to shape as though he'd never sat there. "It's all right," he said, "all right, no sweat, I'll go."

"Stay—"

"No—" He felt her hands on his cheeks but could not bring himself to look at her. She was kissing him fully, her mouth open to his, unbuttoning his shirt, brushing his chest with her lips, drawing him to the floor with her. The phone's shrill ring cut between them.

"Hello . . . hello . . . hello."

There was life at the other end. Their ears, sharing the receiver, could hear the breathing. Dulcie held the instrument out, but he refused it, as he refused to meet her challenging, inquiring eyes. She hung up the phone.

"You can't be sure it was my mother . . ." but in the corruption of the moment he was sitting up, desperate fingers fumbling with recalcitrant buttons, awash in a sea of humiliation. It was like watching a man drown and Dulcie couldn't let it happen. "Wasn't there ever anyone—anyone, Ron—who made you want to break loose?"

"Once . . ." he admitted. "Once," and told her about the picture; how, when he'd found it, the girl was cut off. Just himself, standing there, grinning like an idiot, his arm around nothing. Air. "Fourteen years, and Geegee cut the poor girl right out of the picture. Evelyn . . ." It startled him. "Evelyn . . ." the name so buried came back so easily now, and with it a face. "Evelyn Beatty—and I saw her," he remembered, "a couple of years ago—in a store—she had children with her—two—didn't see me—her boy dropped the oranges and they were all laughing. Her hair was short, used to be long . . ." He stared into space, unaware of Dulcie reaching to him, touching him. The recitative of deception so long concealed could not be denied. "I saved two thousand dollars to get married—stole it from myself—lied to my mother

172

about my salary, my bonuses, lunches—All these years, it's still in my closet—hidden—can't spend it—my mother'd smell it out—kept it in the bank, long time, till they started sending notices of interest earned. Tried a safety deposit box, but a renewal bill came to the house —told her I'd got the vault to hide her surprise birthday present—been making payments all along on a new dishwasher for her birthday—had to go out and buy her something valuable, personal—got her a Navajo squashblossom necklace—it turned out to be stamped Made in Japan—I kept the money in a hat—a hat. . . ." The way he got to his feet, tightening the noose of his necktie, spoke his emptiness. "What would I spend it on anyway?"

"Stay, Ron."

"No, I couldn't. Not now. Anyway, why would you want me?"

"I don't know. Maybe it's the way you raise one eyebrow, that's not bad for starters . . ." Her arms locked around him, her face raised to his. The disruptive phone rang again, pulling him to heel. Aubie at the grave raced through his mind, but Dulcie held him in the present with the touch of her lips, the demand of her body. Even now, here, his mind counted the arrogant, insistent, rings. Again. Again. On the fourth ring, Dulcie drew him back to the floor with her. The fifth she aborted. The ring died in her hand. "Go to hell," she said into the phone and put it back on its cradle. Without pause she reached to her hem, pulled her dress over her head and dropped it. They came together, and Dulcie led him away from the torment.

Morning came, bringing December with it. A gray day. Fallible winter let its presence be known even to the dogs who stood outside the door of the gallery, pawing their desire to be let in. The chill seemed to have penetrated the thick adobe walls of the old house. The furnaces, duty bound, had obeyed their thermostats at dawn but couldn't thaw the freeze at the breakfast table.

Habit chained them together, but Ron had structured a wall of the morning newspaper. The long, sleepless night had left Geegee haggard, and he didn't care about that any more than he was affected by the old, faded chenille bathrobe she wore as sackcloth and ashes. It was all trick and he knew it. A weapon of war. But for once he wasn't unnerved by it. His mirror had shown him a face that was alive. He ran his hand through hair that was still damp from being under the shower with Dulcie.

Geegee put a match to her third cigarette and invited his protest. When none came, she exhaled heavily and watched the smoke billow up and around him. He fanned it away, then turned the newspaper to read an inside page.

He could hear her chewing. She always made that slightly moist sucking sound when she was trying to out-wait him. The first one who talked would lose, and the score had always been heavily on her side. What she'd expected this morning, after his being out all night, was a hangover and guilt; for him to say he wasn't hungry, to leave the house with only a mouthful of coffee and his guts in a knot.

Not this time, little mother. . . . Slowly, deliberately, and with appetite, Ron ate his breakfast. He could hear her break her crisp toast.

She was winning, she figured, when his hand appeared from behind the sports page and shoved the butter, arm's length, to her. She refilled his empty cup, certain he heard the coffee pouring even though his head didn't appear with a thank-you nod. A little cream, a carefully measured half-teaspoon of sugar. Stir. When she put the spoon down it was the loudest sound in the room.

She waited. He remained behind the wall.

She got up and let Aubie in, pressing her thigh against the door to keep Lady on the outside, then sat down again, tantalizing Aubie with a piece of bacon which she kept just out of reach of his salivating mouth.

Tease him, go ahead, devil the poor dog, I don't give a damn.

You're not going to get a rise out of me. Ron went to the door and let Lady in, remembering a game he'd played as a boy, only now he felt the winner.

Ronnie, take three steps forward, one scissors, one hop, one giant step.

May I?

No, you may not.

This time, no *May I?* He had taken the giant step. Without a glance at her, he dropped the newspaper onto the table, picked up his briefcase and made ready to leave the house. Geegee, still teasing with the bacon, broke the silence. "No num-nums for you, bad dog . . . after what you did on your mother's grave."

The sledgehammer blow, as she knew it would, as she had planned it through the hate-filled, waking night, hit Ron at the base of the skull and spun him around to look at her: to face the detestable fact that she had known all along. All the hell he'd gone through, and she'd known. Saved it to use against him.

Why don't you die?

14

WHY shouldn't she die? Murder was commonplace . . .
an everyday occurrence. Going to work, before he
reached Highland Avenue, didn't the news casually feed
him a missing person found in an azalea bed? Before the
parking lot there was a wife killed by poisoning. At the
catering wagon, some secretaries, sweetening their coffee
with a front-page item, were more disturbed that the
word "mistress" was male-pig-journalistic-chauvinism
than the fact that a woman had been stabbed in bed. And,
in the elevator, the stainless steel doors had been van-
dalized with a Nazi swastika scratched on top of a Star
of David. An elevator full of people rode to the ninth
floor with six million dead and nobody said a word.

There was no way to avoid Kemper. Ron tried to back
into the corridor, but both were forced to the same side
of the doorway as the file cabinets rolled by on the heavily
laden dolly. "Top set o' files got my prospect lists,"
Kemper told the office boy who was doubling as moving
man. "Take care of 'em, make sure they get in my new
office." A nod to Ron. "Gohdiener."

"Kemper."

"This whole moving thing's a pain in the ass." In this
tight arena, Kemper had the neutral ground of logistics

to retreat to while Ron had nothing but the brutal memory of the parking lot.

"Haven't been avoiding you. Busy—you know—"

"About that crack I made—I talk too much."

"My fault. Don't want any bad feelings. . . ."

They agreed it was one of those things. They would run into each other. After all it was the same business, just different offices; reassured each other that they were bound to meet. Bowling, if nothing else. But the relationship was over. Ron knew. The look on Kemper's face told him Kemper knew, too.

"See you."

"You know it."

For years, everything had been in the same place. Now all the framed charts, pictures, licenses were gone from the walls and the faded spots were like windows in the land of the blind.

Ron was looking around at what suddenly seemed a strange atmosphere, and didn't realize he had stopped at Ruth's desk until he turned and saw her, still wearing her coat, cleaning the last paper clips from the middle drawer, putting her personal belongings into a large carton.

"Today. . . ?"

"In about ten minutes, Mr. Gohdiener."

"I see."

"It's a very nice office in Century City, but I'll miss this one." He nodded, to both points. They agreed that this office needed a paint job, what with all the empty spaces, and she told him that she had made arrangements for a new secretary for him from the building pool. He kept nodding, to assure himself that he knew what was happening, where he was.

"Did you bring the forms in, Mr. Gohdiener?"

"Forms? What forms?"

"For the computer. The manila envelope I gave you."

"Oh, no, no, they're still in my car. I'm sorry, Ruth."

"They've got to be turned in. . . ."

Arlene's desk was completely empty, too. Cleaned out. "When did she move?"

"Arlene? Oh, she quit. Last week. Strangest thing. Wouldn't give a reason. Just called in and quit, for no reason."

"Nice girl," he said. "Really nice girl . . ." he repeated aimlessly as he turned into his office. "Nice girl," he said to the city outside his window.

"Mr. Gohdiener . . ."

"Yes, Ruth."

"Good-bye." She was having trouble hanging onto her smile. "You've been nice to work for."

"Thank you, Ruth."

"Well . . ." she said, finding the doorknob, "like they say on the bumpers . . . have a nice day."

"You, too, Ruth. And a better one tomorrow."

She closed his door. For a moment her image stayed in the frosted glass, then it was gone.

Things were ending. Kemper. Ruth. The way he felt about Geegee. He ran his fingers through his hair, but it had dried. Tried, but couldn't remember Dulcie's number. Searched pockets until he found the scrap of paper. Dialed, but there was no answer. Sat for a while and admitted the temptation to call Geegee and tell her he wanted her dead. . . .

Still no answer. *Was there no Dulcie? Had there never been a firm, tanned, eager body meeting his on a mass of Persian pillows? A body, free, that invited him to partner that freedom?* The erogenous response the memory engendered convinced it was real, and recent, and present. Not one of his fantasies that offered little satisfaction, that only drove him, on occasion, into his bathroom and darkness.

Sweat on the nape of his neck brought him out of his chair to stand in the open doorway and watch files, desks, people, go. In a week or so he would be companioned by a massive computer. Like his own life, this scene of shifting population. No lasting friendships. The first time ever people were moving away from him. He could never remember living in a neighborhood long enough for another family to move out before they did.

Dulcie . . . Geegee . . . out of sync . . . discordant.

He tried to work, but couldn't. His ledgers, with their reality of figures that always added up no matter how he fractioned them, were enemies to solace. He closed the ledgers and did something he'd never done in all the years he'd worked for the Meader Insurance Agency. Walked out. Simply walked out of the office with no special destination. Not to the commissioner's, not to any important client's. Just out and walking with a sense of self he'd never felt before.

Dulcie . . . He saw her in store windows. Smiled at the smog-laden air and fought the temptation to speak to strangers.

He remembered having told Dulcie of that impulse while they lay curled together, covered with a fur throw. "I'll be walking down a street," he had shared with her, "all alone, and I'll suddenly want to go up to somebody and say, I'm Ron Gohdiener, did I go to school with you? Did you live in the next block . . . downstairs, upstairs . . . did we ever kick a ball between us . . . play ringaleevio. . . ?" She hadn't thought it crazy. He had told her a lot about himself through the early morning hours. How he lived in his head. He remembered doing a lot of talking, and she had stroked his hair, his body, with her wonderful hands. And there were dark places in his head, too, that he couldn't let himself look at. He told her that, but he didn't again mention Geegee. Or his father. Or the Borsalino.

Standing at an outside phone booth that was like the hub of a wheel on a small concrete island, he reached her. She sounded breathless, as though she'd been running.

"Where've you been?" and realized it sounded possessive. "I've been calling you all morning."

"Just got back from taking Kevin to school, their bus broke down."

"Have you got a pencil?"

"Sure."

"And a street map?"

"Why?"

"You said last night you didn't know L.A."

"I don't."

"Okay. Hollywood Freeway to Highland to Wilshire, then left." He gave her time to write it down. "Will you have lunch with me?" He told her how to reach the Egg and the Eye, right across from the L.A. County Art Museum, she couldn't miss it. She promised not to, and would he give her an hour? He spent that time walking, replaying every word, every inflection of the brief conversation, understanding fully his head-on attack about pencils and maps and directions: to help get him past the questions he wanted to ask and was afraid to . . . *last night, was it because you felt sorry for me, or because you really like me . . . today, have you thought of me?*

The last fifteen minutes he spent at the La Brea Tar Pits, studying the rigid, lifeless mastodon family standing in the tar that has oozed from the bowels of the earth since time began, and wondered what did they do about mothers in those days? He stared at the still-burbling, black, gummy fluid now sprinkled with cigarette butts, rotting ice cream cones and crumpled paper cups, and a gull that had strayed from the freedom of the ocean breeze to be trapped and die senselessly.

Held in check by a red light on his way to the restaurant, he slew a saber-toothed tiger and made himself a loincloth of the hide.

It was in this mood that he met Dulcie. "Are you glad I called?"

She was glad, she told him, as they went up the narrow stairs lined with posters advertising avant-garde films to the omelet emporium that looked down from a balcony onto an eclectic array of ethnic art, hand-crafted fabrics and jewelry. "Fabulous," Dulcie called it, and it pleased him to have chosen so well. But in his eagerness to find

180

just the right setting, he had overlooked the fact that his enthusiasm for the place was shared by half of the businessmen on the Miracle Mile and a full compliment of luncheon-going wives. Making the reservation, he had envisioned the two of them, *intime* on a banquette. Once he'd dined here with Geegee, but that had been late afternoon of the winter Sunday they had done the museums. Then the tempo had been easy, with candles glowing on all of the tables. He'd never lunched here before, having usually eaten with Kemper, and this was hardly Kemper's style.

The maître d' was apologetic: There would be a considerable wait, would they care to go to the bar. . . ? which to Ron didn't appear too promising, since bodies were stacked three deep in there. However, the maître d' suggested he could serve them sooner if Mr. Gohdiener and the lady wouldn't mind sharing a table with another party. In spite of their willingness to do this, they spent fifteen minutes at the bar—at least, in the same county with the bar. Ron ordered two Bloody Marys, which came just as they were informed their table was ready.

"I'm sorry it's so crowded," he said to Dulcie above the buzzsaw of conversation, as they shouldered through.

"I don't mind," she smiled.

"I really wanted to talk to you."

"Well, I've got a six months' lease; I'm not going to move away."

The seating available to them was at a small wall table, on chairs whose backs were in the aisle, putting them elbow to elbow with diners crowding both sides. Their tablemates, on the banquette opposite, were two women whose sole concern was why doesn't Givenchy make up his mind about hemlines.

Since Ron commended the caviar, he and Dulcie both ordered omelets Kiev.

To be seated on the banquette was what he wanted. Even with the heavy luncheon crowd, it would have been better. That way, they could have turned inward, toward

181

each other, spoken privately. Touched. Just not possible on these damned chairs. And it set up in his mind the tremor: What if she wouldn't want to touch him, that last night was last night and this was today. . . ?

At least if they were opposite each other, their eyes could meet. He wanted to ask her, Did you sleep after I left you? Do you like me; do you really like me? Instead: "How's your omelet? Pretty great, hmm? They make the best omelets in town." The party of four at the next table was leaving, but there was already a replacement moving in. Ron determined to keep his eyes open.

"How far is your office from here?"

"Just a few blocks. Did you have trouble finding this place?"

"No, you give good directions."

"How's Kevin today?"

"Fine, he likes his school."

Not a word uttered about Geegee. He wondered if she wondered what happened after he got home.

"I wouldn't want this to get out," came from one of the women across the table, "but Picasso leaves me ice cold." Ron looked over his fork at that moment to see them reaching for their purses. It was now only a matter of artful maneuvering. In order for their luncheon mates to leave, the small table had to be pulled out, and Ron was in first position.

"The lady and I will have our coffee over here," he informed as he moved himself and Dulcie to the ban-quette side of the table. And it was as he had hoped. She sat with one foot curled under her, her pant-covered knee touching his, voice low in his ear.

"Are you tired?"

"I'll never be tired again."

"You sure you're not in advertising, after a line like that?"

"Insurance."

"Wasted."

"Will I see you tonight?"

"No."

"Oh," he said, and prepared himself for rejection.

"I thought tomorrow night."

"Why not tonight?"

"I'm taking Kevin to Venice, where we used to live. There's this lovely lady there, Mrs. Leopold, used to baby-sit sometimes for me, always wanted Kevin to spend a night with her. . . . I thought tomorrow night might be a good time for him to be away." Her eyes took up the narrative and gave him assurance of what fulfillment would be possible in the house alone, and in that flash he saw her reaching down to pull off her long, skinny dress, and under it there was only Dulcie.

"Can't you take him down this afternoon, then you'd be free tonight?"

"I couldn't do that to Mrs. Leopold, just take him and drop him. I called, and if I know her, she'll be cooking all the rest of the day. I really have to spend the evening there. I want to."

"How long will he be gone?"

"Kevin? Two nights, maybe three."

The excitement so overwhelmed him he felt the entire room must be aware, and fell silent. The conversation of two businessmen seated opposite was all about a stock split, and from an adjacent table came, "I know she's right because her brother is a Chinese dancer."

Ron retreated to what could be safely overheard. "So that's where you got that great tan, Venice."

"Oh, we were only there a short time, but I've always lived by the ocean, I love it. . . ."

"If I'd known that, I'd have taken you someplace near water for lunch. We'll do it tomorrow."

"Lunch? Again?"

"Absolutely."

Before he stepped out of the car in front of his office, she leaned over and kissed him. He stayed at the curb and watched her VW blend into traffic and disappear.

Geegee was not going to cut this picture in half. . . .

The switchboard operator informed him there were no messages. That surprised him. Nor did Geegee follow her normal pattern of calling at least once in the afternoon. She had to call first, or he couldn't go home. Wouldn't go home. She had to call first or going home would be walking back into hell. That day at the grave, the anguish he'd felt, how he'd protected her from Aubie's gross act . . . and all the time the incident was just another weapon in her armory. The fault in their relationship was exposed now, like a festering sore.

Dulcie's little red car ran over Geegee in the streets of his mind, and he thought ahead to tomorrow. At ten of five the phone rang. There were bristles in Geegee's voice. "Bring home some of that ready chicken, I'm not cooking."

"I won't be home for dinner," the tone of her voice decided for him. "I'm working."

"You're a damned liar. You don't have to work tonight; you've got a date with that slut." He hung up hard, catching his finger between the phone and cradle, creating a blood blister. Since he was the only one still in the office, the switchboard operator left his line open, in case he wanted to make or receive any calls.

"I'm sorry, sir, but there's no listing for a Mrs. Leopold or any Leopold in Venice."

"Thank you," he told Information, and hung up. The three lost working hours from the early part of the day demanded his time. He worked without letting his mind stray. At a quarter of nine the phone rang again. He hoped it was Dulcie.

"Sonny . . ."

"I wasn't lying; I told you I'm working."

"I opened a can a' tuna."

"Well then eat it and don't bother me."

Nowhere to go and nothing else to do. Even the reading left on the reception room table wasn't worth the eyestrain, but the decision not to go home until she was in bed held fast in his mind. The empty offices echoed his footsteps. He stopped at the huge window that had served up the city to Mr. Meader. A tower clock told him it was ten forty-five. Was that his phone ringing? He walked, heel to toe, slowly, deliberately. *Ring around the ring around the ring around the rosie. . . .* The twelfth time he picked it up, "Hello."

A click at the other end. She would do this again and again, he knew, like a persistent jackhammer. She would try to drive Dulcie away as she had driven away Evelyn Beatty. To create his own life was like climbing a long, steep, bald hill; slipping, losing his footing, clinging with bloodied fingernails, and now, this moment, he was finally achieving the summit. He was standing on a pinnacle, his vision extending into infinity.

Geegee had to die.

There was no pretense of quiet as Ron came into the house, yet she continued to feign sleep. Even as he opened the door to her bedroom and the light from his room found her on the bed, she didn't move. It would be so simple to walk over there, press a pillow hard to her face . . . and hold it. . . .

And that's how you found your mother, Mr. Gohdiener. . . ?
Yes, Lieutenant, this morning, she must have suffocated. . . .
Are you trying to tell us, Mr. Gohdiener, that your mother, an able-bodied woman, not under the influence of alcohol or any other drug, not forcibly detained in any way on the bed, could have suffocated herself. . . ? That's true. . . . I'm taking you in, Mr. Gohdiener. Murder one. You have the right to remain silent, you have the right to a lawyer, you have the right to—

Ron closed the door and broke the routine of his life

185

for the second time in recent weeks. He hung away his Thursday suit, and took out for tomorrow's luncheon date casual jacket, slacks and sweater.

Geegee must have a good, a special death. He would have her laid out in the jellaba with the orange flowers, which was so kind to her skin, a casket smothered in gardenias. . . . Now that would be a special death, to be smothered in gardenias. How many would it take? Probably tons and tons, he thought. And cost a great deal. No, he knew what agony it was to want for air to breathe. He couldn't do that to her.

Death should come easily to Geegee. Without warning. No need to frighten, to worry her. Since she had to die, it seemed unnecessarily cruel to waste the last part of her life worrying.

To die dancing the tango. Now that ought to appeal to her. To glide, to dip, and then at the most ecstatic moment of music, all of the crepe paper decorations to wind around her neck and snap it.

But where was he in all of this? All he could see was Geegee all alone.

Who is that lying dead in the coffin wearing an eyepatch?

That's my mother; have you ever seen a more beautiful mother?

The eyepatch. He hadn't thought of that since the night he ran away from Soldier. What a phony. Probably never won those medals, either. But he shot so straight. Right on target, five times in a row.

Soldier fired the gun and Ron jumped up from the bed, realizing he'd been asleep, and the moving targets were Geegee.

So much had happened, and only ten minutes had passed since he last looked at the clock.

The next morning Aubie killed a crow.

15

FROM under his pillow, Ron heard it happening. The agonized plea for help hardly seemed different from any other crow's raucous protest at having its food stolen or being dispossessed from a tree by a rival.

The alarm clock offered eleven minutes, but the morbidity penetrated the blanket of sleep. He felt the adrenal jolt with Geegee's first scream, "My God, Sonny, my God, oh, my God, he's killing it!" He had to pull her vicelike fingers loose from the handle of the steaming coffee pot.

In that fugitive moment, the mortal struggle had ended.

If only Geegee would stop screaming. Couldn't she see it was over? Through the gallery window, Ron saw it clearly. The head that fell back from the broken neck had long red hair, the pallid flesh was lusterless, the full breasts seemed shriveled in death. The jaws that held her were not jaws, but arms. *His.* And the face above the lifeless body was calm, without remorse. *His face.*

"Take it from him," Geegee was shrieking, "before he eats it!"

Aubie sat in the backyard, proud of having awakened to a primeval instinct, jaws grinding at the bones of the fragile black-feathered corpse, depositing his offering in

187

front of Lady before Ron could organize himself to reality.

"*She* made him do it—that bitch!—get rid of her, get her outa here, I won't have her here—" Geegee's hysteria stayed with Ron while he buried the hapless victim in the farthest corner at the side of the house. As he fought the hard soil with the posthole-digger and lay the wrapped bird deep into the ground, he fought the tyranny of his mind.

> Little fly upon the wall
> ain't you got no home at all?
> ain't you got no mama?

The hands that smoothed the earth over the grave were trembling.

"Finished?" Geegee called from the kitchen when she heard the door open and close. "Sonny . . ." The coffee cup in a large ashtray moved with her into the gallery. "Answer me. . . ." But the only response was that of the innocent transgressors, Aubie and Lady, whining from the service porch for parole.

"Sonny. . . ?"

He heard her above the sound of the ball bearings as the medicine chest mirror rolled back to show him all of the bottles. Bottles that promised sleep, calm, death's stillness. Labels that held up caution's hand—*Take one at bedtime—Not more than 6 in 24 hours—Poison—Beware—If symptoms continue, call physician.*

"Sonn-neee . . ."

He heard but didn't answer.

"Where are you? I know you came in . . ." She felt cold, even as she swallowed the hot coffee, rid herself of the cup and hurried across to his empty bedroom. "Sonny . . . answer me; I'm not up to games this morning. . . ." Could he have left for work, such an inconsiderate thing, without saying good-bye? Then she remembered he wasn't dressed; he was still wearing his robe and slippers.

"Sonnnneeeee . . ." The house felt full of doors, darkness in daylight, not a drape pulled to let in the day. An unnatural night that unleashed a runaway anxiety. "SONNNNNEEEEEEE."

The sound of rushing water found him for her. "You crazy? What d'you think you're doing?" Every drawer was open. Her bathroom counter looked like a cut-rate drugstore bargain table. He was feverishly disposing of pills, capsules, fluids, the bowl changing color as the dye from one medication married that of the next until the heavily scummed liquid waiting to be drained away wore the bruised purple-black of the murdered crow.

"You want to wake up dead some morning?" His tension committed him to apology again, and that wasn't what he wanted. He was already burdened and trying to free himself of the debt incurred by the images of death. Why couldn't she recognize that instead of standing there, yelling that she needed her goddamn pills. . . ?

"Geegee, you haven't been to a doctor in over two years—"

"What do I have to be—sick?—just to take a tranquilizer?" There was no question in her mind what he was up to, trying to twist her around, make her forget what happened this morning with this phony concern, *You'll take the wrong pills, Geegee, you'll kill yourself. . . .* Why couldn't he be honest with her like she always was with him? Going on that half the bottles didn't have labels, and how would she know what she was taking, when what he was really after was to take her mind off what that bitch had turned Aubie into. Sonny had that same look—same guilty look—like when he made plans to run off with that other girl, or the first time she caught him with his hand inside his pajama pants.

She let him take the cigarette from her and dump that, too. *You don't fool me, little boy. Nothing gets past Geegee. . . .*

"I let you keep her . . ."

He could hear Geegee as each dressed in his bedroom.

"I let you have your way. You don't know what it's like, you're at work all day, I'm home with them. . . ." She kept at him, even as she counted vitamins C, E, and complex into his hand and poured his orange juice, "You don't have to put up with it all day. . . ." Before he took his coffee, he opened the service-porch door and let the two dogs in. The gallery became a noisy racecourse. "See? He's crazy. He was never like that. Eat your breakfast."

"I don't want any." He drank coffee, standing, watching the two dogs as they played, rolling on their backs, twisting their bodies, pawing the air. *So Aubie killed a crow.* . . . There had been a crow convention on their lawn almost every day for the longest time, and Aubie would just sit and watch them. Once a bluejay chased him and he ran, yiping, into the house. Now he had become the hunter. Surprise, surprise.

"Get away from me—" For a minute there, Ron thought Geegee was going to kick Lady who was being her most appealing, bowing her front end, wagging her tail, offering herself on a platter. "Get away, I don't like you. You made Aubie do it, smelling around him all day, licking him. It's disgusting."

"What do you want from the poor dogs? They're only human."

Geegee heard the words but not their warning. "Save your jokes," she said. "If she comes into heat, I'm not going to be responsible."

"That's true, you won't. Aubie will."

"I won't have that, I won't have that here—"

"You hear that, Aubie? You better keep it down, buddy."

"That's dirty, Sonny!"

"Ron." The warning bell sounded again.

"Ronald!"—that's smutty, just filth—" Geegee's radar caught the blip. "Somebody opened the gates."

"Ron!"—it's time you called me *Ron!"*

"Somebody opened the gates—!"

The antagonism between them stopped the dogs' play

and brought a growl from Aubie. The threat of it seemed menacing even to Lady, who backed off. It was a volunteer at the door, collecting for the March of Dimes. Ron gave a dollar, explaining he'd made a donation at the office, and went back into the house only long enough to pick up his case and leave. After the door slammed, Geegee realized he was wearing a tweed jacket and bright yellow sweater. She got a terrible chill and had to run to the bathroom.

Everything was gray. The day, his mood. The sun, which rode fitfully with him along the freeway, finally hid behind a cumulus bank as leaden as his depression. A violent headache had him in its grip. The crow death had left him badly shaken, as did the knowledge that he'd held the means of murder in his hands—all the pills and poisons—and found himself unequal to the task. A drizzle engaged his windshield wipers and kept his concern on the pavement made treacherous by moisture on oil. By the time his car turned into its parking space, he felt very negative about the weather as well.

Immediately upon reaching his desk, he phoned Dulcie. Waiting out three rings, he anxiously studied deep mole-colored clouds rolling up formidable layers over the city. Her voice came on, "Hi, guess I overslept . . ." and he felt himself beside her in the bed.

"We're having lunch today, remember?"

She did. They talked awhile about her evening in Venice and the weather. It was decided she would pick him up. That way it would be simpler, just in case it rained. No, she didn't mind the rain, she loved it. He loved it, too, he said.

By the time they met there was a deluge. Collar turned up, Ron had waited in the lobby of the building by the door for at least fifteen minutes, eyes following each moving spot of red through the blurring downpour, ready to race across the thirty feet to the curb. Dulcie had forgotten to unlock the passenger door and he was soaked by the time he sat into the car.

"Here . . ." Reaching over into the back, she came up with a beach towel, and slowly pulled back into traffic.

"I'm sorry about the weather . . . nothing's right today. . . ." His dejection was an interloper to whom Dulcie refused passage. "Come on, you said you loved the rain. . . ."

"I had a place in mind at Santa Monica," he said as he squirmed out of his jacket and hung it on the back hook, "but I don't think we'll make it today."

"I figured that." On Dulcie's back seat was a hamper of food. She made a right turn off Wilshire onto a side street, parked, and there, ignoring the violent rush of waters that covered the curb, their vision limited to the nose of the car where rain bounced and steamed off the hot headlights, they ate. In the middle of the city, cut off from everything and everybody by a wall of water, uncoerced by outside pressures, calm began to prosper. The knots in Ron's stomach eased.

"We really should have taken my car. It's bigger."

"Okay, next time."

They ate in silence, their looks exchanging the pleasure of each other.

"I can't get over it . . . you fixing all this food."

"Neither can I, prices being what they are." They laughed, Dulcie recognizing his laughter wore a cloak that darkened it. "We don't know each other too well," she ventured. "I suppose that sounds funny, after the other night—took me four years with a shrink to get my head together—but I'm trying to understand about you. . . . I'm no Lucy Brown, come to my stand, for a nickel I'll analyze your troubles, but—how come you never left? I mean, got your own pad? Maybe I should change that and say why *don't* you leave? Your mother looks capable, I'm sure she could take care of herself. . . ."

"No, Geegee can't take care of herself. No, she can't.

She looks like she could, but she can't. If I left her, she'd come apart. I'm making no excuses for her, she can be a bitch on wheels—I guess you know that, the way she took after you—but without me, she'd be better off dead. . . ." (That got away from him; he hadn't meant to say that.) "Now . . . I don't mean . . . what that sounds like. . . . Look, I've got to tell you I lied to you the other day . . . that wasn't the truth about the Colorado River . . . if I explain you'll understand better about us, I mean Geegee and me. . . . My father didn't die there. I don't know where he died . . . or if he has . . . might still be alive, for all I know. . . ."

For an instant Dulcie felt a sense of trepidation, that perhaps she had opened a gate she didn't know how to close. "It doesn't matter you lied," she placated. "I've done my share. . . ."

"He left us . . . walked out on us . . . left Geegee to raise me by herself. . . . She was . . . a dancer, not too good. . . . We had to move where the jobs were, never stayed any place long enough to make friends; it was always just the two of us. . . . I promised her, soon as I got old enough, she'd never have to work again and she hasn't. . . . I remember her coming home, late, tired, beat, I'd wait for her at the bus—a kid—I was scared stiff myself, but I couldn't let her walk the dark streets. . . . I've got to tell you, though, she was great company, you know? Always trying to make fun, and things were tough for a long time . . ." The reel was spun out. "We . . . uh . . . well, I guess, with time we just got comfortable. . . ."

"It's really none of my business—"

"No, no," he urged. "Please, I want to tell you, want to talk. Do you think you love me?"

The question was unexpected, and not really welcome. Dulcie slid her hand from his and pressed against the door. "I don't really know about that."

"But you slept with me. . . ."

"Oh, I liked that part of it. Like a lot of things about

you, Ron, but love. . . ? That takes, well . . . time . . . time. I jumped into that undertow once without thinking. . . ."

"My mother won't hurt you; she won't do a thing to hurt you, I promise."

"It's not me, Ron. I'm not afraid of her. I just don't want anything to hurt you."

"She won't. Never again. Ever. She'll never hurt me again. I'll see you tonight? We'll make love?"

"I told you I like that part."

For no reason he began to feel uncertain. His eyes darted to the back of the car for an instant, to reassure himself that Geegee wasn't there. "Dulcie, it's not just because you feel sorry—"

Her fingers touched his lips to silence him. "Learn to believe me when I say I like you, I like you."

He looked at his watch. "Is it time?" she wanted to know.

It was time. She drove him back to the office. Mid afternoon the rain slacked off and stopped altogether before five. The decorating crew came in to prepare the offices for painting that night. Ron wasn't looking forward to going home, but Geegee had left the message they were out of margarine and coffee.

An explosion burst on him as his key turned and he came through the door. Geegee, in violent red; sequined; fringed; shimmying in a dress that fit her twenty years and twenty-five pounds ago. Shaking it up to brassy, jangling, rickytick music of another time.

"Baby-baby-baby . . ." she sang, ground and bumped.

Pathetic, he thought. Obsolete. Extinct. Stale. And pulled his eyes from the sausage of white flesh that thrust through the gaping zipper. Why couldn't she lose weight like she'd promised? "It doesn't fit," he said.

Raaaaah . . . rasped unmuted fat trumpets, and a drum was pulse to her body.

"IT DOESN'T FIT."

Wah-wah-waaaaaaah the sound strung out even after he lifted the needle and went into the study, leaving the groceries on the front table. She couldn't make up her mind whether to run to the bathroom again, as she'd been doing all afternoon, or to follow him.

"It was just a gag, Sonny. . . ."

He didn't look up from the desk where he was vaguely sorting the mail of the day. "Get rid of it."

"I found it today—thought it was good for a kick since you and me been havin' such a bad time. . . ."

"Take it off."

"I heard a lot of that in my day."

He didn't join in her nervous laugh but concentrated on opening the manila envelope he'd brought into the house.

"I was just doin' what you wanted, hon—ordering up the closets—when I found it. . . ." Geegee was frightened. He could hear it, see it. First time ever. He worried the moment: Was she crawling through his head again? "And I cleaned up the galleria, put all that junk away in the back room. . . ."

"Burn the dress."

"Sure, baby, I'll change—just give me a sec, sweetie, I'll get us a drink—make ya a double, huh?" The fringe on her hips jellied wildly as she hurried from the room. He picked up the phone and dialed.

"Dulcie?"

"Ron," her voice sang over the wire. The long cord stretched to the window. These nights it got dark early. He could see her house lighted up and reawakened to the excitement of being locked in her thighs.

"I can't tell you how much I want to see you."

"There's no set time; come on over, I'm here."

"Is ten okay?"

"I don't understand, what's wrong with now?"

"Well, I'm home . . . you know. . . ."

"Ron, we're grown up. We don't have to play come out wherever you are."

195

"Dulcie, I *can't!*" He slapped a hand over his mouth to smother the violence he felt erupting.

"That's a bad trip," she was saying, "a real bring down. You're too old to hide the car around the block. For your sake"—through the phone he could feel her hand reaching to him—"just tell her you're going out and walk across the street. . . ."

"I'll work it out—work something out—my mother seems very upset—later," he said, "when I finish up here."

"*Now*, Ron—it has to be now. I can't play it any other way but straight out. . . . Just open the gates . . . cross the street. Just one step . . . everybody's got to take the first step. . . ."

"Later—I'll call you—please, please, Dulcie—Wait for me. . . ."

When Geegee came back into the room she was wearing the jellaba he liked with the big roses, the one he'd dreamed her wearing in her casket. She was pale, a toothmark in her lower lip where she'd bitten it. As he reached for the ample double she'd poured for him, some spilled on the desk blotter. He touched her hand and it was trembling.

"What's the matter, Geegee?" he asked quietly.

"Nothing." He felt the anxiety in her to pull away from him. "Dinner's ready." The gulp of vodka hit him like a sudden mouthful of ice cream eaten too fast. There were darts of pain above his eyebrows. He tried to rub the fermenting horror from his head as he followed her.

"Geegee . . . we've got to talk."

"About this morning—I'm sorry . . ." She tossed the salad. Incessantly.

"Not only this morning . . ." Lady, hearing his voice, ran in from the kitchen, stood up on her hind legs with her front paws against him. "It's every day, our whole life, the way we live . . . it's wrong. . . ."

"You can see I'm sorry; I was mean, everybody gets mean. . . ." *She hadn't heard him. Not one desperate word.*

196

"Mothers get mean sometimes; now can we sit down and eat?"

Mothers . . . the same answer for thirty-five years. *Mothers get mean.* . . . Lady pawed at Ron, demanding attention. He scratched her head. "Geegee, if we don't work things out, something terrible's going to happen. . . ."

"We're not perfect; nobody said mothers were perfect. We do the best we can. I did enough, believe me. . . ."

"Where's Aubie?"

"You want French or roquefort?"

"Aubie—where is he?"

"Oh, didn't I tell you? At the vet's. Why don't you put on some music?" She began to dish up the meatloaf.

"Sick? You didn't call me."

"Didn't want to bother you. I took a taxi. Now can we sit down?"

"He was okay this morning. . . ."

"I'll turn on the music." He grabbed her arm as she moved to pass him. "Please . . . I have to go to the bathroom. . . ."

"What's wrong with Aubie?" She tried to twist loose, but the trap of his hand held her. "I asked you," she pleaded. "I told you not to bring that bitch in; he was after her all the time; you know what that does to me; you wouldn't pay attention. Sonny, please . . ." she begged, "you know my problem, I'll wet my pants—"

"Dammit, what happened to Aubie?"

"*I . . . had . . . him . . . fixed!*"

A stabbing pain fired Ron's groin. He bellowed like a mortally wounded animal. Like a leopard, a rhino, leaving a trail of pain, he sought refuge. In the dark, in his room, alone, the frenetic beast calmed.

Geegee deserved to die.

16

WHAT the hell was he keeping the stand open for anyway. . . ? The waterfall of rain that strained the overhang
laid it out clear for Soldier. It was time to pick up the
dice with that bimbo in back and tell her to blow. No way
he could keep her on. Even the occasional free lay wasn't
worth it. Return the camera and the rest of the equipment, and pick up a few bucks on the unused film; that's
what he'd do. Maybe even turn back a few rifles.

What if it kept raining? That was the trap of California
here I come—somehow you never figured it to rain by
the barrel. When he first bummed in from the East, after
the war, he remembered coming off the road, dirty and
draggin', into a clean, white city and all those palm trees
and oranges, and a job was easy to get. Now all that was
gone. Where did he fuck up? If things kept on the way
they were going, he'd be walking around with a tin cup
selling pencils. Why couldn't it rain easy for an hour and
stop, instead of flooding two, three weeks every goddamn
winter, keeping people home?

His stiff back kept telling him he really shouldn't live
by the ocean anyway. Gets in your bones.

Hell, he'd just go back there and tell her to get her
ass out. He stayed under the eaves as he came out from
the stand and moved sidewise along the battered, clap-

board building. One thing about the rain, though. With no business, nobody coming around, he didn't have to wear the patch. After a few hours that damned elastic band always hurt his forehead.

It took all his weight against the rain-swollen door. Even before he was fully into the sleazy cubicle, the smell of hash burned the inside of his nose.

"Told ya, f'Chrissake, no grass back here. I don't want no trouble with the cops. I break my ass to keep the whole operation legal and you—"

Soldier's bimmy looked up from the unmade daybed, eyes vacuous as though trying to figure out who the hell he was. A smoldering joint seemed glued between her thumb and forefinger as she took a deep, hissing drag and shifted the ancient threadbare bathrobe, haphazardly held together by a safety pin. From the wall, she smiled down on herself from half a dozen over-lighted, glossy photos; grossly seductive, bait to the lonely, the distorted, the misinterpreted.

"C'mon, get your ass up, get outa here, you're goin'—right now—blow—"

"Whaddja say?"

Any higher, Soldier thought, she'd be walkin' on'a ceiling. He dragged at her arm, got her to unsteady feet and undid the safety pin. The bathrobe fell to the cold cement floor. Ignoring her artless nakedness, he was on his knees, pulling out a suitcase from under the bed. While she fumbled into jeans, sweater, sneakers, he checked out the camera equipment to get it ready to send back.

"Where the fuck are the lenses? And the film? There was a drawerful o' film."

"Why don't you shuddup," she growled.

"You cunt, you sold 'em, didn't you? Don't you know I'm accountable? I gotta return all this equipment to the rental place—and I was gonna pick up some scratch by turnin' back the film—get outa here—get out!" His voice bellowed after her as she slogged away in the rain, carry-

199

ing her suitcase, and disappeared in the soup that was fog, haze and God knows what all.

Holy crap . . .

The drink he needed led him back outside to the stand. He belted a couple from under the counter and began to realize the rain was letting up. What the hell, might as well stay open, he needed every penny. That crazy, hopped up broad. . . . By the time he fixed the hinges on the shutter that the stinging wind had torn loose, he was hungry and a little loaded. He made his dinner. Salisbury steak with onions and French fries, his own dollar-eighty-five special. Before he sat down he chalked in a new price on the blackboard: Two twenty. As he ate, he looked around hopefully for that rare customer to interrupt him, but winter had really moved in. Soggy days, cold nights. Not till April could he hope for it to pick up and not a helluva lot then. Look what happened to the old amusement pier. They dressed it up, called it Pacific Ocean Park, got a lot of smart money and now it lays there. Dead. Like a bombed-out city. The skeleton of the roller coaster against the sky always depressed the shit out of him, but now that it had burned down he missed it. Where were people? Where was fun? Where the hell was he?

The reflection of the lights bordering the pier fell into the water and stared back like robot eyes. Soldier tried to close the frayed, six-button cardigan against the cold, but it wouldn't stay. He'd have to remember to sew the buttonholes smaller. He looped the buttons through twice to lock them and cut himself a wedge of hardening pumpkin pie.

The solitary, unexpected footsteps brought a pause in his chewing. From his pocket he quickly retrieved the patch and put it on. Once in awhile some oddball walked the pier alone at night and sometimes he was worth a buck, buck and a half.

"Dog? Burger? Wanna shoot?" Soldier's face furrowed like a plowed field as he looked at the man standing just beyond the light. "Hey, ain't you the guy? I remember you—sure—Patton, right? Your old man, right?"

He didn't move. He could smell the chalk as he stood in the corner of the room. The blackboard was all his left eye could see. A photograph of a painting of General Grant in the field filled the periphery of his right eye. He didn't answer when the teacher, Miss Reed said, You can leave the corner now and sit down, Ronald. . . . You may sit down now, she repeated impatiently. . . . How could he leave the corner? How could he face the class? "Your mother goes bare-ass naked; my ole man saw her in a skin show. . . ." Wait'll he got that guy after school. Nobody's gonna pick on Geegee. . . .

"Hey—not gonna run again, are you?"

Ron shook his head and moved into the confines of the stand and sat across from Soldier, for whom the prospect of company warmed the air, even if the guy's name did happen to be Sonny. "Coffee's my treat," Soldier insisted. "I remember some stories about Blood and Guts after I seen you that time; maybe you know if they're true; maybe your old man wrote some letters, huh? I heard he was a great swimmer, the general—know about that?" Soldier could tell this guy wasn't with him. "Look, if you come for dirty pictures, I had to let the broad go, couldn't afford to feed her no more." No rise, so Soldier went on, willing to oblige. "If you're lookin' for some special kink, I can steer ya—but I don't get nothin' for it—" It irritated Soldier the way this guy just sat, looking at him. "What the hell do you want? I don't like flakes hangin' around. . . ."

Ron stirred the coffee until the whirlpool in it was cup-deep, then watched as the surface calmed again. He knew he couldn't sit there much longer, silent, swallowing coffee that seemed to get more bitter every time he put the cup to his mouth.

"Your eyepatch is a fake!" he blurted.

"Yeah, 'at's right." With relief, Soldier pulled it off and

201

stuck it into his pocket, "I could say I get a headache from it, but it's really a pain in the ass," and laughed at his joke. "Usta be good for business. People walkin' by—me wearin' a soldier's cap, my medals, wounded veteran . . . people usta care about things like that."

"The medals phony, too? You buy 'em? Or did they come with the stand?" Ron heard his own words, like listening to a stranger; never before had he spoken so aggressively to anyone. He thought for a minute Soldier was going to come across the counter at him.

"Listen, you sonofabitch, I earned those medals, every goddamn one. . . ."

"You really kill as many as you told me?"

"You damn right."

"Didn't bother you any?"

"How can it bother you, you don't know 'em? It's nothin'. . . . You just see 'em and pull a'trigger."

"Think you're still a pretty good shot, huh?" Ron pressed.

"The best. Little side bet?"

"Yeah, sure. Why not?"

"Okay, what'll you bet. . . ?" Soldier came from around the stand to the front of the shooting gallery. Ron waited while he took off the padlock, rolled up the clanging steel overhead door, turned on the lights and pulled the switch that brought the targets to life.

"Ten dollars you can't make five in a row."

Five in a row, Soldier thought, that's a sweat. All he had in his pocket was about nine bucks, and he'd have to come up with the bread for those lenses, maybe a coupla hundred. "Four out of five," he countered, "and make it twenty bucks."

"You're on."

"And I get a coupla practice shots."

"Fifty, if you don't make the practice shots."

"I haven't got fifty," Soldier told him. "The bet's off."

He reached to turn off the switch. Ron grabbed his arm.

"Oh, no, no . . . tell you what . . . no bet, okay? If you hit four out of five, I'll pay you twenty. . . ."

"That's the kind of shootin' I like." Soldier put the stock to his shoulder, thinking the guy's a nut. What was the geek after? Soldier knew what *he* wanted: the twenty. Sighting down the moving row of clay pipes, he fired. Hit. Fired. Hit. Hit the third one, missed the fourth. Put the rifle down a moment. Pressing the stock back against his shoulder, he took a deep, wheezing breath, held it. Fired, shattering the fifth clay pipe.

"I'll take the twenty."

In the dream there had been five perfect shots. . . . Ron stepped out of the cocoon of light into darkness. From what he could see, the pier was desolate, empty, just himself and Soldier and nesting gulls. They were alone. It was time to take the chance. Exchange the nightmare for reality. He stepped back into the light. From his inside jacket pocket, brought out a packet of money that he laid on the worn linoleum counter.

Soldier knew what a twenty looked like. Two tens, four fives, even twenty singles didn't make that thick a wad. He picked it up, riffling it with expertise. "A grand?"

Ron nodded till his throat opened and he could speak. "And another thousand when it's done."

Soldier pressed the money between his hands. He owed for everything. Camera . . . the lenses . . . booze . . . rent . . . he'd never crawl out of the hole . . . two grand, two big ones. He could blow it off here, start again.

Why didn't the man quit staring at him? Ron wanted to scream. *Would he have to say it? Would he have to hear it out loud?*

"Who do you want me to kill?" Soldier finally asked.

"My mother."

It was a beautiful night. The day that had started so dismally had a full moon and clean, crisp air.

Soldier was impressed by the neighborhood. He hadn't

been up to this North Hollywood area in all the years he'd been in L.A. He knew everything around the pier and the arcades downtown, and once, about ten years back, he'd been hired with his guns and medals for a rally in Culver City for some politician that was out to get the American Legion vote. Outside of that, all he knew was the coast towns like Laguna Beach and Oceanside and San Clemente. Lot of old people there now, and the President, too. He didn't like old people. There was one little town he did like, though. It was called Cardiff-by-the-Sea. He might go there when this was over. Or maybe go someplace in the Midwest—some small town, where medals still meant something. But it was probably better if Ron didn't know where he went. They both agreed to that.

"Turn right." Ron leaned through the camper window into the pickup and directed him. "Two blocks, then right again." It had been a rough, smelly ride in this airless sardine can and Ron would be glad when it was over. "Stop right about here."

Soldier braked, pulled against the curb, and put out all the lights. Nobody would likely pay any attention to a weather-worn cab-over parked on a dark residential side street. Happened all the time.

For Geegee, the sound of the gates was reprieve from purgatory. Hell's fire would be better than what she'd been through these last hours, wondering if she'd lost Sonny for good, and trying to understand what made her do that to Aubie. . . . Lady understood, and had come to her when she was lying on the bed, crying her eyes out. Had nuzzled the icebag off her forehead and licked her face.

"My God, Lady, what did we do. . . ?"

The gates swinging open brought Geegee from the bed, into her dressing room for a spray of cologne, a dab at her eyes, a quick survey in the mirror. Grateful that the dim light of the living room would be kind to the puffiness in her face, she waited beside the door. *Forgive me, Sonny—I'm sorry, sweetheart—it was stupid—you know Mother didn't mean it. . . .*

But the sound of the familiar engine on the semicircle of driveway didn't happen. No car lights swept the living room.

The gates were open. She could see that when she moved the drape aside.

"Who is it?" she called anxiously through the grilled peephole. "Who's there?"

Fingers lacing into Lady's fur, she carefully opened the front door, a bit at a time, then, seeing no one, ran across the veranda and the driveway, heart pounding, hanging onto the dog, to close the gates.

Damned hippies, no respect for private property . . .

"Clear shot," was Soldier's comment when he saw her through the windshield. Slumped in the seat so that anyone even five feet away couldn't have seen there was a man there, he closed one eye and sighted down his finger. Good street for it, he assessed. Lotta bushes and no one walkin' around at night. He had the perfect piece, he told Ron. A Luger and no way to trace it. Lifted it off a dead kraut officer, kept it cleaned and oiled all these years. He could get her from here easy, but it would be better if he parked closer so he could make it back to the truck after opening the gates.

"Monday." Ron was anxious, wanting to rid himself of the sight of Geegee, standing there, a perfect target. "Has to be Monday—about ten's a good time—I bowl Monday nights, never get home till one." The scene had played over and over in his mind from the moment he took the money off the shelf. He would come home from bowling and there would be police cars in the street. Dulcie would come out all upset and want to comfort him but he would wait for that—and he would start leaving his gates open. . . .

"I don't go in nobody's house," Soldier voiced a definite condition. "She don't come out for the gates, I don't go in."

"She'll come out," Ron assured. "She hears those gates no matter what."

After Geegee went back into the house and the gate lights went off, Soldier turned the ignition key and pulled away. Four miles later, under a walnut tree near the on ramp to the San Diego Freeway, Ron got out of the back of the camper and into his own car. He had deliberately not looked at the registration in the camper as he now averted his eyes from Soldier's license plate. It was better not to know who had killed your mother.

> Little fly upon the wall
> ain't you got no home at all?
> ain't you got no mama?
> ain't you got no papa?
> wanna go to God?
> SPLAT—go to God.

Soldier's pickup angled upward onto the freeway, joining the stream of tail lights, and disappeared. Ron drove home.

Soldier held the thousand dollars in his hand and stared at the money till the sweat from his palm saturated the top and bottom bills. He spread it out onto the small table in his camper and moved away to get the Old Hickory half pint, his eyes never leaving the green that was his ticket to freedom. How long since he'd seen this much at one time? Another deep belt and the tough gristle over his memory melted away. He remembered nine hundred bucks once, when that kid he had—what the hell was his name?—Ignacio something, fought and won a main event at the old Santa Monica arena. "Should never a' sold his contract," Soldier said to no one in particular. Then he took another swallow, corked the bottle with determination, put it away in the nest of rags that filled the lower cupboard drawer. And brought out the Luger.

Dulcie's house was dark. He could see that. There was no use parking and walking to her door. She would understand. He would call her tomorrow, tell her he was busy for the weekend. Then Monday, when it was all over . . . no, better Tuesday, he'd wait a day. Or after the funeral, that would be best. . . .

Geegee came running out of the house and walked the last few feet alongside the car before it came to a stop, telling Ron how glad she was to have him home, and of her fear when someone opened the gates before. She moved in little half steps as he closed and latched them, giving him the feeling that she wanted to be near him for protection.

"Probably just some kids, Geegee."

"I've been waiting hours, Sonny, to tell you what I did was terrible, a terrible thing."

"We won't hurt each other anymore." How easy it was to smile at her, now that everything was settled. She moved in front of him, into the house, walking backward as a child does, promising she would never, never again ask where he went, and she would even go bowling Mondays if he wanted.

"Not this Monday, Geegee." It pleased him that he was being so kind to her. He let her kiss him on the cheek. "Good night." As he was about to close his bedroom door, she remembered he had gotten a phone call, ". . . from that woman Ruth, that works for you."

He would contact her tomorrow, he said.

"It's about some forms—" She slid her hand in to keep the door from closing as she imparted the urgency of the message. "She said she gave you the wrong date. They should'a been in today, but could you please get it in first thing tomorrow morning, even though it's Saturday, she said she'd come in for it. . . ."

Normally, a thing like this upset him, but he found

himself extremely patient. Amenable. "Well, guess I'll have to do 'em now."

"I saved dinner, if you want to eat something." She trailed him back through the house to the study. "Or a drink?" He patted thanks on her shoulder, shook his head no, and settled at the desk, loosening his tie and taking off his jacket before he unfolded the forms.

Read carefully. Print legibly.

"It's not like he was a young dog," Geegee said tentatively from the other side of the desk.

"It's done, Geegee. Settled. Everything's settled," he told her with gentle finality.

"You know I love Aubie. I wouldn't hurt him. . . ." Ron looked through the desk drawers for a ballpoint pen or hard lead pencil the forms demanded. "Lady was very sweet tonight," she said. "I think she likes me."

Ron's eyes raised to hers. Geegee stood waiting, hoping for his face to tell her that she was blameless. He offered no alms to her poverty but turned back to the form, pen in hand.

"Name," he said, as the pen printed each letter in its proper box: Ronald (space) Colman (space) Gohdiener. He looked at the twenty-three little square boxes that held his label and shook his head with a lifetime of heartbreak at the bitter joke. "Worn it all my life, still can't believe it . . . Ronald Colman Gohdiener . . . always gives me the feeling I should be walking around with a bag of buttered popcorn."

"How can you say that?" she defended. "It's a beautiful name; he was a beautiful man. Remember I took you to see *Lost Horizon*; you were five; then I bought the book and read it to you; we read it together—"

"And you bought me his hat and raised my eyebrow. Mother's name—" Again his pen filled the boxes: Grace (space) Gohdiener. "Mother's maiden name," he asked pointedly, looking at her. "Well . . . what do I put down? I can put down Grace Gohdiener . . . that I'm a bastard . . ."

208

"Put down same as last time. My grandmother's name. Trayco."

He'd sell this house, after it was over. "Father's name?" *Get a nice small modern house, maybe with a pool.* "They want to know my father's name, Geegee."

What was happening in this room was strange and somehow frightening to her. This man behind the desk was someone she didn't know. Instinct told her to fight.

"I could'a given you away. I could'a, I didn't. I let my mother call me a whore. . . ."

"Father's name, Geegee?"

"There was a lawyer offered me money, but I kept ya—"

"Father's name . . ." He slammed the phone book across the desk at her. "Pick one—go on, pick one—which one? Who made it? Who scored, Geegee? Who hit the bull's-eye?"

Geegee sensed she was fighting for her life. She picked up the pages of thousands of names and numbers and began tearing at them, page by page, screaming back at him, "You don't forgive me for being raped? *You* don't forgive *me*? My *father* was going to forgive me. I was on the streetcar, going to see him, but he died—"

"I'm not interested in *your* father—"

"Who're you, you little bastard, not to forgive me? That bitch across the street tells me to go t'hell—I could'a left you in a garbage can and she tells *me* to go t'hell—"

"Which one, Mother?" His smile was a knife turning in her. "You must've remembered something about one of 'em, didn't one of 'em lift his eyebrow?"

"You wanna grind me in your computer? Okay, baby, go ahead, put it all down, see who yells I give first. Go on, write. Gang-bang, basement Ogden Avenue, January 6, 1932, Happy New Year, Gracie Gohdiener. Go on, write it all—mother's age, thirteen and a half, too damned ignorant to know she's knocked up till it's too late. . . ."

He was beginning to tire under her assault and wanted

to finish, get to his room. He was writing faster now. Father's name: George (space) Gohdiener. *Living or deceased?* He fought the pen and x'd the dead box. It was *Date and Place of Father's Death* that blunted his effort.

"I don't remember. . . ." He looked up, suddenly lost. "Geegee, what'd I put down when I first went to work there? What'd I put down?"

The need to help her Sonny dissipated her anger. "Didn't ya say . . . didn't ya say. . . ?" her jaw opening and closing like a puppet's, but her brain felt wooden, with no answers.

"I've got to know," he cried. "They've got my other records. If it's not the same, then the whole office'll know I lied, that I'm nobody. . . ."

"Sweetie, I don't know, don't remember. . . ."

"Get out! Get away from me—"

She felt the upheaval in him but stood rooted, unable to cope. "Baby . . . we always had so much fun. . . ."

If he didn't escape the forms, his mother, his life, he would choke to death. He started around the desk. She ran to him, clinging, her arms claiming him. "Baby, baby, don't want ya to be hurt, didn't mean t'hurt ya. . . . I love ya, love ya. . . ." He struggled against her hold but couldn't find the will to break from her, from her warm, soft body pressed so close to his. "Love ya, baby, love ya. . . ." She was kissing his face. He stood rigid, resisting.

"Why didn't you give me a father?"

"Love ya, love ya. . . ."

"I'm nobody. . . ." he cried in the dark of desolation.

"Couldn't stand anybody else touching me . . . only you, Sonny. . . ." Her tears salted their lips and the door to the forbidden room in his mind opened wide. "I'll die without you, Sonny, die. . . ." She slid to the floor, her arms still circling his legs.

"Stop crying," he demanded. "Stop it!"

"Not a whore not a whore not a whore . . ."

"Geegee, get up . . . stop it, stop crying—"

She didn't hear. She was in a basement on Ogden

210

Avenue, six animals at her. "I hurt I hurt I hurt, I'll die, die . . ."

The plaintive whimper brought him down to the poor raped child at his feet. He held her, soothing, cradling, rocking her. "You won't die, Geegee; you won't die . . ." If these words came through to her, they had no special meaning. Only his touch spoke to her. "Sonny's here, don't cry, nobody's going to hurt you, nobody nobody nobody . . ." he kept repeating until their mouths met, held, and kissed into silence.

17

IT was a quiet morning. The water lapped the shore with a tenderness that made the rise and fall of the tides irrelevant. The sun that was trying to clear the morning clouds hadn't yet drunk up the dew. Moisture heavy enough to pose as rain ran in tiny rivers on the rusted fenders of Soldier's pickup.

"Yeah?" His voice, rough with sleep, came muffled. " 'Sta minute." Looking as stale as the smell from inside the battered vehicle, Soldier, in long johns, sweat shirt, unshaven, peered out, "What'n hell you doin' here? Y'crazy? Come on, get in."

Ron took the one step into the rat's nest that Soldier called home, but left the door open for air. Soldier knelt on the open bunk and pulled the door shut.

"It's off," Ron said. "I don't want you to do it."

Soldier dug sleep from the corners of his eyes and looked with suspicion at the pinstriped man. "You don't get the money back, whaddya pullin'? We made a deal, the grand's mine."

Ron told him to keep it and laid the other thousand on the rumpled sleeping bag.

"Don't bullshit me—nobody gets nothin' for nothin' . . ." but Soldier made certain to stuff the bills out of sight.

212

"Just keep it," Ron told him, "and go away, that's all you have to do. Disappear. Don't come near me. I don't know you. I never saw you."

Soldier agreed that he never saw him. Never in his fuckin' life. But he had a parting word as Ron stepped out of the camper. "I'll tell you somethin', fella . . ." he leaned close to emphasize the point, "I don't like ya, see? Didn't like ya from the beginnin', but I like ya better now, know what I mean?" Ron didn't. "Well, what I mean—any guy that'd kill his own mother . . ."

The epithet stayed with Ron all the way back to his car.

He handed in the forms, leaving some of the spaces open. If there was any problem later with the computer, he'd simply say he forgot and ask them to check the old records. After all, he'd committed no crime.

On his way home from work he picked up Aubie. The vet told him that, of course, the dog didn't know what had happened to him. He was just a dog. He would likely be uncomfortable for a few days; then, since he'd never been mated, he would just forget. Just a dog. When he had to stop suddenly, Aubie slid off the seat and yiped like a puppy. Ron drove the rest of the way with his arm around the dog whose agate eyes seemed filled with uncertainty. "The hurt will go away, boy; it will go away."

When Aubie got out of the car, free to run in the front yard, he concentrated on marking off his territory from any intruders, leaving a drop here, a drop there. Ron stood at the gates, resting his head against a garland of rusted-iron roses and looked across the street. The red VW was in the garage. The drapes were open in the living room, where pillows cluttered the floor and a sewing machine lived like a piece of sculpture.

"Sonny . . ."

He turned. For a moment, for the fraction of an instant as Geegee looked at him, the stirrings of memories from day one surrounded him. They were displaced by the same feeling she'd had the day of his anger when he

213

found the cut picture. She remembered her terror when she seemed not to be in his eyes, but the layers of time ran over the fear and, like lava spewing from the earth's depths, cindered everything before it. Besides, he would never go across the street now. The gates were closed. Geegee relaxed and finished what she had started to ask him:

"What'll we do on Sunday?"

Ron hammered the latch into place with the heel of his hand. He would have to learn to live with that house across the street. Might be better to start coming in and out of the other set of gates. He looked across just once more and thought of Persian pillows. Then he joined his mother and they went into the house.